PU[illegible]S
STRINGS

MIKE PENISTONE

ISBN: 978-0-6486929-8-0

Book design, composition and artwork by Robyn Greathead, Treehouse Type & Art Workers. www.treehouse.com.au

---

CHAPTER 1

PRESENTATION EVENING: THE AFTERMATH

COLIN PUNTER IS A BORING MAN. HE'S A SELF-PROCLAIMED boring man. For over 30 years he's edited *The Community Advertiser*, a local rag, a free paper. He's known locally as 'Punter the hunter' for the way he stalks shopkeepers in pursuit of an advert. At six-foot-four and pencil thin, he enters shops in stages: arms first, upper body, then legs. Always popping up with this week's latest advertising offer, he has a 90% success rate, based more on the shopkeeper's desire to get rid of him than the quality of his presentation. Only Mr Woo finds time to berate him, usually over the spelling of noodle, not noodel or nooder.

Colin knows his place in the community and has come to terms with his role. Tonight he's sitting in the back row of the school hall waiting for his nephew Gerald to receive an achievement award. Gerald is the jewel in Colin's crown. Colin nestles his zoom lens camera on his lap, in preparation for Gerald's appearance on stage.

As the night unfolded, turning from order and tradition into frenzy and chaos, Colin sensed an opportunity and began clicking away merrily, securing enough content for at least three future editions. He went up and down the aisles and no one was spared. Some even sought him out. Doreen pouted this way and that. Fred gyrated like a geriatric on steroids. The cast on the stage swayed left, then right. Colin was energised beyond his years: above the waist he was struggling to keep in touch with his fast feet, his tentacle arms projecting the camera up close and personal. Maybe I should get on the stage, he thought, and take some shots of the seething crowd pushing forward. The more locals I can photograph the more likely an increase in sales. People like looking at themselves, especially Doreen who had already suggested an adult only section in *The Advertiser*. Naively Colin had agreed without really understanding the implications, especially the half-price introductory offer.

The euphoria began to die down. Eric had pressed every conceivable button to quieten Rod Stewart, but too late as the mob had already learned the words and were singing loudly. The under-50s showed some rhythm, the over-50s an uncoordinated apology for bygone years. They stuttered across the stage, sporting stupid grins of embarrassment. Eventually energy levels began to subside and they drifted towards the exit.

Colin wrapped an arm around Gerald and, guarding his camera like the crown jewels, ushered him out.

Members of staff hugged each other. Potter stood in isolation, but Mr Bartholomew glowed like a proud father. Never in the school's history had there been a presentation night of this magnitude. Total interaction: parents, kids, staff — at times completely out of control. The only unifying voice was Rod Stewart's, but there are only so many times you can sing "If you think I'm sexy and ..."

Bartholomew shook hands with everyone as they left the hall. A group led by Billy the postman had harangued Mr Woo into opening his noodle shop. Mr Woo sensed a killing and had already phoned ahead. "Three for two nooder," he cried, and the mob cheered loudly. Fred began "For he's a jolly good nooder, for he's a jolly good nooder, and so say all of us!"

The trail of staff and parents stretched from the hall to the school gate, like migrants leaving a beleaguered city.

Danny was momentarily isolated as his teenage troupe cavorted across to the other side of the hall. Janice recognised his aloneness, just as she appreciated the connection that had taken place between them. She turned to fire a look of laser intensity and like a sniper's red spot, it hit Danny between the eyes. He couldn't ignore it ... for now.

Danny, the maestro, had lost control of his orchestra, and he needed to think quickly and reposition himself, physically as well as mentally. Potter glared down from the stage like an eagle eyeing its prey, preparing to launch. Danny cast a knowing eye at him, and Potter accepted the challenge and began to cross the stage, but to no avail as the last group of disco freaks embraced him and submerged him in "If you think I'm sexy ..."

Then Danny headed towards Janice and friends, but not before casting a wry smile in Potter's direction. The contest will resume, he thought, but not tonight.

"I'm opening the café, lads, if you fancy a late-night coffee," Fred chipped in.

"There could be a late-night cabaret!" Doreen mocked.

"Better make the coffee strong, Fred," said Chris. There was a loud cheer and a chant of "Fred's, Fred's" echoed around the hall as they passed an exhausted Bartholomew.

Potter shrugged off the last Rod Stewart impersonator and glared down the hall, knowing his chance for revenge would have to wait till next term.

The final day of term was for the staff only. They came in to tidy their rooms and place orders for books or stationery for the start of the new school year.

Bartholomew invited them all into the staffroom just before lunch for drinks and a thank-you. There was only one topic on the agenda, and as Bartholomew stood to make his address the excitement grew.

"What can I say, what can I say? Our finest ever presentation evening. My inbox is bursting to capacity with comments from satisfied parents and guests. Inspirational, exciting, intoxicating, sexy are just a few of the messages. My personal thanks to all of you who somehow managed to ride the waves of uncertainty and keep the show on the road, especially Miss Whittaker, who rescued me on several occasions. I can't seem to get that Rod Stewart song out of my head," Bartholomew concluded.

The staff laughed and there were several nods of agreement. Potter stood motionless on his own. Nothing he could say would count. There was nothing he could do. He now had six weeks of holiday to prepare for Danny Carver's final year.

Miss Stanger, in a strained attempt to reassert her status and authority, suggested drinks down at the Dog and Gun. Eric the technician thought the Railway House pub might be a better choice as some of the kids used the Dog and Gun.

"Railway House it is then. First round on Mr Potter."

Loud cheers broke out as the staff headed for the car park.

Potter winced; he was trapped in the moment.

CHAPTER 2

FRED'S CAFE

THE MORNING AFTER THE NIGHT BEFORE, DANNY HAD arranged to meet the boys in the park just off the precinct. Better to be out of sight than bump into anyone. The revelry at Fred's had gone on long into the night. Janice had latched vice-like onto Danny's arm, and Sato was encircled by Asian beauties begging to know how the whole evening had been planned. Jeff and Kevin chatted away in a corner. Chris was on the hunt, but he was too enthusiastic for most of the girls, apart from Gillian, a Year 10 girl with buck teeth.

Doreen eyed the crowd for any available men, preferably alone or slightly detached from their wives. She slipped her business card (Doreen 0467 561 950) discreetly into their hand or pocket followed by a knowing look and occasional wink. She played the numbers game. If she gave out 20, she might hook one client. And she did. Billy the postman slid past and whispered "Get on the 442 at 9.30 tomorrow morning. Stops outside the post office and we can arrange a time and place. I'll be on the top deck."

Doreen was taken aback, but quickly assumed her role. "I'll be wearing high heels and a black dress," she whispered. Billy started to feel uncomfortable below and decided to go over to the bottle cooler, his face glowing like a spring lupin.

Danny extricated himself from Janice's grip and headed to the toilet, just long enough to text his team where and when to meet the next day.

Slowly, one by one, Fred's cafe emptied, Billy and Doreen managing to avoid one another, each wondering if the other were serious.

Danny nodded at each of his crew and they acknowledged receipt of his text, so he and Janice slid out into the night and began the slow walk home.

CHAPTER 3

REGROUP

REAL WINNERS IN LIFE LEARN QUICKLY FROM EXPERIENCE and then move on, and Danny was no exception. The presentation night had not gone strictly to plan, but the outpouring of support for each video clip suggested a lucrative return might be just around the corner or, more specifically, in Colin Punter's office.

The crew all slumped down onto the park bench, Sato unflappable, Chris and Jeff bleary-eyed.

Danny spoke: "Let's look at last night's positives. Firstly, it was a raving success. The staff and parents loved it. Most of them hadn't a clue what was going on, but they loved it. I don't think there will be any comeback when we start Year 12. Only Potter remains a threat. We have six weeks before Year 12 starts to cash in on last night."

Chris and Jeff raised an eyebrow, Sato a sardonic smile.

"There must have been over 300 people there last night," Danny started. "If we sell to half of them, that's a healthy profit. How do we cash in?"

Chris and Jeff looked at each other, searching for an answer. Sato broke the ice: "We still have the porno movie. That's what you mean, Danny, eh?"

Chris and Jeff lightened up.

"Sure is. We just have to find a way of getting the message through to all of them."

"Use that tall skinny bloke with the camera," said Chris. "You know, Punter the hunter. He runs *The Advertiser*. He was in Fred's last night. I saw him talking to Doreen, up close and personal. She was fiddling with his jacket even."

Danny's brain slipped into overdrive. Everyone reads the local rag, he thought.

"When's the next edition due out?" he asked.

"Thursday, and it'll be full of photos from the presentation night," Chris continued.

"Is Punter married?"

"Yes, his wife works in the butcher's next to Woo's. She's a brute. She's like a Viking when she chops the meat." Chris had them laughing now.

"So, we need to get a free advert in the rag before Thursday's edition?"

"Doreen was slipping her business card into men's jacket pockets," Sato said.

There was a deathly silence.

Danny held everybody's attention. "We need Doreen to ring Punter and get amorous with him, threatening to tell his wife if he doesn't play ball."

"How are you going to get Doreen to phone Punter, Danny?" asked Jeff.

"I'll make her a sub-agent," Danny replied. "Let's go down to Fred's and check her out."

"No point," said Chris. I saw her getting on the 442 around 9.30 this morning. Dressed up, she was. I bet Fred didn't know."

“I need to chat to Doreen,” Danny said. “Let’s meet at my place tonight and go over the plan.”

One day on from the greatest ever presentation night and Danny was already hatching the next stage.

CHAPTER 4

A ROMANTIC TRYST

DOREEN HOPED SHE WAS AT THE FRONT OF THE QUEUE AS the 442 arrived. She needed time to negotiate the stairs in her high heels, and thought of asking the driver to delay his departure until she had arrived at her seat, but decided not to. She took her ticket and made a dash for the first step, but the driver pressed the accelerator and she missed it. Her right knee crashed into a sharp iron edge and a ladder shot up the right thigh of her stocking. A man sitting in row three reached forward to help but didn't know what to do when Doreen's stocking top and suspender belt appeared. Doreen's muffled "bollocks!" made several passengers look the other way, trying not to smile.

Billy, dressed like a 1970s country and western singer, had seen Doreen at the bus stop. He heard the commotion and for a moment thought of going to her aid, but he was near the back upstairs and didn't want to risk his hat falling off.

Doreen, somewhat flushed, appeared at the top of the stairs.

The bus turned right sharply and she stumbled left even more sharply, crashing into an elderly man on his own. He groaned a weak obscenity and she pushed herself up, looking for Billy. There were six people between her and the country and western singer, who Doreen guessed was Billy, despite the brown Stetson covering most of his face. She carefully negotiated the three metres to his seat, plonked herself down next to him, and the other passengers gave a sigh of relief.

"Didn't know it was a fancy-dress meeting!" she whispered.

"Can't risk being recognised," said Billy. "That elderly guy at the front asked for my autograph when I got on."

Doreen seized the moment as the bus was only three stops from the depot and everybody off.

"It's $150 an hour and you pay for the room hire or I come to your house," she whispered confidently.

Billy started to shake. The question required an answer and Billy was trapped, shoulder against the window. Doreen had crossed her legs revealing her inner right thigh and suspender belt.

"Agreed," he mumbled.

"To what?" asked Doreen.

"$150 and the room hire," said Billy.

"I'll need a deposit," she said.

Billy fumbled in his pocket. He had gone this far and he couldn't back out. He opened his wallet and Doreen, bold as brass, took it off him and withdrew a $50 note.

"Text me when you've booked the room. Allow 30 minutes for travel," she said.

She gave him back his wallet, and the other passengers cowered as she staggered past, pausing only to steady herself before negotiating the stairs.

Billy looked as though rigor mortis had set in. He had to get off the bus as it had pulled into the depot, but his legs were trembling and seemed out of touch with the rest of his body.

The elderly man at the front muttered "Give us a song, Elvis," and the remaining passengers laughed and filed forward and down the stairs.

Billy rose and the numbness in his legs began to ease. Tentatively he walked down the aisle.

"About time," said the driver. "This lot want to get on."

Billy jumped the final step, and his Stetson caught the edge of the driver's cabin and spun off, landing at the front of the queue.

"Look, it's Billy the postman!" cried a voice from the back.

"Hope you sing better than you deliver mail," called another.

The queue burst into laughter as Billy grabbed his hat and made a dash for it.

CHAPTER 5

EXPANSION

ONE BY ONE, DANNY'S TEAM ARRIVED AND, AFTER FENDING off the usual inane comments from Eileen and Gerald, locked themselves in his bedroom.

They knew Danny would have a strategy and want their input, even if it made little difference to his original concept. And they all knew that, whatever the plan, Sato would be instrumental in its application. There had to be no comeback, no trace back to source.

Danny opened: "Let's look at our current position. We have a successful porno video, which clients can access via a 4-digit code on their mobile phones, so thanks to Fred we have a small but regular income. My thoughts are that we build a network of Fred's who act as sub-agents, each believing they are the only agent, unaware of any others."

Jeff interrupted "So, it's a similar model to the drug dealer I had a problem with?"

"Yes," said Danny. "It's also quite foolproof. If one sub-agent is caught or found out; it doesn't affect the rest of our operation."

Chris, a little slow on the uptake, asked "because they don't know of the existence of the other sub-agents?"

Danny and Sato swapped glances and Jeff hid a mocking smile.

"The question is," said Danny, how do we expand our operation?"

Sato, to avoid the frustration of a long wait as the penny dropped with Chris and Jeff, said "We need additional sub-agents and free advertising."

"Punter for the advertising, Danny," Chris jumped in.

"Doreen as the next sub-agent," said Sato.

The crew looked at Danny for confirmation. He was ahead of them, but it was satisfying to know that the troops concurred with the general.

"Fred doesn't know about Doreen's work on the side, so to speak," said Danny.

"Or on her back," quipped Chris.

There was a long pause before Danny giggled and shook his head.

"Correct, Chris, well said."

"That's where she's vulnerable, Danny. She knows that if Fred found out he would end their relationship and she would have to find a new base to operate from," Jeff clarified the position.

"You need to talk to Doreen, Danny, but not at Fred's," Sato suggested.

"I got one of her cards," said Jeff. "You could text and start a conversation about using her services, then meet her at the motel just outside town, The Griffin."

Sato immediately handed the neutral mobile to Danny, and Jeff passed Doreen's card over.

Danny mused for a while, then began to text.

He put the mobile back on the table and tension and expectation filled the room. There was an uneasy quiet — in a war film they would be waiting for the device to explode.

Sato suggested "She may be working."

Then a ping, and all eyes focused on the mobile.

Danny reached forward slowly and confidently, but not before glancing at the others with that twinkle in his eye and a hint of a smile.

CHAPTER 6

DANNY MEETS DOREEN

DANNY EDGED HIMSELF OUT OF THE UBER AND THANKED Mohammed for the ride. He was a few minutes late, a ploy designed to create anxiety in the person waiting, in this case the expectant Doreen. Danny acted best on instinct. No need to loiter outside preparing yourself — go straight in and make it happen. He did however enter through a side door. The receptionist noted his arrival, but his attempt to make contact was brushed aside.

Doreen was sitting at the bar facing the main entrance, her back to Danny, right leg crossed over left, wearing a tight-fitting black skirt, thigh-length.

Danny tapped her on the shoulder.

"Doreen," he started, "thanks for answering my text, can I buy you a drink?"

Doreen was lost for words. Was Danny the client or was he there by accident?

"Tonic and lime, please. Never touch alcohol when I'm working."

"You're not working, Doreen."

"Your text was not about my services then, Danny?"

"No, it was about a mutual friend. A friend I care for and have known through some difficult times."

Doreen picked up the thread. "You mean Fred?" she asked.

"I do." Danny looked her in the eye.

"I know he's very fond of you, Doreen, and assumes you are fond of him." Danny demanded a response.

"I am." Doreen squeezed out the words.

"He assumes you have given up your past and want a life with him, running the café." Danny made the conversation more intimate and sensitive. Doreen hesitated, sensing he had an ulterior motive for this meeting, and her late-night senses, sharpened from years of standing on street corners, knew Danny was moving in.

"You can see my concern, Doreen? I don't want to see Fred hurt."

Doreen's hard edge began to surface.

"I make my living how I want, Danny. I always have and always will."

Danny switched on a more diplomatic tone. "I appreciate that and don't want to instigate a confrontation. I merely want to offer a solution that might benefit all parties: you commercially, Fred harmoniously, and of course me." Danny eased back as wheels began to whirr in Doreen's head.

"What do you mean by commercially?"

"Well, we sell a short porno video through a small number of sub-agents of whom Fred is one. This is done with a 4-digit code sent to a private mobile number. Each sub-agent works independently and is unaware of the existence of any other sub-agents. It is very personal and lucrative. All you do, Doreen, is include the cost of the video in your charges. The video costs $25 and you keep $15. On a fortnightly basis you pay my team our share. If you don't pay, we cut off the mobile connection. We will know how much you owe because you will be the only one with that digital code. This way all parties are happy. You can stay at Fred's. You make additional income from the same client, and I can feed you any other products that I think you may be interested in." Danny sat back, sales pitch over.

Doreen thought about it. Additional income from the same client meant less work and less risk.

Danny tried to clinch the deal. "Let me give you the 4-digit code and mobile number as a gesture of good faith. You can also keep the $25 from your first client."

Doreen had an easy way in, but didn't agree immediately.

"Okay. I'm not saying I'm going to run with this, but I'll test your plan on my next client. Give me the code and number."

She reached forward. Danny pulled a small white card from his pocket, handed it over, stood up and left.

Doreen sipped her tonic and lime and stared at the card, thinking about what he had said.

And, as she put the card in her handbag, her mobile rang ...

CHAPTER 7

FRED'S CAFE

DANNY TEXTED THE CREW TO MEET AT FRED'S IMMEDIATELY, and made sure a table was set in the corner where Fred could not hear them. When Fred placed the tray of drinks on the table, Danny did not suggest he join them.

"Well, did she bite?" Jeff asked.

Then, as though pre-rehearsed, a loud ping sounded from Sato's pocket. He dug out the phone.

"Yes, she did," Danny said.

Jeff and Chris rocked in their seats, laughing out loud, and Chris gave Danny a high five. Danny explained that this was a free trial, designed to lure Doreen into the realm of sub-agents. Sato sent the link and Doreen was in the money.

Fred sensed a way into the jocularity and offered a second free drink.

"Good news?" he asked.

"The best," said Danny. "By the way, Fred, any sales to report?"

"Just the baker, Phil. He gets paid on Thursday."

"More good news. One a week is a good start. Then you can start to look for potential buyers among your customers. Three a week and you can treat Doreen to dinner or the movies and, who knows, maybe a holiday in the sun."

Fred suddenly had a vision of himself and Doreen strolling along the Costa Fortune like the rich and famous, arm in arm taking the sea air. Doreen would love that, he thought.

"Fred, Fred! A customer wants serving!" Chris woke Fred from his daydream.

Then the phone in Sato's pocket pinged again!

Chapter 8

Strategy Meeting

IT WAS NOW ACCEPTED THAT THE CREW MET AT DANNY'S every Thursday evening. Gerald was at the club and there was nothing to hide from Eileen, who was still basking in the glory of Danny's presentation. She descended into a transcendental state frequently, always with one hand grasping the musical egg timer Sato had given her, trying hard to hum along with the music of Bach, or maybe jazz.

Danny opened the proceedings in his usual positive manner.

"Now we have Doreen on board, where next?"

Chris answered first: "Advertising, Danny. Punter the hunter."

"Okay, so how do we play it?"

The crew knew Danny had the answer, but they also knew he expected their input.

"We need to get him dependent on your help, Danny," Chris suggested.

"In return for free advertising," Jeff chimed in.

"Who benefits from the free advertising, Danny?" Sato quizzed.

"Our main sub-agents," said Danny. "Doreen and Fred."

"So how do we get the Punter dependent on you for help, Danny?" asked Jeff.

Danny held the moment, then began to reveal his plan.

"The Punter took Doreen's card, yes? Nods all round. What if I talk Doreen into leaning on the Punter for business, suggesting he wouldn't want his wife to find out about his seedy goings on?" Danny paused for a reaction.

"Will she do that?" Chris asked.

"For free advertising she would," Jeff said. The last thing the Punter would want is his wife finding out. I've seen what she does to meat!" The crew laughed, and Danny nodded his approval.

"I'm going in to see the Punter on Friday to congratulate him on all the publicity and photographs of the presentation evening he has put in this week's edition. I'll thank him personally and on behalf of the school. I'll also emphasise, in my new role as school captain, I could be of help to him in generating more sales for *The Advertiser*. Plus, on a more personal note, because of my local status I may be able to help with any personal issues.

"When did you become school captain?' Jeff asked.

"Next term," said Danny. Sato smiled and Danny continued "Next I have to meet with Doreen and sell her the plan."

"That won't be a problem," said Sato. She's already sold three videos.

"Pass me the phone. I'll set up another meet at The Griffin."

CHAPTER 9

DANNY MEETS DOREEN: TAKE 2

DANNY CAME THROUGH THE MAIN DOOR. DOREEN WAS IN her usual spot: sensual pose, sexy attire. He sensed from the bartender's look that her drinks didn't cost much.

"Like a drink, Danny?" Doreen asked.

"Just a Coke, please."

"Coke, Roger, please, and don't put it on my account," Doreen ordered.

Danny was impressed with Doreen's confidence. The look on Roger's face suggested he might be in possession of a certain video.

"I see business is good, Doreen. Our records show you have sold three videos. Well done." Danny smiled.

"You can have the money now."

"No, let's stick to our agreement. Friday will be fine." Danny, ever the businessman, cooled the situation. "I would like to take our relationship to the next level. How can we make your business more efficient?"

Doreen thought for a moment as Roger pushed Danny's Coke across the bar. "On the house," he whispered. Doreen smiled and winked at him.

"Well, I give out lots of cards and they cost me money to print. Most get thrown away," she said.

"So, if we could find a way of reducing that cost and increasing the number of potential clients, it would be good for both of us?" Danny asked.

Doreen mused for a while, then nodded in agreement.

"My crew noticed that you slipped one of your cards into Colin Punter's pocket after the presentation night was over, when we all descended on Fred's." Danny was about to proceed when Doreen interrupted.

"That Punter was looking at me all evening, even in the school hall. He couldn't keep his eyes off me. He almost molested me at Fred's. That's why I gave him my card. There's a time and place for everything."

This was all music to Danny's ears.

"I think Punter's enthusiasm deserves free advertising, don't you?"

"That would save me money, Danny."

"I have to make a couple of phone calls. Would you excuse me for a moment?" Danny asked.

Doreen nodded. Danny knew full well that Doreen would be mulling over the prospect of free advertising.

Danny turned at the door and suggested "Maybe we can think of a way to exploit Mr Punter?" His look was enough to ignite Doreen's creative juices.

After several minutes, Danny returned and looked into Doreen's eyes.

"Most men are all talk, Danny. When you come on strong, they wilt and back off."

"But we don't want them to back off, do we? Wilt yes, but not back off. Maybe if we, or should I say you, put some pressure on Punter he might wilt rather than back off. What would be the worst that could happen to a man who was seeing a lady of the night, Doreen?"

"Easy, his wife finds out," Doreen confirmed. "Do you think I should go in there and threaten to tell his wife, Danny?"

"Not directly, Doreen, but I admire your enthusiasm. You see, I have been to see Mr Punter and offered him my help in times of need, both practically and personally. He is aware of my status both at school and in the local community. We, or should I say you, need to put him under increasing pressure to visit you for your services, ultimately threatening to tell his wife if he doesn't. You know she works in the butcher's next to Woo's?"

"Bloody fearsome, Danny, that one. Have you seen the way she cuts meat?"

Danny smiled. I must pop into the butchers for a look, he thought. "The more pressure you exert, the more likely he is to come to me for help."

"Then we get the free advertising for me — and Fred?" Doreen winked at Danny, who nodded approval.

"Here, this is Punter's number." Danny handed over a slip of paper. "Maybe you could start a conversation today?"

Doreen reached for it as Danny stood up to go. "Another lime and tonic, Roger, please, and this time put some gin in it."

Danny smiled as he headed for the door, but not before casting a sly glance and wink at Roger.

CHAPTER 10

MISSION ACCOMPLISHED

DANNY CHANGED MEETINGS FROM THURSDAY EVENING AT his place to Fred's on Friday afternoon. The crew knew why. It was revenue day.

They sat down at their usual table. Fred winked; Doreen winked at Danny, then disappeared into the storeroom and reappeared with two poached eggs on toast. She winked at Danny again as she went past.

"Why are they winking?" asked Chris.

"They want to pay," said Sato, "and neither wants the other to know. The important thing is we are about to get paid ... somehow."

Danny smiled. He liked it when the crew worked things out for themselves.

"Yesterday I had a successful meeting with Doreen. In a couple of days, I expect to get a phone call from Punter asking for help. Doreen is on board and can see the benefits of free advertising. We may have to revamp her advert, Sato, to include words such as 'wellbeing' and 'counselling'. Doreen will be able to filter out the time-wasters. Fred will also get free advertising, so that will improve his customer flow as well as giving him more potential clients. I expect our free drinks to continue," Danny concluded.

The crew loved it when Danny talked positively like this, full of authority.

At which point Doreen bent to whisper in his ear as she came past.

"Order take-away toast when you leave, Danny. I'll put the money between the slices."

The crew heard, and Jeff bit his wrist to delay an outbreak of hysterics. Chris almost bit through his bottom lip. Danny just nodded calmly. Doreen disappeared behind the counter and into the back room.

Seconds later, Fred appeared and took an order for two coffees from an elderly couple whom Danny recognised from one of his cabaret performances. He squeezed past the boys and served the coffee.

When he came back, he bent down, cast a furtive eye in the direction of the back room and whispered in Danny's ear "Order three take-away rolls, Danny. I'll put the money in the brown one," and moved off.

This was too much for Chris and Jeff to cope with and they both headed for the door.

Sato remained stone-faced but exploding inside.

Several minutes passed before Chris and Jeff returned.

"Are we all okay now?" Danny asked.

They nodded.

Their orders were duly placed, and minutes later packets of bread and toast were on the table. Sato cast a sneaky look inside and nodded at Danny.

"Okay, let's go. You deal with the money, Sato. I'm off to the butchers to see a lady."

Chris and Jeff looked puzzled. Why would anyone want to see Punter's wife?

Sato sensed Danny had an ulterior motive but, for once, couldn't see it.

Danny walked past the butchers and looked inside. Punter's wife was easily identifiable. At around 170cm and 90 kilos, sporting a white bandana and brandishing a glistening silver chopper, she was indeed a fearsome sight. If she was waving her chopper and had sausages in the other hand, you always ordered sausages, even if you didn't want them!

When a gap appeared at the counter, Danny went in. Punter's wife turned, chopper in hand, but Danny beat her to the punch.

"Danny Carver from school — just thought I would pop in and thank you for supporting our school presentation evening. I hope your advert in the school magazine has generated extra business. With your charming personality, I feel sure it will have. May I leave you my introduction card? All my contact details are on there and, who knows, when we hold the new school term barbecue, maybe we could order some of those sausages you're holding."

Mildred put down the chopper and reached for Danny's card. She was a little lost for words. Danny sensed it and moved closer.

"Are those sausages beef or pork?" he asked. "They look tasty. Could be what we're looking for."

"Beef, and yes, they are very tasty. I suppose you want to try some?"

That was quick, Danny thought.

"Well, that is exceedingly kind of you. Sorry, I didn't catch your name," he said.

"Mildred. Mildred Punter."

Danny shuffled his hand. "Punter, that rings a bell. You're not Mr Punter's wife, are you?"

"Yes, I am," Mildred smiled.

"Lovely man, Mildred, so humble and hard-working. He deserves a lady of your quality. Tell me, have you thought of wearing different coloured bandanas? You could carry it off."

Mildred was touched by Danny's compliments. He glanced at the sausages and she asked "Will eight links be enough?"

Danny nodded, and the giant chopper did the rest.

Mildred wrapped the sausages in white paper before putting them in a brown paper bag. Danny picked it up off the counter and thanked her for her time and generous contribution.

"I'm sure this is the start of a mutually beneficial arrangement." Danny backed away from the counter and winked as he left.

Mildred was a little bemused. Maybe I should buy some different coloured bandanas, she thought.

Danny went straight to Fred's.

"Here, Fred, some sausages — enjoy!"

"How much?" Fred asked.

"On the house," said Danny, as he left.

CHAPTER 11

DOREEN'S CAMPAIGN

DOREEN'S BLACK BOOK OF TRUSTED AND SAFE CLIENTS took on extra value. Not only could she trust the clients, but she now had an additional way to extract money from them. She did however realise that they could only be stung once so to speak. She needed new clients, and now she had the time to scrutinise them to ensure they met her criteria:

1. They had money.
2. They were local.
3. They were married.
4. They could be regulars.

She sat at the bar of The Griffin and Roger asked if she would like ice with her gin and tonic. Doreen gestured, and Roger slipped in the ice. She had Roger's work roster and knew exactly what time he started and, more importantly, when he finished. Hence, he was at her beck and call, and she asked him for the full rota with the names of the other bartenders.

The Griffin was a safe harbour, and Roger wasn't the only boat in port. The male receptionist also needed some attention, both physically and commercially, so the room rate was reduced ... but that was for another day.

Colin Punter reclined in his seat, his long legs stretching out underneath and beyond his desk, his arms clasped behind his head. He was contemplating his life. He ached for some excitement, but the chopper-wielding Mildred limited his horizons. In fact, there were no horizons.

His long sigh was interrupted by the ring of his mobile phone.

"Colin Punter," he said confidently.

"Hi, Colin. You are Punter the hunter. But now I'm hunting you." Doreen was firm and suggestive.

Colin froze. He pulled his legs in and sat upright. He glanced quickly round the shop, but no one was in.

"Who's this?" he whispered.

"You have my card, Colin, and I have your number," Doreen continued (thanks, Danny).

"Colin's brain was racing. Number? Card? Then the penny dropped, just as Doreen continued "Friday wasn't the time or place, Colin, even though I appreciated your attentions. I certainly didn't see it as sexual harassment."

Doreen paused to let the words sexual harassment register, then continued and shot straight from the hip.

"I appreciate Mildred may be a little concerned if she receives a complaint about her husband's behaviour, especially if it's supported by a visit from the local constabulary." Doreen paused again. "I'm sure I don't need to expand any further, Colin. "You have my number. Please give me a call in the next couple of days, and by the way can I suggest you look at The Griffin motel on the edge of town? Very discreet." Doreen rang off.

Colin pulled open his desk drawer, and there were Doreen's card and number. His heart was pumping and his brain racing with a host of options. He got up and put the 'Back in 15 minutes' card in the shop window. The last thing he needed now was a client. Suddenly the excitement he craved was here. How did she know about Mildred though? Sexual harassment — was that a threat?

He clicked on his desktop computer and googled The Griffin. There it was on the outskirts of town. Fortunately they were not advertisers, so no one would know him. What would happen if he didn't phone her back? The thought of Mildred finding out mortified him. Was he about to be blackmailed?

His mobile rang again. Colin froze, but had to pick it up. He felt terrorised. He clicked receive and waited.

"Hi, Colin, it's Danny."

Danny heard Colin's sigh of relief.

"Just thought as I'm passing I might pop in and we could discuss advertising for school next term, especially the welcome barbecue."

Fred had gone to the wholesalers. Doreen looked across the counter as Danny made the call. She marvelled at his casual manner. How could the Punter refuse?

Colin pulled himself together, then hurled himself emotionally at Danny.

"Be great to see you again, Danny. Ignore the 'Back in 15 minutes' sign — just walk straight in." Colin obviously had a problem and Danny knew it.

"See you in 10 minutes." Danny clicked off.

Danny and Doreen looked at each other for a moment, then Danny stood up to go. He raised his eyebrows and winked, and for a moment Doreen fell into his trap, then pulled herself together.

CHAPTER 12

THE STING

COLIN ALMOST TRIPPED AS HE RUSHED TO SHAKE HANDS with Danny, who was barely through the door.

"Come in, take a seat. Would you like a coffee?"

"Just a glass of water please, Colin." Trying to slow the whole process down.

"Have you had a good morning? You look a little stressed?" Danny asked.

"Just the usual morning. A few general enquiries. But I did get this strange phone call which is bothering me a little." Colin began to open up. He didn't want to ask for Danny's help outright, didn't want to appear too desperate.

Danny decided to divert and build up tension. "I bet you get a few dodgy calls from customers whose advertising didn't work?"

"No, it was nothing to do with advertising, Danny. Remember that woman with Fred at the presentation night, the one in the black skirt and high heels? It was her."

“She’s a bit naughty,” said Danny. You seemed to be getting on okay with her when we went back to Fred’s though.”

Colin froze for a moment. Who else had noticed him and Doreen at Fred’s?

Danny acted dumb. “Did she want to place an advert?”

“She never mentioned an advert, Danny. She wants me to use her services.” Colin squeezed out the words.

“I hope you declined,” Danny said.

I did at first, but then she talked about sexual harassment and even mentioned Mildred.”

“Mildred!” Danny exclaimed. “I’ve seen what she does with sausages. She’d kill you if she found you’d been harassing a lady of the night. What did Doreen want you to do?

“She wants me to book a room at The Griffin,” Colin explained.

“The one on the outskirts of town?”

“That’s the one. I didn’t know it existed.”

“That’s why she’s chosen it. Discreet and not far away. Have you booked the room yet?” Danny asked, knowing full well Colin hadn’t the nerve.

“No, I can’t risk it, Danny. My whole world would end if I were seen leaving a room at The Griffin.” More desperation in Colin’s voice.

“But your world will definitely come to an end if you don’t go, especially if she tells Mildred.” Danny tightened the screw. “How much do you charge for a quarter-page advert, Colin?” Danny focused on an outcome.

“Monthly $60, for four weekly slots.” Colin looked slightly confused.

“Did Doreen indicate her charges?” Danny asked.

“No, only that it was by the hour.”

“Does Fred advertise with you?”

“Yes, he does — alternates weekly between a quarter and an eighth, depending on how flush he is.”

“So, if Fred found out you were seeing his girlfriend and buying her services, you would certainly lose his business and perhaps a lot more as well." Danny stirred the pot. "He buys his sausages from Mildred. I saw a receipt on his counter yesterday afternoon. How long before you have to let her know about booking the room at The Griffin?"

Colin nearly choked on the words: "Two days, she said."

"Can I have a few hours to think about this Colin? You're a friend and I'd like to help you. Will you be here tomorrow morning?" Danny offered his hand.

"Yes, I can be. I usually call on some clients on Gregory Boulevard, but I can see them next week." Colin sensed a possible solution.

"Okay, leave it with me. I'll pop in tomorrow around 11." Danny was gone before Colin could shake his hand.

He wandered back to Fred's, who was back from the wholesalers and had his arms wrapped around Doreen. Customers smiled as Fred occasionally burst out with the Rod Stewart song, "If you think I'm sexy ..." Danny smiled and sat down at the table in the corner.

"Go in the back room and tidy up, Fred," said Doreen. "I'll get Danny a coffee."

Doreen put the coffee down in front of Danny and stared at him earnestly.

"He's petrified," said Danny. "I said I'd go back and see him tomorrow around 11. I think we can get free advertising for you and Fred. A quarter-page for you and an eighth for Fred. I'll get Sato to rewrite your advert so it's more professional with words like 'wellbeing' and 'counselling'. You can lure people with your other pursuits once you meet them. Maybe make The Griffin your meeting place for clients? Always have a room booked on standby. Is the receptionist a client yet?" Doreen's hesitation led Danny to assume not. "Do you think you can make him a priority?

The Punter spent a restless night. Every time he glanced at Mildred, every time he closed his eyes, he could see the silver chopper.

"Stop walking around the room, Colin, you're making me nervous," Mildred cut in. "Go make dinner. There are some sausages in the fridge."

The last thing the Punter wanted was sausages. His stomach was in knots.

CHAPTER 13

CLOSING THE DEAL

11AM, 11.05, 11.15 ... THE PUNTER WAS BECOMING MORE AND more anxious with every second. Where was he? Would he come?

Danny put down the paper he was reading at Fred's, checked his watch and set off, sure the pressure would make the deal easier to seal.

The 'Back in 15 minutes' sign was on the door, and Colin almost leapt out of his chair as Danny strode in.

"God, I thought you weren't coming," he exclaimed, breathing a sigh of relief.

"These matters can be difficult to resolve, Colin. We're dealing with a lady hardened on the street corners of life. A whimpering client is of little consequence — money counts." Danny created a picture that petrified Colin.

"I've talked to Doreen about the importance of cutting costs when running a small business, even one as risky as hers. To compel her attention and, more importantly, counter her threat to inform

Mildred and the police, can you think of any way you can help her financially, Colin?" Danny knew that if Colin could see a way out, he would feel happier with any financial arrangement.

"Well, I haven't got much cash. Everything is tied up in this business," Colin said.

"How about Mildred? Has she got any?" Danny knew the answer but needed to close all avenues.

Colin didn't even reply — he just raised his eyebrows and frowned. "All I've got is this advertising business."

"All you've got, Colin?" Danny was moving in for the kill.

'You're not suggesting I involve Doreen in the business to keep her away, are you?"

"Not exactly," Danny replied.

Colin mused over the word, exactly. Then the penny dropped.

"You mean offer her free advertising?"

"And Fred."

"Free advertising is worth a lot more than a horny afternoon with you. No disrespect meant, Colin, but Doreen is a business-woman of sorts. You would only be one client. Free advertising could produce many more. Give Doreen a quarter-page and Fred an eighth and everyone's happy. I'll get one of my crew to write Doreen's advert so there are no direct links to her nocturnal activities. Once she gets clients it's up to her to seduce and promote her special qualities." Danny eased back and stared hard.

"That's a lot of money, Danny." Colin tried to take a commercial route.

"Mildred and sexual harassment would cost a lot more, if you survived the silver chopper." Danny sealed the deal.

"Do you think she'll agree to that?"

"Let me speak to her over the weekend. I'll ring you back." Danny knew Colin would not last the weekend.

"Any chance you could see her today, Danny?"

"Okay, I'll drop into Fred's on the way home. Let's hope she's there." Danny headed for the door but turned round to suggest Colin could add 20% to the school advertising invoice as a commission.

"Consider it done, Danny," Colin agreed.

Danny thought it wise to ask the crew to meet him at Fred's. He didn't want Fred suspecting he and Doreen were an item — perish the thought.

The crew arrived a little perplexed. There was nothing on the agenda, or so they thought, although Danny was always ahead of the game.

"Doreen and Fred are to get free advertising in the local rag," Danny started.

"We will get 20% commission from *The Advertiser* for all the advertising invoices the school pays. The free advertising for Fred and Doreen should increase video sales and enhance that revenue stream. Sato, you'll need to write a suitable advert for Doreen, a quarter-page in size. Include the words we discussed: counselling, wellbeing, etc. I'll go tell Doreen and Fred now. Stay put, I'll be back."

"Hi guys, a quick word if I may. In return for your wonderful hospitality over the years, I have agreed with Colin Punter that you can have free advertising in his paper. You get a quarter-page, Doreen, and you an eighth, Fred. Doreen needs more, Fred, because of her work counselling and promoting wellbeing. Sato will write your advert over the weekend, Doreen, and subject to your approval, I will deliver it to Punter on Monday. All happy?" Danny smiled, staring at them. Doreen winked and moved off to serve a customer. Fred was doing the maths.

"That will save me over a $1,000 a year, Danny. What can I say?"

"Drinks on me, will do for now, Fred." Danny was smiling as he returned to his crew.

"Just need to ring — no, I'll text — Punter and we can conclude this project."

The Punter's mobile pinged. His reaction was quick as a rat. He snatched at the phone. "All agreed. Relax and have a pleasant weekend ... Danny," he read.

Colin slumped back in his seat. He had survived the worst 24 hours of his life.

Chapter 14

Summer Recess

THE NEXT STRATEGY MEETING WOULD BE THE LAST BEFORE the new term started. Gerald and Eileen glowed with pride as the boys arrived.

"Just to think you will be in your final year, boys. I remember when you first started — you were all dressed in short pants, so cute." Eileen was about to carry on when Danny stepped in.

"Time to plan our learning program for Year 12," ushering the crew up the stairs.

Gerald smiled. He knew the score. He also appreciated how much more relaxed life with Eileen was since the boys had got the Community Award.

"Time to suspend our program for a few weeks now. We have three revenue streams in operation. Can you call in at Fred's on Friday, Sato, and do the collections? I'll let Fred and Doreen know. If you can't, let me know and I'll step in. Have you written Doreen's advert yet?"

Sato passed it over.

"Reads well, thanks. I'll pop in and see the Punter tomorrow. By the way, how much do we have in our account, Sato?"

"$565 in my name now, Danny. We need to think about separating the money into more than one account. Schoolboys don't usually make that much money so quickly."

"We each need our own accounts, but a joint account for all of us might work. I'll look into it. I suggest we meet in three weeks' time, a week before school starts. I'll text you the date. Until then, stay under the radar and enjoy the holidays." Danny rose to his feet and the others followed.

Chris and Jeff had said nothing. Both felt in safe hands with Danny's planning and Sato's technical brilliance. Jeff reflected on how different things might have been.

Chris ran his fingers through his hair and smoothed his shirt. He knew where he was going, and so did the others.

Danny stood on the doorstep as his crew sauntered down the path. He was glowing with pride, but you would never know it from the outside. Just as you would never know the planning and scheming already fermenting inside his head.

As he closed the door he thought, maybe I'll text Janice ...

CHAPTER 15

TRANSITION TIME

DANNY SPENT THE THREE WEEKS THINKING ABOUT HOW to take advantage of his inevitable new role as school captain. His reputation had been greatly enhanced by the presentation evening, not only along the corridors of power at school, but also in the local community. Everything was in place for greater progress, but firstly he had to become school captain. However, the position was voted by the senior members of staff, and Potter was one of them.

Danny mused over a Donald Trump-style approach: brash and forthright, in every one's face. He needed support — and where could that come from? Too easy to be shot down if I go down the Trump route, he mused. No, I need to use my strengths, and those are my crew and members of the local community.

We have a database of community members, who not only loved the presentation evening but benefitted from it financially. Time for repayment. Danny moved up a gear. Everyone had to send a written submission to Bartholomew in support of Danny's appointment as school captain. Now, how do I get them to do that, he wondered? Bartholomew must welcome their interest and at the same time see a benefit for the school. Although not commercially minded, Bartholomew appreciated the value of money, and the school could always avoid unnecessary bureaucracy if private sponsorship were forthcoming.

Danny began to consider the idea of a school community supporters club.

One week from the start of Year 12 and Danny texted the crew: "My place Thursday at 8.30pm, guys. Hope you've had a good break."

CHAPTER 16

THE PLAN

DANNY LAUNCHED STRAIGHT INTO HIS IDEAS FOR PROGRESS. He had no time for small talk or what did you do during the break. "The way I see it, our primary concern should be my appointment as school captain." He looked for acknowledgement and duly got the nods and raised eyebrows.

"What are your thoughts, Danny?" asked Sato. "You know we have a database we could use."

"What do the people on our database really need?"

"Most of them run small businesses in the precinct. Other than passing trade, they don't have much income," Chris said.

"Apart from Fred and Doreen," Jeff laughed.

"True. The question is how we link the two: my appointment as school captain and benefits to them commercially?" Danny knew the answer but wanted the crew to grasp his thinking.

Sato smiled and watched Danny. Jeff thought hard and suggested "Maybe we should look at how the school can give them extra business — increased income from charging the school for their services." He looked at the others, but Danny had heard enough to take over.

"Agreed. We need to get an email out to all our database, Sato, asking for their support in my attempt to become the next school captain by contacting Mr Bartholomew personally. But before that we need to send an email out to the same group outlining my plans for their businesses. More and more school orders will be directed to their businesses and I think we need a two-pronged approach. Sato and I will compose both emails tonight. Jeff, you and Chris take the database list and begin walking around the town tomorrow, canvassing by explaining how I'll help them. It's important they agree to email or write to Bartholomew immediately. This will coincide with my email. Sato will print the list out tonight before you leave and add Bartholomew's email address." Danny glanced at Sato who nodded, and glanced at Chris and Jeff whose faces lit up as they understood their roles.

"Let's meet at Fred's tomorrow at 7am," Chris suggested to Jeff.

"Good idea. We can pick up a free coffee and bacon cob." Chris, ever the one for self-indulgence, hit the spot.

Danny smiled.

"Okay, go downstairs and talk to Eileen and Gerald while Sato and I write the two emails, and Sato prints off your list.

"Should we get your mum and dad involved?" Jeff asked.

"Wouldn't do any harm to get them to send an email saying how pleased they would be if their son became school captain," Danny agreed.

The boys left and Danny looked at Sato.

"Can the Asian girls help?" he asked.

"They all use Woo's, Danny, so that shouldn't be a problem. I'm sure Bartholomew would welcome a visit from Sanjira, who represents the Asian girls, to say how happy they would be to have you as school captain. Fortunately, you have always been considerate and respectful to them."

Danny appreciated that last comment. Out of regard for Sato, he had always set aside the commercial value of exploiting the Asians at school, rich as they were.

CHAPTER 17

STAFF DAY

BARTHOLOMEW STOOD BY HIS PRINTER, WHICH WAS almost smoking as minute after minute support for Danny Carver as school captain rolled off the machine. Much as he tried to ignore the commercial suggestions from local businesses and private benefactors, the dollars multiplied in front of his eyes. He piled the printed emails on his desk and prepared to greet the staff, many of whom were new. He was also aware that the senior staff had to meet afterwards and agree or disagree on the new school captain. There were several candidates, but only one stood out.

The usual pre-term attitude pervaded the staffroom. Bubbling excitement from the new young teachers and cynicism from the old and weary, who'd seen it all before. A few were prepared to mention the presentation evening, but that was history now and even Potter sensed there was little value in stirring an old pot. Little did he know the stack of papers under Bartholomew's arm would drive him to the point of insanity.

Bartholomew went through the traditional greetings and introduction of senior staff. Over the years he had exhausted his small repertoire of jokes and one-liners, and since the presentation evening he had been reluctant to get entangled in any casual frivolity. Miss Stanger sensed this and was on hand, just in case ...

"In conclusion, my final words to you all are from Albert Schweitzer. Several members of staff stared open-mouthed. Miss Stanger prepared to intervene but left it too late.

"Success is not the key to happiness; happiness is the key to success." Bartholomew stared forward and upward.

There was a stony, bewildered silence until one of the new-comers began to clap, prompting embarrassed support. Miss Stanger said "Could all senior staff meet in Mr Bartholomew's office in two minutes, please?"

"Lovely quote to finish with Mr Bartholomew." She sought to relax an obviously anxious headmaster.

"Thank you for sending your recommendations in for the next school captain," Bartholomew began. "There are several interesting candidates and I'm pleased to see Sanjira's name amongst them. However, there has been a groundswell of support from the local community," at which point he raised his hand waving the emails, "for Danny Carver." Potter was about to explode, but Bartholomew carried on. "It would seem a community school support group has been formed to not only promote the school in its many facets, but also help commercially with any school projects that require financial support, and Colin Punter is the chairman."

Bartholomew hesitated just long enough for Potter to ask: "Don't tell me this is all dependent on Carver becoming school captain?"

"That's very astute of you, Mr Potter." Bartholomew thought diplomacy might appease Potter.

"Well, maybe it's as a result of the best presentation evening the school has ever witnessed," Miss Stanger pointed out.

"He was behind all those shenanigans." Potter said.

"Can't be sure of that," said Miss Stanger. "He stayed in his seat throughout, then left with Janice from Year 11."

"He didn't need to leave his seat. He arranged and orchestrated it all well in advance. I'd bet my mortgage on it." Potter was edgy and beginning to tremble.

"With both the volume of support and prospect of financial support, how can we ignore the voice of the public?" asked Bartholomew.

Potter stared at the others, who looked elsewhere and nodded in support of Bartholomew.

"All agreed then. Danny Carver is the new school captain. I'll announce it in assembly tomorrow morning." Bartholomew reached for the door to usher everyone out. Potter tried to stay behind, but Miss Stanger wrapped an arm around his shoulder and pulled him away.

"Well done, Headmaster. A few tricky moments, but safely manoeuvred. Potter will calm down now the decision's been taken. Maybe we should open the cabinet and have a quick short one? Pass me the key. You get the glasses." Bartholomew felt he shouldn't, but he wanted to stay at school until everyone else had left, especially Mr Potter.

"Well, Headmaster, what a to-do. Time to relax. Have you any plans for the rest of the afternoon?" Miss Stanger crossed her legs and stared wantonly at Bartholomew, who suddenly wished Potter were still around.

CHAPTER 18

YEAR 12

DANNY SLUNG HIS SCHOOL BAG OVER HIS SHOULDER AND strutted down the road.

"Make them have it," shouted Billy the postman. "You're the man!"

Harry the bus driver slowed and sounded his horn as he went past. "Great night," he yelled through the open door.

Danny waved and acknowledged both comments. There were challenges ahead, but today he was the man. His appointment as school captain was sure to be announced in assembly. Only Potter remained a threat to his total control. The laboratory man had to be dealt with and Danny knew it. And the secret to Potter's demise might even lie in his own laboratory. Something had to happen there to bring about his downfall. Danny dwelt on the thought as he swept through the school gates. The crew slouched against the wall straightened up.

Several kids recognised Danny and moved away after a cursory glance. Danny ignored them. Only Janice, standing outside Hut 6, 40 metres away, got a half-glance. She smiled to herself and went inside.

Bartholomew stood at the lectern.

"And I'm pleased to announce that, after much care and consideration, Danny Carver will be our new school captain. Jeff and Chris, carefully placed apart, began to clap. Several younger boys who had been threatened immediately joined in. The level of applause grew, and Danny saw an opportunity to join Bartholomew on the stage, prudently taking the opposite path to the one Potter was blocking. Several members of staff froze in disbelief, but others smiled in recognition of a smart operator. Mr Trumper said to himself "That's my boy."

In an unprecedented move, Danny shook hands with a startled Bartholomew. Potter thought of moving onto the stage to remove him, but the weight of applause deterred him. Danny turned to face the audience. He raised his hands for quiet. Silence was immediate.

"This is our school, mine and yours. Look around you. Applaud the men and women who have chosen to care for and nurture our development." Danny gestured in the direction of the staff. More applause. He raised his hands again and there was silence. "This is our school, mine and yours. Come to my office with your problems, boys and girls. My door will always be open. I am and always will be for you." He turned to shake hands with a stunned Bartholomew before a slight gesture to the audience and a controlled walk off the stage. The applause reached a crescendo as Danny returned to the rear of the hall. Janice, two rows in front, managed to get a knowing look through to Danny, who felt it land, and calmly acknowledged her with a slight nod.

Potter was incandescent with rage. What did Carver mean, my door is always open? Is this is a school assembly or a presidential rally?

Several members of staff tapped Danny warmly on the shoulder as they left the hall. Better to have Danny Carver as a friend than an enemy, they thought.

Bartholomew pulled Danny aside and asked where his office would be.

"I thought I'd convert the small storeroom two doors down from your office, sir. I'm sure I can deflect much of the triviality you have to deal with. Should free up some of your time, sir. I've taken the liberty of ordering a nameplate for the door: Danny Carver, School Captain. May I submit the supplier invoice to school accounts please? It's only a moderate amount."

Bartholomew, initially wary of such a move, warmed to Danny's explanation and the benefits to his office. Removing trivial issues resonated with him. "Yes, you may submit the invoice. Give it to Miss Larkins in the office, and she'll pay it immediately. By the way who are the suppliers? Let me see."

"S. Ato, suppliers? They must be new — and local, judging by their bank details. Hand it in this morning. She does supplier payments tomorrow." Bartholomew gave the invoice back to Danny and sought refuge in his office.

Danny suppressed a smile. "Have a good day, sir."

Next stop Mr Atkins in woodwork. I need this sign up today, Danny thought.

Alan Atkins was the staff lecher. There wasn't a female member of staff he hadn't propositioned at some point. He preyed on the new and first appointees. Despite his fawn work coat, he always wore a tie and occasionally a dickie bow. The coat disappeared when he slid into the staffroom for recess. His introductory line was embroidered with an offer to help with any domestic issues a new arrival might have.

"That's very kind of you, Mr Atkins, how do I contact you?" asked a nervous young target.

"Call me Alan, please, I feel we will be seeing quite a bit of each other. Here's my card. I rarely give it out, so rest assured I will have time to solve your problem very quickly. 'Have tool bag, will travel' is my motto!"

Those in proximity cringed as Atkins spun his tacky tale.

Danny hesitated outside Atkins' workroom and glanced through the small window in the door. He was alone, fiddling with a drill bit. When Danny walked in, Atkins lifted his safety goggles and welcomed him enthusiastically. He saw a little of his own character and personality in Danny.

"What can I do for you?"

"I need my name plate on my office door, sir. Today would be ideal."

"Very busy today, Danny, maybe tomorrow." Atkins dismissed Danny's urgency.

"You know I wouldn't come here unless I could reciprocate your generosity." Danny sought Atkins attention.

Atkins glanced up, curious to hear more.

"Do you recall the presentation evening, sir? The lady with Fred from the local café on Ward street?

Atkins interrupted "Who didn't spot her — couldn't keep my eyes off her. Really sexy that one!"

"Well maybe I could help with an introduction?"

Atkins processed Danny's suggestion.

"What about Fred?" he asked.

"Not a problem. Their relationship is purely platonic, although Fred tries to convey it isn't." Danny approached the finish line.

"Go on." Atkins wanted more.

"I can arrange a meeting between you and Doreen at a safe venue close by." Danny backed away to let Atkins consider the statement, then followed up: "Do you know The Griffin motel on the edge of town? They have a small secluded car park and a comfortable bar area. You could call in for a drink. I'd arrange for Doreen to be at the bar. A favour for a friend in return for some office help."

"I'll come after recess. Where's your office?"

"Two doors down from Bartholomew's. I'll be there when you arrive. In the meantime, I'll check with Doreen and maybe have an answer for you."

Danny headed for the door, turned and winked, and Atkins acknowledged it with a nod and a smile. The new term was starting well.

Danny texted Doreen and she suggested Thursday evening at 6pm.

Atkins knocked, and entered before Danny had time to answer. Danny glanced down at his tool bag and said "Thursday, 6 pm at The Griffin. Doreen will be at the bar. I suggest you get there about five minutes past."

Atkins stared, then walked out of the room, shutting the door behind him.

Danny waited for a moment, and smiled as he heard the drill whir. Atkins was hooked.

Must check Doreen has got The Griffin receptionist on board. I don't want Atkins too much out of pocket, Danny thought.

Fifteen minutes went by, and the silence suggested Atkins had gone. Danny opened the door and there it was: Danny Carver, and underneath School Captain.

Maybe Janice could help with the interior design, he thought. He texted her "Check out my new office over lunch break?"

Danny hoped for a prompt response, but knew Janice was more likely to just turn up.

At lunch, several members of staff raised their eyebrows as they passed the school captain's office on their way to the staffroom. Some thought it could work. Some thought it was too much power in the wrong hands. Potter thought it absurd, although the words he used could not be printed. He was alone in his disagreement with the appointment.

"I'll have my day," he muttered.

Janice duly arrived and scanned the room with a knowing smile. Danny held back, waiting for a comment.

'It's a bit dark and dingy. You need some bright colours on the wall or light paintings, and maybe a corner lamp to make it cosy. You only have one chair. Where do your visitors sit? This rug is a bit tatty too."

"Can you help?"

Janice, turning to leave, said "Leave it with me."

The door shut and Danny relaxed in his chair. I like this role, he thought.

CHAPTER 19

PLANNING A STRATEGY

THEY ALL MET AS USUAL AT DANNY'S ON THURSDAY EVENING and after initial pleasantries with Eileen and Gerald, the boys trooped upstairs.

"Do you remember when we first met here, Danny, all struggling to get a good view?" asked Jeff.

"That's almost a year ago. Look where we are now," added Chris.

"Always tomorrow," Danny said. We never go back or look back. Talking of looking back, how do we open a joint account at the bank, Sato?"

"The Central Bank is in the precinct, Danny. We need to decide on a name, and each of us becomes a signatory. It's all confidential. We nominate two people who can make withdrawals. We can all make deposits. Most of our deposits will be cash, apart from the 'S. Ato' payments from the school, which will be cheques. I can pay them into my account, then transfer the money across. I'll tell the bank it was a spelling mistake. We just need to find time to visit the bank together. I can phone the manager and get the paperwork ready. We don't want to be in there too long as a group. By the way, the manager's son is in Year 7," Sato said.

Danny twitched at the news of the manager's son.

"Monday after school, meet at Fred's at 3.45 and then we can walk up to the bank separately." Everyone nodded.

Sato said he would go to the bank at lunchtime on Friday and ensure all the paperwork would be ready for Monday

"Oh, what about a name?"

"Everyone happy with 'Always Tomorrow'?" Danny asked.

Chris and Jeff smiled, and Sato wrote it down.

"What's the manager's son called, Sato?" Danny asked.

"Timothy Wilson."

"Can you two check him out?" Danny looked at Chris and Jeff who nodded, aware Danny would want a detailed social and financial report.

"Great. Let's meet at Fred's Friday afternoon and collect the fortnightly revenues. Remember, stay cool at school, and don't draw attention to yourselves. By the way, Doreen's meeting Atkins tonight at The Griffin. Watch this space!"

Even Sato joined in the laughter.

CHAPTER 20

DOREEN MEETS ALAN ATKINS

ALAN ATKINS' CAR SLID INTO THE GRIFFIN CAR PARK. HE backed in close to the entrance next to a white van with 'You mow it, we'll move it' painted on the sides.

Alan laughed — everyone's got to make a living, he thought. He had one last look in the rear-view mirror, straightened a thinning quiff, took a quick breath and got out of the car.

As he went through the main door, the receptionist said "Good evening, Mr Atkins, Doreen is at the bar in the cocktail lounge, just through there" with a sleazy smile. Atkins slowed down, but then composed himself just as James Bond would have done. Unconcerned, he thanked the receptionist and headed for the cocktail lounge.

Doreen was at the far end of the bar. Black, her colour of choice, stockings not tights, high heels, tight fitting top, hair pulled back — a cynic might say mutton dressed as lamb.

"Ah, Mr Atkins, I presume. Come and take a seat." Doreen exuded professional calm, remembering at the last minute to cross her legs slowly and breathe out.

Atkins tried to match Doreen's class. "Can I perhaps share some champagne with you, maybe a bottle of your choice?"

Doreen looked at Roger the bartender. "Take Mr Atkins' credit card and hold it behind the bar, please, then open a bottle of bubbly — not the cheap stuff — and two glasses please, Roger."

Atkins' eyes widened a little as he reached for his wallet. Roger took his credit card and a bottle of good champagne, and they all giggled as the cork ricocheted off the ceiling. Roger poured the champagne slowly so not a drop spilled and handed a glass to Doreen. She took a sip while Roger held the bottle, waiting for confirmation. Doreen held the moment, then shook herself sexily and said "Just what we need, Alan. Pour on, Roger." She stared at Alan, now in a drooling sexual trance. He had the same look as the receptionist, a look all Doreen's admirers seemed to adopt.

'Pull your stool a little closer, Alan. Time to relax. No need to rush, unless there's somewhere you'd rather be," she teased.

Alan cleared his throat and, in a strong voice, confirmed his manliness, "Not at all, my time is your time, Doreen. Let's enjoy." At that he raised his glass. Doreen, with a clink of glass, crossed her legs and noticed Alan's eyes head south. I might even enjoy tonight, she thought.

It was 3am when Alan woke up. He was alone, although the sheet and blanket formation suggested someone else had been there. Without raising his head from the pillow, he stared at the clock radio on the bedside table. The room was unfamiliar. He raised his head, his misty eyes began to focus. I can remember being at the bar with Doreen, but the rest is a mystery. How did I get here, he wondered? No point going home now. May as well hang on for breakfast. He gulped down the contents of a water bottle strategically placed at his bedside, and then slumped back on the pillow. As he put the bottle back, he saw a white envelope on the edge of the table and propped himself back up, flicked the blankets off and moved shakily towards it. The envelope had his name in the top corner and he opened it tentatively, almost fearing the contents.

"Hi Alan, thank you for a memorable evening. I'm sorry I had to leave early. Leslie at reception has your credit card. Just collect and leave. Breakfast is included. Enjoy, and I hope to hear from you soon, Doreen."

Alan felt both relieved and sceptical. How much had the evening cost, he wondered? Too late to ask now. He slumped back on the bed and dozed off.

At 7am, showered and dressed, Alan set off for breakfast, assuming he would be the first down.

"Hi, Mr Atkins, sleep well?" Leslie asked with a smile on his face.

Alan heard the voice but couldn't see Leslie until he peered round his desktop computer.

"I have your credit card," he whispered. "Would you like a printed receipt?"

Alan hesitated, and Leslie continued "I'll put it in an envelope for you. Here you are. Enjoy your breakfast." He handed the envelope to Alan who was still functioning in slow motion, both physically and mentally. Did Leslie just wink at me, he wondered?

The breakfast room was a buffet apart from the tea or coffee, which a waitress took orders for. This suited Alan who was still struggling to put sentences together.

When the coffee arrived, a single sip gave Alan the confidence to open the envelope. He was heartened to read "Thank you for making use of our promotional offer. But his heart started to pound as he read 'Total $615' at the bottom of the receipt.

Details were limited. A personal service heading, which fortunately could cover a myriad of things, included film hire, etc.

As a single man, Alan felt no guilt, but the amount shocked him, especially as he couldn't remember most of what had happened. Surely, he hadn't been drugged?

The receipt said D Services with no mention of The Griffin.

Doreen's expertise and man management now included the receptionist and bar staff. Key support staff had to be kept on side so, once she received the $615, two small sums went to Roger and Leslie. Leslie was saving for a facelift; Roger had a drink problem. Plus, there was Danny's commission.

Alan finished a basic fried breakfast and decided to put the whole event down to an expensive experience.

Danny arrived at Fred's first on Friday after school for an update from Doreen. Fortunately, Fred was at the wholesaler, so he sat down at his usual corner table. This time Doreen had put the money in an envelope — definitely a step up from a bread roll.

"Thank you," Danny said. I'm assuming everything went well?"

"Perfectly, he was a real tiger."

"Will the tiger be feeding again?"

"I'll ring him next week."

The others arrived on time, and Danny handed the envelope over to Sato.

"I can bank this on Monday, Danny, when we go to the bank," he said.

"I'd prefer you do it now. You'll be back before Doreen serves the drinks. If Fred comes in, we can bank his on Monday."

Sato nodded and left. The point was not lost on Chris and Jeff. Carrying money around can be risky. Discretion and integrity were the foundation of Always Tomorrow.

When Sato got back, Danny told them the Atkins and Doreen evening had gone well, and that prospects looked good for an ongoing relationship.

"Now we need to consider expanding our operation. Thoughts please?" he asked, as Fred walked through the door.

"Do we need more sub-agents?" asked Chris.

"Only if we know a lot about them," Jeff replied.

Sato stressed that agents were a no-cost revenue stream with once-only clients, so there was a minimal risk of exposure. Danny agreed and suggested considering what was on the doorstep.

"You mean the kids at school, Danny?" Chris asked.

"And the staff?" Jeff added.

Danny was impressed by their immediate contributions. "Correct. How can we make use of both groups?"

"Well, we know the bank manager's son is in Year 7," said Sato.

"How can we exploit that situation?" asked Danny.

"All we can hope for is a better savings rate on our group deposit," Sato replied.

"He won't give us a better rate just because his kid goes to our school," Jeff said.

"We need something on him," Chris suggested.

"Okay, let's shelve that suggestion for now. I'll investigate the bank manager's background. Maybe you and I can sit down and hack some personal information about him, Sato? There may be something in his past or current behaviour that we could exploit?" Danny said. "Chris, can you and Jeff get some background on his son, Timothy Wilson? In fact, can you investigate all the boys in Year 7 and see if there's anyone else of interest? No rush, we're only looking for the odd one or two candidates."

"Let's meet at the bank at 4pm on Monday," Sato said.

"We don't want to meet outside. Let's enter separately and meet inside," Danny said. "No point in drawing attention to ourselves."

Fred meandered across the café floor, careful not to bump into any tables and taking time to say hello to customers.

"I've put some rolls in a bag for you, Danny. They're in the cooler. Just take a Coke and the bag. Know what I mean?" Fred winked, and the entire crew winked back, then glanced at the cooler.

"Go get it, Sato, before MI5 come in." Danny smiled and got up to go. The others stood up too, smiling. Sato took out the bag and waved his Coke can at Fred, who confirmed "On the house, boys."

CHAPTER 21

THE BANK MANAGER

DANNY HAD SUGGESTED THEY SHOULD STILL MEET AGAINST the playground wall in the mornings to avoid drawing attention to themselves in his new office.

"All set for later. Meet at the bank at 4pm. I'll be inside. Better if we arrive one at a time. No need for anyone to see us going in as a group. I'm free for the first period so I'll be in my office." He was still getting used to saying that, but loved the ease with which it flowed, and so did the others, who all left with a smile until Chris and Jeff noticed a scuffle developing between two Year 8 boys, one of whom was particularly loud-mouthed.

"Who's the fat kid?" Jeff asked.

"Johnny Archer," said Chris. "He's turning into a bit of a bully."

"Maybe we should have a chat with him," Jeff suggested.

"Good idea, I'll get Sato to hack his timetable."

Danny unlocked the door marked School Captain and took in the sight. There was a pot plant in the corner, waist high, that resembled a triffid with bottle-green leaves and long stalks. He quite liked the pot too, a dusky shade of orange. A wickerwork chair with a beige cushion was positioned opposite but slightly to the side of the desk. Too confronting to have guests sit on the other side of the desk, especially the headmaster. On the desk there was a photograph of the presentation evening with Danny and his victorious crew receiving their award on stage, and next to that a slender glass vase contained a single red rose.

Leave it with me, Janice had said. Wow this was fantastic, he thought. Before he could close the door, Mr Bartholomew leant out of his room and suggested a meeting in 10 minutes. "I'll come to you," he said, and winked at Danny. Danny smiled and nodded.

When there was a tap on the door, Danny responded with an quiet "come in" and got up to shake Bartholomew's hand.

"I see you've settled in, Danny. I like the pot plant — bit like a triffid."

"My thoughts exactly, sir." Danny thought it wise to address Bartholomew respectfully.

"As you'll be aware, your appointment was not universally accepted by senior members of staff. However, I'm quite sure that between us we can placate them." Bartholomew held the stare.

"I'm sure we can, sir. "What's the number one problem we need to deal with, sir?"

"Prefects, Danny. I'm not sure they understand their role, and some may be running some mild sort of extortion racket, taking sweets, etc., from younger pupils. My time is precious, and I don't want to be involved in sorting these problems out. Do you see what I mean?"

"Of course, I do, sir. Rest assured they will be taken care of with the minimum of fuss. Do you have any names?"

Bartholomew took a slip of paper out of his pocket and gave it to Danny. He let the names register, and then with an "Enjoy your day" left the room.

Danny looked at the names and began to text Jeff and Chris: "I want as much info as you can get on these three boys in Year 10 please, by Friday afternoon at Fred's."

Another knock on the door, this time more hurried and deliberate. Danny barely had time to say "come in" before Alan Atkins appeared.

"Hello, Tiger," said Danny, which immediately took the wind out of Alan's sails.

"What do you mean Tiger? he asked.

'I bumped into Doreen at Fred's. She said, she had a charming and tigerish night with you at The Griffin."

Tigerish and charming — the words altered Alan's whole demeanour.

Danny leaped in with further praise and support. "Don't worry, sir, it will go no further. She did say next time she'd buy the champagne. Wow, you're a class act, sir. Champagne. I can certainly learn from you. When's pay-day? You might get a discount if you book another appointment in advance."

Atkins began to relax and wallow in the praise.

Danny pushed, "So when is pay-day, sir?"

"Two weeks on Thursday," Alan said, just as the school bell rang for the next lesson.

"Got to go, speak later."

"Have a good day, sir. Oh, and remember to book early." Danny smiled and fell back into his chair.

The day had already provided him with several issues to resolve as well as some commercial opportunities.

CHAPTER 22

THE BANK

DANNY APPROACHED THE RECEPTION DESK IN THE BANK and spoke softly "I'm waiting for some colleagues as we have a meeting with Mr Wilson at 4pm. Do you mind if I wait inside?" A pert young thing glanced at her desk diary and said "Not a problem, sir. There are some leaflets on borrowing over there. You may find them interesting." She smiled.

"I'm sure I shall," Danny agreed.

She watched him cross the room slyly. Nice shape, she thought.

Danny wasn't sure which was Wilson's office, but suspected it might be the room on the far side, so he picked up a lending leaflet and wandered over, sharing a slight smile with the receptionist, and found the Bank Manager sign on the door.

As if by fate, the door opened and a bespectacled man, slightly balding and with a protruding shirt front suggesting a weakness for food or drink, came out. He exuded a certain old school confidence — a trained, relaxed confidence, developed over a career at the bank.

Danny suspected Wilson was camouflaging a weakness, and therein lay his vulnerability.

He watched as Wilson moved along and behind the row of tellers, all young women. Occasionally he stopped to comment. With Teller Number 3 however there was closer contact and a whisper. Wilson's hand lay gently on the girl's shoulder, and his comments raised a guarded smile and reddened face. As he moved away, he tapped the girl lightly on her bottom. She smiled and glanced sideways to see if anyone else had noticed.

Danny had noticed, and decided he needed the girl's name. The receptionist was engaged with an elderly couple, so Danny walked across to her.

"Good morning, the receptionist is busy. May I have a bank business card, please?" He smiled.

"Certainly, sir, please take mine."

Danny smiled and took the card. Too easy, he thought.

One by one the crew arrived, and Mr Wilson came out to invite them into his office. After a very professional meeting, he stood up and shook hands with each of the boys, thanking them for opening the 'Always Tomorrow' account. As they filed out, Danny turned to ask one final question. "What's the interest rate on our savings account, Mr Wilson?"

Wilson was taken aback. "2.5%," he said.

"Hmm, Danny mused. "I'm sure we can improve on that." He gave a humourless smile and tapped his bottom as he left.

Wilson stood there confused. Strange behaviour, he thought. Who is Danny Carver? Must find out.

The boys walked down to Fred's to discuss the meeting and look at the week ahead.

Sato asked the first question. "Do you think you can improve on the interest rate, Danny?"

"I saw Wilson getting over-affectionate with one of the bank tellers. This one." Danny handed over Helen Walker's business card.

"Can you fish around for some information on her, Sato? If we can lean on her and Wilson's son that should be enough to raise the rate. Banks don't tolerate sexual harassment."

Now I suggest we step back and settle in at school with a minimum of fuss. Bartholomew is fine with me and wants me to investigate the behaviour of these three prefects, whom he thinks may be running a small extortion racket, exploiting younger kids. We either need to stop it or control it ourselves. Take this and find out what's going on, you two." Danny handed the names to Chris and Jeff.

They were leaving when Fred waddled over.

"The egg man's coming in five minutes, Danny," he said, winking feverishly.

The crew all winked back and stood up.

"See you Friday, Fred, and can we have fresh bread rolls?" Danny suggested.

CHAPTER 23

SETTLING IN

DANNY HAD MET MOST OF THE STAFF IN HIS NEW ROLE AS school captain. He invited the new first year teachers in for a chat "next time you pass by." Some of them looked so young they could have been in Year 12, and some of them were attractive and might require further attention, but not just yet. Besides, Janice was still in the process of decorating his office.

He sent an official invitation to Mr Trumper to join him for coffee Friday at lunchtime. Trumper smiled and accepted, knowing there had to be a hidden agenda, but that Danny was and would remain a cheeky challenge. He secretly wished he were 40 years younger and a member of Danny's crew. The memory of the presentation evening would stay in Trumper's mind forever, and had left a warm glow, especially on those late quiet nights when he sat by the fire with a soothing brandy.

There was a loud knock on the school captain's door and Alan Potter stormed in. The scene was electric, and it could have been two heavyweight boxers meeting for the ref's final comments before war broke out.

Potter never blinked "I don't know how you did it, Carver, but I'll find out before I retire and bring you down."

Danny sensed Potter trembling slightly and responded in kind "You'll be dead before it happens."

The tense situation came to a head when Bartholomew went past and recognised Potter's voice, although he could not hear what he said. He invited him into his office and further angered him by saying "Good to see you popped in to chat with our new school captain. I know you were a sceptic when he was appointed, but I think we can use him to our advantage." He waited for a response, but only got a blank expression.

Danny put Potter's name at the top of his to-get list. He knew the two of them would not survive the year unscathed, and he needed a master plan to get Potter out of the school.

The next scheduled meeting was at Danny's on Thursday evening. They were all working hard, but Danny sent a text message to Sato suggesting that whenever they took an exam the results should be hacked and grades raised half a point to ensure respectability. Members of staff would miss the small adjustment, swamped as they were in volumes of marking.

Sato's immediate response was "Agreed, but if the results are poor, I'll raise them by a full grade."

Danny texted "Yes."

And so the days passed. The boys moved from lesson to lesson, and often went their separate ways knowing that on Thursday they would have to provide Danny with the information he wanted. Pre-school and lunch breaks were spent watching what was going on, who was talking to whom, were any groups meeting in the same places, and what the three prefects were doing.

CHAPTER 24

THE SCHOOL GOVERNORS

BARTHOLOMEW HAD BRIEFLY MENTIONED TO DANNY THAT at some point he would have to meet the school governors. A note signed 'Headmaster' was slipped under the new school captain's door with the date. Danny responded with a polite handwritten acceptance. He knew it would be a nauseating handshaking meeting with polite laughter and no skirmishes. Still, he had to go through with it, and perhaps an opportunity for further commercial enhancement would present itself.

The governors were:

Sam Johnson: self-made businessman, a car dealer who had sold most of the staff their cars. He was a former pupil, occasionally brash and outspoken, and sponsored several school sporting events. Whatever the event, Sam Johnson would have a car or cars on show. He never missed an opportunity, and his blonde model partner, several years younger, was usually in attendance. Sam was cringe-worthy — more rotund than athletic with a receding hairline, and tolerated because of his donations, not his catchphrase "You'd look good in a sports car."

Joan Webster: self-appointed secretary, very prim and proper, who took the minutes. Joan had a thing for Mr Bartholomew and owned the local florist, 'The Power of the Flower'. She despised Sam Johnson. Never married and in her early 50s, she wore glasses and trousers, not skirts, and would bring a vase of flowers to every meeting and plonk it down in the middle of the table.

Gerald Trapper: in his early 70s and on the local council. Very status conscious and known as 'Too late Trapper' as he never arrived on time. With Trapper the penny dropped eventually, but always minutes after the rest. He wore a tweed jacket and sleeveless sweater. Occasionally he would fall asleep in meetings. He had asked Joan Webster out for dinner on several occasions, but without success.

Headmaster Bartholomew and Deputy Headmistress Stanger represented the school, Miss Stanger conscripted to ensure Bartholomew did not commit to any foolish requests.

The school captain was always asked to represent the main body of the school. Whatever he said was politely listened to, but seldom acted on. The new incumbent, Danny Carver, was warmly welcomed and replied politely when Johnson asked "What colour car would you like?"

"The one you're selling, Mr Johnson, I'm sure." Danny had them chuckling.

Bartholomew spoke highly of Danny, and then asked the committee to be patient for a few minutes as a new member had been held up in traffic but was in the car park. Joan Webster poured out glasses of water, and Sam Johnson added a drop of liquid from his hip flask to two of them.

The door opened and in walked an apologetic Carol Whittleston. The committee smiled and began to take their seats as Danny moved into Carol's view. Their eyes met, and an electric spark fizzed –

briefly, but long enough to send out a thousand messages. Danny seized the moment.

"Doesn't seem five minutes since we last saw each other at the careers meeting, Miss Whittleston. I really valued your advice and maybe we could talk briefly before we leave tonight?" That elicited a knowing look from Miss Stanger as Carol replied "I'm sure we can, Danny." Sam Johnson's partner nudged him as he was about to make a crass comment.

Joan Webster handed out the agenda, and Danny and Carol fought to avoid eye contact.

The meeting followed the usual pattern. Sam Johnson volunteered sponsorship money. Joan Webster offered to decorate events with flowers, and for once Gerald Trapper stayed awake.

Mr Bartholomew brought the meeting to a close and Danny edged to the side of the room. Miss Whittleston had no option but to go and speak to him. Secretly she wished she had left the tight-fitting black skirt and high heels at home. Danny wished he had put on his white T-shirt and denims.

"Don't be long, you two, the pub shuts in 30 minutes," Sam shouted as his partner pushed him through the door.

Danny broke the ice "Let's meet soon, otherwise the next electric shock may be even more obvious."

Carol saw a way out and suggested, a little too loudly, meeting the following Thursday when she would be in school.

Danny responded "Shall we say my office at 12.30? Two doors down from Mr Bartholomew." He shook Miss Whittleston's hand politely and left.

Carol was momentarily stranded in no man's land, but quickly thought of a reason to talk to Joan Webster about flowers.

The meeting ended at 10pm.

CHAPTER 25

FORWARD PLANNING

DANNY WANTED TO KEEP CONTROL OF EVERYTHING THAT was happening, both live and potential, so he had Sato draw up a list of discussion topics to be kept hidden on his laptop.

Tonight's topics for discussion:

- Johnny Archer in Year 8
- Three prefects
- Betting slip
- Chemist's son
- Mr Wilson the bank manager
- Potter
- Doreen to contact Wilson
- School Sports Day
- Girls.

"Okay, let's start with Johnny Archer in Year 8. What do we know about him?" Danny looked at Jeff and Chris.

"He's been a bully since primary school, Danny. He probably has a complex about being fat and takes his frustration out on younger, vulnerable kids. There's no extortion, he just pushes them around. Even so, many are afraid of him and some parents have been to see Bartholomew," Chris reported.

"What do you suggest?" asked Danny.

Jeff said "Remember the lad in Year 11, Danny, the one you saved from expulsion, Jordan Smith? He owes you. Why not get him to frighten Johnny and make him write a letter of apology to Bartholomew?"

"Great idea. Get a message to Jordan, will you? I'd like to see him."

"Now what about the three prefects? What are they doing?" Danny was pushing hard on this one as Bartholomew needed a solution quickly.

Chris took the lead. "Quite simply, they are stealing food and in some cases money from Year 7 boys — offering a protection service in return for food and money."

Sato stepped in with a possible solution: "Why don't I send them a threatening email, saying each of them will be exposed and reported to the Board of Governors for expulsion if they continue to extort money and food from Year 7 boys? If that fails, we send Jordan in to scare each one individually."

"Can you do that without their knowing who sent the email?" Danny asked.

"Not a problem," Sato confirmed. "We will also be able to receive a reply from each of them."

"I want to cut corners on this one," Danny said. "Can you get the email out tonight, Sato?"

"I'll do it now." Sato sensed the urgency and the need to score points with Bartholomew.

"Let's take a break for 10 minutes. Mum's made a cake. I'll bring some up while you send out the emails."

Danny left the room and spent some time with his mum while

the boys completed their tasks. He complimented her on the cake, saying how spongy it was as he sliced it into eight portions — and ate one himself before heading back upstairs.

The remaining seven pieces did not last long. Nobody focuses better than a teenage boy devouring food. The room went silent, and not a crumb was left.

Then the silence was broken by the sound of an email on Sato's laptop. Then another.

"What do they say?" Danny asked.

"I can't say the words, Danny, they're too rude. Here, have a look." Sato handed the laptop to Danny, who frowned.

"Any reply from Jordan?"

"Yes, he says he has a free period in the morning and will come to your office, Danny." Chris got a mocking smile from Danny, who suggested one more issue before calling it a night.

"I found this betting slip on the floor in the languages room, Danny."

"How much is it for?" Danny asked

"$150," Chris replied, "made out to John Foster, the French teacher."

"Interesting. See if he goes out at lunchtime tomorrow. He's the one with the little yellow Renault," Danny said.

He saw the boys out and gave the cake plate back to Eileen. And went upstairs to make one last phone call.

CHAPTER 26

ACTION STATIONS

DANNY STROLLED BACK TO SCHOOL, ACKNOWLEDGING several people en route. Harry the bus driver tooted his horn and he waved back. Just before he turned into the school driveway there was cheering and raucous laughter, and a large group of pupils were standing by the school gates. There, hanging upside-down from the top of the gate, was Johnny Archer, his face red with embarrassment, his body writhing as he tried unsuccessfully to unhook himself. The more he tried the greater the cheering. Danny calmed the mob.

"Well, what have we here?" Danny investigated Archer's upturned face.

"I think your bullying days are over, Johnny. What do you say? We'd all like an apology, or do we leave you here for a while longer?" Danny spun Johnny around and the mob laughed.

A tearful Johnny uttered a quiet apology, and Danny indicated to Chris and Jeff to get him down. Just in the nick of time as Miss

Stanger had begun to march towards them across the yard.

"No issues, Miss. Just some light-hearted fun. It's all over now." Danny looked squarely at Johnny who nodded in agreement, his face a lesser shade of red.

Danny escorted Miss Stanger to one side and confirmed that a little bullying had been going on, but it was over now and wouldn't happen again. They walked side by side across the yard towards the staff precinct, and to a casual observer Danny seemed to be a member of staff.

Back in his office, Danny sat down and glanced around. Janice certainly had a flair for décor.

Just then, there was a knock on the door. "Come in," he replied.

In walked Jordan Smith, a somewhat bedraggled youth. He didn't have any tattoos, just handwritten names and numbers in black pen on his wrist. His hair needed combing and he should probably have started shaving.

"Danny," he muttered.

"Good idea this morning, suspending Archer from the school gate. Worked a treat." Danny started with a compliment, but Jordan remained impassive.

Danny slid an envelope across the table and Jordan put it in his pocket without saying a word.

"I have another job I'd like you to help with." Danny stared at Jordan and held the moment.

Jordan looked back with an expression that suggested he knew what was in the envelope and was interested.

"Mr Bartholomew is having trouble with these three prefects." Danny slid a piece of paper across the desk. They are extorting money from Year 7 boys and several parents have complained to him.

"Jordan, you and I don't need Bartholomew on our backs. I'd like to think you see some potential in a relationship. Do you think you could put an end to this petty prefect racket, and quickly?"

Jordan shuffled his feet and made for the door. He turned and, with a poker face, said "Be done by tomorrow. I'll come back Friday morning."

"I'll look forward to seeing you then," Danny replied, and relaxed back into his chair knowing he now had the necessary muscle for any dirty work.

Now what to do about the gambling French teacher, Mr Foster?

The day passed without incident. Miss Stanger gave Bartholomew an overview of the Archer episode, and Bartholomew felt it wise not to pursue the matter further although he might have a quiet word of thanks to Danny. However, he kept this to himself. No need for Stanger to know how close he was to Carver.

Chris and Jeff watched Foster's yellow Renault leave the yard at lunchtime and made a note of the time he went out and came back — approximately 20 minutes. Just enough time to consider the form and place some bets.

"Not really what we expect our teachers to be doing at lunchtime," Chris suggested.

Chapter 27

Bartholomew's Delight

BARTHOLOMEW TAPPED ON THE SCHOOL CAPTAIN'S DOOR. Danny guessed it was the headmaster and stood up to welcome him.

"Just thought I'd say a quick thank you for dealing with the Archer incident yesterday morning, Danny. I've had a note from Johnny apologising for his behaviour. I feel we can close the door on that. Any news about the rogue prefects? I'm introducing a new group of prefects to the school in assembly this morning. I'd hate to think they were a wing of the Mafia." Bartholomew gave a wry smile.

"The matter should be resolved today, Headmaster, hopefully before assembly." Danny said.

"Good, let's hope so." Bartholomew turned to leave but hesitated long enough to say "I noticed you and Miss Whittleston talking earnestly at the governors' meeting. Is everything okay?"

"Not a problem, sir, just sharing a passion for the future." Danny thought a confusing answer might deter any further questions.

Bartholomew raised his eyebrows and left the room. Danny

had survived a tense moment and now realised that behind Bartholomew's scatterbrain appearance lurked a streetwise man.

Alternate rows of boys and girls filed into the assembly hall in military manner. As school captain Danny had a seat on the stage facing the school and Janice at the end of the first row of teachers. Danny tried to avoid her stare, but Janice had got under his skin and they both knew it.

"And now I would like to invite our new group of prefects for the coming year on stage." Bartholomew began to read out their names, and each one stood up and made his or her way towards the stage, 12 in all.

Danny sat back as they filed by. He nodded to each as they came up the stairs, especially numbers 3, 5 and 6. 3 was sporting a black eye, 5 a large lump on the side of his nose and 6 needed assistance because of a leg injury. Bartholomew raised a worried eyebrow but decided not to comment. Chris, Jeff and Sato nudged each other knowingly.

Potter searched for an answer to the injured trio but could not find a link.

Janice could tell by the expression, or lack of expression, on Danny's face that something had happened, but despite her intense stare could not get him to look her way.

Bartholomew introduced each prefect by name and polite applause followed.

When the new prefects left the stage, Danny assisted the one with the leg problem, wrapping a supportive arm around his shoulder. Potter winced; this was too good to be true, he thought.

Once the staff had left, Danny marched down the aisle, winking at Janice as he passed her. She saw that as an invitation.

Bartholomew popped his head around Danny's door to thank him for his help with the assembly and was about to mention the injured trio, but then had second thoughts. Danny held his stare and thanked him. Janice arrived to relieve any tension, greeted

Bartholomew, and closed the door behind her. The headmaster knew that, despite Danny's bravado and cunning, Janice was a restraining force, and smiled as he went back to his office.

"What do you know about those injured prefects?" Janice asked.

"Almost embarrassing wasn't it, watching them come up to the stage or attempt to?" Danny deflected.

"Just as well. Me and the girls don't like them. Always staring at us. The one with the limp is a real lecher." Janice sided with Danny, and the tension between them eased.

He sensed an opportunity for a closer connection with the senior girls through Janice, knowing he had to find a commercial angle. In situations like this experience had taught him not to force an issue but to let it evolve, and usually it did. The seed had been sewn; germination was sure to follow. After all, there were almost 150 girls in the senior school worth exploiting, and with Sato's Asian connection this was too rich a market to be ignored.

Friday arrived and Jordan Smith poked his head round the door. Danny welcomed him and immediately slid an envelope across the desktop.

"Thanks, good work. I'll be in touch." He nodded at Jordan, who stuffed the envelope into his pocket and left.

Danny was searching for a way to make greater use of Jordan's services. Jordan had limited skills, but they were effective. Maybe some sort of protective services for the Year 11 and 12 girls? Maybe he should chat to Sanjira and Janice?

CHAPTER 28

THE VULNERABLE

DANNY HAD BEEN A SECRET FAN OF OLD MOVIES FOR A LONG time, especially the ones that involved some form of scam. *The Sting* was one of his favourites, featuring Paul Newman, Robert Redford and Robert Shaw, where a couple of professional grifters con a mob boss. The film was both complicated and daring, and Danny knew that the scope of a scam like that at school was limited, however Sports Day might afford an opportunity to raise some light-hearted revenue.

He looked down at the betting slip bearing Mr Foster's name. $150 is not a small amount, Danny thought. Chris and Jeff had noted he'd gone out at three lunchtimes that week.

So, he's obviously an enthusiast. I'll pick up the morning paper tomorrow and check the daily race meetings. Then I'll invite Mr Foster round for a private chat, Danny decided, putting the betting slip away in the desk drawer before he left for an English lesson, and stopping off at Mr Foster's class on the way.

Mr Foster was sitting at his desk fingering another losing betting slip. A man of certain moral values, this was his only real vice, however it was beginning to take a hold and make inroads into his monthly salary.

Danny poked his head round the door and apologised for interrupting the lesson. "Someone has handed in a note of yours, Mr Foster. I have it in my office. Please pop round and collect it. I'll be in at lunchtime." He didn't wait for a response. Foster was about to ask what the note might be, but couldn't get the words out quickly enough.

Relaxing in his office, Danny opened the morning paper at the horse racing pages and spread them out over the desk. He ringed two horses in red pen, Flaming Cheek in the 1.30 and Secret Vice in the 3.30, tipped by Phil the drunk in Fred's café.

Mr Foster looked furtively down the corridor, then knocked quietly on Danny's door.

"Come in, sir," said Danny.

Foster came in and Danny stared intently at the horse racing. "Yes, they're the two for me," he said, "Flaming Cheek and Secret Vice."

"Sorry, Mr Foster, my apologies for not welcoming you in. It's just that I got these two tips from a gambler in Fred's café and was hoping to put a bet on. I love horse racing. Oh, by the way, this betting slip was handed in to me by a close friend, and your name is on it. I thought it wise not to let Bartholomew get his hands on it. My family have always loved horse racing, sir. Bet sensibly, and it's great fun. Occasionally you can get a good win. These two aren't favourites, but they are well fancied. Here, have a look, what do you think?" Danny turned the paper round and Foster leaned forward to study the form.

"Both were placed last time out so they could be on the improve. They have good jockeys on board and Secret Vice is from a top stable. Might be worth two single bets and a double," Foster suggested.

"Sensible bet, sir. Are you going out this lunchtime? Maybe you could put $15 on for me?" Danny slid the money across the desk. Foster picked it up without hesitating and turned to leave.

"Don't lose the betting slip!" Danny said as Foster closed the door. The perfect scenario would be for both to win, but a single win would suffice for now.

Time to give some thought to Sports Day. Maybe Foster could run a book on some of the races. The thought of staff betting on schoolboys running races on Sports Day amused Danny. He would need a cut of course, but now the seed had been sewn he would come up with a scheme. Maybe Chris and Jeff could get data on the sporting prowess of the best athletes and then set the odds? I just need Foster to have a few wins. He's the conduit to the staff. Danny's office could be the bookmaker. Staff could pop in and place bets. Sato could hold all the information on his laptop. Always Tomorrow would keep all losing bets and take a small management fee out of any winnings. In the event of a potential major loss, Jordan Smith could threaten the winner.

Danny sat back in his chair, content with a new model for success.

CHAPTER 29

UPDATE MEETING

THIS THURSDAY AT DANNY'S WAS TO BE THE LAST MEETING. His organisation was moving along nicely and productively and he was confident of his crew delivering whatever he asked. Fred's remained the favoured meeting place — earthy and close to the public was how Danny liked it. After all, Danny relied on the community for income and didn't want to distance himself.

Sato opened the meeting, outside the agenda.

"Sanjira told me Mr Foster was jumping up and down during their French lesson. He answered a text on his phone and went crazy." Sato looked at Danny puzzled.

"Maybe he had a good win on the horses," Danny suggested.

Chris and Jeff smiled, and Danny handed over some money to Sato. "For the bank," he said.

"Talking of money, maybe it's time to let Doreen loose on Mr Wilson, our lecherous bank manager." "Do we have anything on his son Timothy?"

"Nothing, Danny, he's Mr Perfect and even tipped to become a school prefect and possibly school captain."

"Wow, that's good," Danny thought.

A sceptical Sato wondered what they could get out of intimidating Mr Wilson. Sure, he might improve the interest rate by a percentage point, plus a cut from Doreen's involvement and maybe increased sponsorship of a school event. He put forward a case for including Wilson in their exploits.

"The last thing Wilson would want is to embarrass his son and harm his chances of achieving either status or academic prowess through his own misdemeanours becoming public. I'll chat with Doreen. I'm sure she'd like a customer in such high local esteem," Danny said. "I had a confrontation with Potter yesterday. He stormed into my office. He suspects something. Only Bartholomew prevented the meeting getting out of order. We need to find a way to get rid of him. The school calendar shows a visit by the governors in two months' time. That would be an ideal time to attack Potter. He always takes such pride in showing the governors round his labs. Get Jordan to bring the chemist's son to my office, will you, Sato? Before school tomorrow would be ideal. I have a plan."

The boys glanced at each other, hoping for details, but Danny needed time.

Sato said that of all the teachers at the school, the senior girls, especially the Asian ones, hated Potter the most. He's always leaning over them when they're carrying out experiments, often in the small darker labs, when only a few girls are in there.

Danny raised his eyebrows and closed the meeting but, after the others had left, he texted Doreen "Potential client for discussion, meet Griffin Friday 6pm. Danny."

Chapter 30

The Chemist's Son

JORDAN SMITH KNOCKED ON DANNY'S DOOR AND, WITHOUT waiting for a response, pushed a trembling Oliver Little into the room and left.

"Come in and take a seat, Oliver." Danny offered calm reassurance that maybe everything would be okay.

Oliver sat awkwardly on the front of the seat.

"No need to panic, Oliver. I know Jordan can appear a little threatening. I see you're an academic with a good school record. As you know, I am the school captain and with that comes a raft of responsibilities. I work closely with the headmaster and try and save him from many of the trivial school issues like bullying, petty theft, etc. In fact, you may have seen Johnny Archer hanging upside down from the school gate. I don't think bullying will be on his agenda from now on." Oliver laughed nervously and Danny continued "I am also accountable to the school governors and have to produce a report on many issues that may or may not be a threat to a constructive school environment. One of those issues, and with your background you may be able to help, is the use of social drugs such as cannabis. I believe your father is a chemist, Oliver?" Keen to be involved, Oliver nodded more willingly.

"I don't think we have a drug problem here at school, Oliver, but personally I need to know more about cannabis. I read that a boy at school on the East Coast grew medicinal cannabis in his bedroom. Can you believe that? I need to know more about medicinal cannabis, Oliver. Can you help? Can you let me know everything about growing medicinal cannabis? You may wish to consult your father. One final point, Oliver. This meeting and its subject is strictly between you and me. Strictly between you and me. Do you understand, Oliver?"

At that point there was a knock on the door and Jordan Smith's head reappeared.

"Get back to me soon please, Oliver. Jordan will see you back to your class."

Oliver stood almost to attention and thought about saying something, but Jordan's hand on his shoulder hastened the departure.

Friday's meeting at Fred's was relaxed and jovial. Contaminated bread rolls were in a brown bag — contaminated with cash! Doreen left early, and the crew knew why.

Chapter 31

Doreen's Strategy

DANNY SMILED AT LESLIE AS HE STRODE CONFIDENTLY through reception. Leslie had a knowing look and half-smile that suggested if you're interested so am I. Danny remained firmly on the other side of the fence, but appreciated the expression.

Doreen sat there, typecast in her seductive way. Roger held up a bottle of Coke and Danny nodded.

He pulled his bar stool over to Doreen's. "Do you bank in the precinct, Doreen?"

"No, too close to home, Danny."

"I see. You wouldn't want to bump into too many clients in the queue, eh?" Danny agreed with a smile. "However, there is an employee there I think would make a very suitable client. He certainly has the money and would be the pinnacle of discretion." Danny eased back, knowing full well that he had filled at least three of Doreen's criteria for approach.

"What does he do?" Doreen asked.

"Bank Manager."

"Hmm, we are going up in the world. Why do you think he would be interested?" Doreen wanted more information.

"He has a weakness for female bank tellers, and I have the name of one in his current branch. He was moved here because of a minor harassment claim made by a previous employee at a another branch."

Doreen warmed to the idea.

"So, you are suggesting I make an appointment to move my account and arrange a meeting with him?"

Danny liked the speed at which Doreen spotted an opportunity.

"What else do I need to know? Opening an account dressed like this might get his juices flowing but not clinch the deal."

"He is currently over-affectionate with Helen Walker, an attractive young teller. Do you need any more information?" Danny smiled.

Doreen said "He'll be sitting in your seat within seven days."

Danny took a final sip of Coke, winked at Roger and, touching Doreen's knee lightly, said "Always good to do business with you" and left with the air of a man in control, a man on a permanent mission. He breezed past Leslie without a glance.

Doreen fell for Danny's charisma briefly, before pulling herself together when a ping on her mobile refocused her attention.

CHAPTER 32

OPENING THE ACCOUNT

"COME IN, PLEASE, MAY I ...

Doreen guessed what he was going to say and pre-empted him: "Yes, I prefer Doreen."

Arthur Wilson was immediately on the back foot but had learned over the years that appearing slightly vulnerable often put new clients at ease. However, the high heels, short black dress and plunging neckline posed a problem, especially as the guest chair was too close to his desk. He was already tempted to walk Doreen across the room to look at some savings brochures. Despite his previous misdemeanour, the lecherous wheels in Arthur's head were beginning to whirr, and Doreen could hear them ... loud and clear.

"I see you have a considerable sum you would like to move across, Doreen. May I ask why?"

"No." Doreen stared at Wilson.

"I see. Not a problem. And I notice you make deposits on quite a regular basis. Have you considered a term deposit? The interest rates are quite attractive." Arthur smiled.

"Something we can maybe discuss at a future meeting?" Doreen stood to straighten her dress and then sat down again. Let's open the account first."

Doreen's newfound confidence, because of Danny's involvement and more importantly his ability to provide reliable and profitable clients, tempted her to hook Arthur without any threat of exposing his seedy approaches to Helen Walker.

"Quite. I'll pass your details through to one of my tellers and she'll open your account." Wilson picked up the internal phone and Doreen said "I'd like Helen Walker."

Wilson froze for a moment, and Doreen noticed his brow redden slightly. He pushed a different number. "Could you come through please, Helen, and bring some new account forms?"

A tap on the door, and a trim young teller walked in. Doreen measured the electricity and wondered if Wilson could avoid touching her. Helen handed over the documents and Doreen watched for any hand contact. There was none, but Doreen couldn't avoid a bit of devilment by keeping Helen in the room.

"You'll be looking after my account, Helen", she said. "Maybe accounts if Mr Wilson can tempt me with favourable rates."

"Let's hope so," said Helen before turning to leave.

"Could you please sign here, Doreen, and we can open the account immediately. Then perhaps I can show you some term deposit rates?" Wilson walked across to the brochures at the far side of the office, but Doreen remained seated.

"As I said to Helen, Arthur — sorry, do you mind if I use your first name? In private of course. Let's meet later to discuss term deposits. You can bring the brochures with you."

Wilson sat down and noted her phrase "bring the brochures with you."

"Where were you thinking of meeting, Doreen?" He was intrigued and interested.

"I find it relaxing to use the lounge bar at The Griffin motel on the edge of town for a G&T after the daily grind. It's probably one of your clients, Arthur?" Doreen glanced at the desktop computer on Wilson's desk.

A quick press of a couple of keys and "No, it doesn't appear to be." Wilson frowned, more out of habit than concern.

"Maybe I can help you with that. Let's meet there next Thursday at 6pm." In a twinkle Doreen was heading towards the door, leaving Wilson transfixed and wide-eyed.

"Oh, my apologies — how rude." Doreen walked sexily back and put out a hand. "Maybe you'd like to show me out, Arthur?"

Arthur opened the door and, with a "See you Thursday," Doreen sauntered through it.

Outside she turned sharp left down the alley, reached into her bag, took out a small bottle and had a big swig. Well done, girl, she thought as she gasped the fresh air, then took another swig and went back to the precinct.

CHAPTER 33

THE WIN

JOHN FOSTER GLANCED IN BOTH DIRECTIONS A LITTLE uneasily as he tapped lightly on the school captain's door.

"Ah, Mr Foster, I wondered if you might call. Congratulations on your win. What was the name of the horse now?"

"Secret Vice — 10 to 1. He romped home. I made over $500."

Danny put a finger to his lips. "No need for the whole world to know, John. Sorry, do you mind if I call you John?"

"You can call me Tom Thumb if you want, so long as you keep finding winners like Secret Vice, Danny."

"I made a few dollars too, John — or should I call you Tom?"

Foster laughed and Danny suggested this was not a good time or place to discuss horse racing. "Let's meet at The Griffin on Thursday about 6.30. You know, the motel on the edge of town."

"Great, I'll be there. Where will you be?" Foster was in.

"Leslie in reception will tell you. See you Thursday." Danny rose to usher Foster out.

Wow, he's keen, Danny thought. Maybe it's time to talk to the crew about Sports Day?

Chapter 34

Doreen and The Bank Manager

ARTHUR WILSON HAD MET MANY CLIENTS IN DIFFERENT places, but for some unknown reason he felt a sense of apprehension. He reached for his briefcase, then thought it might be a little less formal to take out the brochures and leave it in the boot. A quick look in the rear-view mirror, and he ran his fingers through his hair and got out. He still needed to tuck the front of his shirt in, but by and large he felt up to the task.

Leslie greeted Arthur professionally. "Good evening, Mr Wilson, welcome to The Griffin. Doreen's in the lounge bar."

Arthur Wilson was impressed. Maybe the term deposit was a favourable play.

Doreen sensed Arthur Wilson's presence before he entered the room. She thought of standing but felt more alluring seated, right leg crossed over left.

"Arthur, lovely to see you again." Roger's ears twitched and he reached for the gin bottle. Doreen, carefully positioned to reveal her stocking top, gestured to Arthur to take a seat.

"Two G&Ts, Roger and not too gentle on the G, please," she giggled.

In all his time at various banks, Arthur Wilson had never experienced an opening move like this. Usually the client was desperate for help and behaved accordingly. Here Arthur was a support player at the behest of the lead actor. It was an unfamiliar role, but he felt quite at ease and, so far, willing to go with the flow.

Roger stood to attention, a G&T in each hand. Doreen and Arthur raised their glasses, clinked them and the bait was taken.

"I see you have some brochures with you, Arthur. Why don't you pop them on the bar, and we'll deal with them presently? I assume you have something earmarked already?"

Arthur was about to begin his sales pitch, but Doreen uncrossed her legs slowly, which diverted his attention and concentration.

"No need to rush, let's relax and get to know each other. Are you comfortable with meeting here?"

"Yes, it's perfect. Only 10 minutes from the branch and, if I might say so, quite discreet."

Doreen looked at him suggestively before saying to Roger "Please ask Leslie on reception to come through. And could you top these up before you go?"

Arthur was beginning to feel like James Bond in the hands of a seductress. He knew what was happening but had no wish to protest. Plus, the gin had a certain freshness about it.

"Ah, Leslie, may I introduce you to Arthur Wilson? Mr Wilson runs our local Central Bank in the precinct. I think he may be able to offer The Griffin some favourable trading terms. Could you provide him with last year's accounts and forward projections? No rush, we'll be here for a while yet."

"I can, Doreen. Pleased to meet you, Mr Wilson." Leslie knew the script.

"Well, you are quite something, Doreen. The Griffin could be an extremely attractive account." Arthur smiled and took another sip. "That hits the spot!" He suddenly began to shake from head to toe — only briefly, but it unsteadied him a little. He smiled stupidly.

"Professional and personal, Arthur. These are tough times, and it would do your reputation no harm at all." Doreen was improving with every meeting. Danny would be proud of her.

"Ah, here's the new school captain. Hello, is it Danny?"

"It is. I think I've seen you in Fred's café," Danny replied. "I know you though, Mr Wilson. Aren't you from the Central Bank? Good to see you again." Danny held his hand out and Wilson shook it, careful not to lean too far forward.

"Must dash, I'm meeting a friend. Have a lovely evening." Danny chose a table where he could sit with his back to Doreen, and his friend could watch her.

John Foster hesitated in the entrance just long enough for Leslie to catch his eye. "Through there, Mr Foster. Danny's waiting for you."

Reassured, he went in and his eyes immediately met Doreen's — only briefly, but long enough for Doreen to connect and cross her legs.

Danny hesitated before inviting John over. "Hi, sir, good to see you again." He played the role perfectly.

"Call me John, Danny, when we're alone and after school. By the way, did you see that woman at the bar? I couldn't take my eyes off her."

"I can see her reflection in the window and she keeps looking over here. I'll introduce you later. Now, let's talk racing. "The way you celebrated your big win suggests you don't win very often, John?"

"Actually, that win got me out of a spot of bother. I was able to pay off a threatening debt."

"Great, let's see if there's a way we can make you win more. By the way, do any other members of staff bet?"

"Yes, there are three others and we often bet together, but I can't give you their names without their permission. I'm sure you'll understand."

"Of course. Do you think we could organise a betting coup on Sports Day?" Danny shot straight from the hip. We could set up the odds on the computer in my office and you could spread the word. Members of staff could place their bets by email and pay you the money. That way we would have a record of the bet and the cash. You would become the unofficial bookie. All in confidence of course. I have some friends who can provide data on the talent so we get the odds right."

John Foster was dumbfounded, but just as he was about to reply there was a crash. Arthur had slipped off his chair and was sprawled across the floor. Leslie dashed in from reception and Danny got up to help, but Doreen gave him a look and he sat down again.

Roger, Doreen and Leslie helped Arthur to his feet and led him out of the room.

Several minutes later Doreen was back and came up to them.

"My apologies for interrupting, Danny, but I know you must be concerned about Arthur. He's had a turn, but he should be okay in a short while. He's resting now. By the way, who's your friend? Aren't you going to introduce us?"

Danny picked up the obvious thread and introduced John. "In fact, could I leave you with John? I just need the men's room."

Doreen smiled and invited John over to the bar.

"Would you like a quick G&T, John?" Before John had time to answer Doreen had placed the order. "Two straight G&Ts, Roger, please. Danny shouldn't be too long." Roger knew what 'straight' meant.

Five minutes later Danny rushed in. "Sorry, but I have to dash, John. A family issue. Please consider my proposal and maybe we can talk tomorrow?"

"I'm free second period. Are you around?"

"I will be," said Danny.

He gave Doreen a teasing look and said "Make sure you look after John. He may need a taxi!"

Danny winked at Leslie in reception and left.

Got it, that one, thought Leslie.

Arthur had been laid to rest, so to speak, in a spare room used only for emergencies. It was 9.30pm when he eventually came round. He had a throbbing headache and only a vague recollection of what had happened. Doreen and John had long since left.

He got off the bed gingerly and staggered a few steps. A bottle of water was on the table and he gulped half of it down feeling like he had arrived at an oasis in the desert.

Leslie saw off some departing customers and went to Arthur's aid.

"Well you look a lot better now than you did three hours ago. I've booked you a taxi. You can pick your car up in the morning. I used your credit card and settled your bill with it too. Doreen says she'll pop in tomorrow afternoon. Take this envelope. It has The Griffin's accounts and projections inside. Here comes the taxi now." Leslie was word perfect. He handed over the envelope and the credit card and ushered Arthur out to the waiting driver.

"Take care, and come back and see us soon." Leslie waved as Arthur left.

A quick text to Doreen and my work is done, he thought. The commission made it all worthwhile.

CHAPTER 35

JOHN AND THE BETTING COUP

DANNY NOTICED A NEW ADDITION TO HIS OFFICE: A COFFEE machine. One of those small unobtrusive ones where you put a coffee capsule in the top and the machine does the rest. A discreetly positioned label read "For sore heads" and was signed "Janice and Sanjira".

Danny laughed and thought of another commercial opportunity, but first John Foster.

"I'm sorry we didn't get a chance to finish our conversation last night, Mr Foster. You'll be pleased to know the gentleman with Doreen recovered and took a taxi home. One G&T too many, I think."

"Not a problem, Danny. I had a lovely hour with Doreen. Did you know her uncle was a racehorse trainer?"

"I didn't, but I hope you arranged another meeting. Tips from the horse's mouth so to speak!"

"Sure did. Next Thursday at 6.30. I like The Griffin." John Foster was well and truly hooked.

"Now let's talk about your plans for Sports Day. I don't have much time." Foster was out of the gates and running fast!

"I can provide you with data and odds on all the runners, boys and girls, in the various events, including the relays. You circulate the odds amongst your betting friends and anyone else you feel may be interested. Sports Day is open to the public, usually parents and friends. All bets will close one hour before Sports Day starts. I will have a computer set up in my office and only you and I will have access to it. I will ensure you have a remote link, so you do not have to keep popping in. All bets will be sent to your bank account and then transferred to this account." Danny slid a piece of paper across his desk.

"Always Tomorrow. I see it's at the Central Bank in the precinct."

"If you don't bank there, Mr Foster, may I suggest you consider moving your accounts? Always good to have a friend in times of need!" Danny manipulated the scenario with gusto and confidence. "I'll have the odds and the computer set up by Monday. You can start priming your friends. And good luck next Thursday with Doreen ... don't go too fast, that's my tip!"

Foster was smiling as he left. This was the spark of action missing in his life: his two major vices satisfied.

CHAPTER 36

THE CREW ARE MOVING FAST

DANNY SCRIBBLED DOWN A LIST OF ALL THE PROJECTS currently in motion, as well as those about to be launched. He texted the crew and emphasised the word update. They knew he wanted answers, and they had to have them!

Meeting in his bedroom now seemed a little old school, so he changed the venue to Fred's café on Thursday after school. Fred had agreed to provide refreshments and put a table in the corner so customers would not walk past them when they left. He realised there was no longer any need for small talk or silly quips. He could just provide the drinks and snacks and back off. Doreen still needed attention though. Danny appreciated her enthusiasm, but not her interruptions.

"Be a good idea to make notes, guys. I don't want to hand out an agenda. These meetings don't happen. We have several projects up and running, and some new ones about to start. I'll work my way through the list, and you contribute when appropriate.

"Okay, let's start with Sports Day: John Foster, the French teacher, has agreed to take bets from fellow staff members and friends. I've supplied him with a contact list of other people who may be interested, mainly those who were at the presentation night.

"Question 1. Have you got a list of the events and the favourites for each event?" Danny looked at Jeff and Chris.

Chris reached into his bag and pulled out a number of A4 pages with the runners and suggested odds against each name. He handed a copy to Danny, who scrutinised the list and handed it to Sato.

"Can you transfer this to your computer, code access, and send it to John Foster? He will begin taking bets and deposit the takings in the Always Tomorrow account. Can you set up an automatic ratification of every bet John places? He is aware that no bet is to be accepted without that ratification. This will ensure he doesn't go rogue and that we are not implicated." Everyone nodded, and Sato said it would be done by end of school the next day.

"Maybe you two should approach our sponsors asking if they would like to take out an advert in the Sports Day program," Danny suggested.

"We don't usually have a Sports Day program, Danny," Chris queried.

"As from now we do. When you have a few promises and adverts, go in to see Bartholomew. He won't be able to refuse the income. Remember, the sponsor makes a payment into the Sports Day account, which I will set up at the bank. We keep 20% and the rest goes into the school account. All this must be operational before you see Bartholomew, agreed?" Nods all round.

"When you see Punter the hunter, get him to ask his wife if she'll sponsor a Sports Day barbecue. Then one of you stops into the butcher and hands Mildred this parcel. Tell her it's a gift from Danny."

Sato broke the silence and asked "What colour?"

"School colours, of course," said Danny.

The penny eventually dropped, and they all laughed.

"Moving on, I expect a visit from the chemist's son on the use of medicinal cannabis. The crew raised eyebrows but knew Danny would explain when the time was right.

"I have a meeting with Janice and Sanjira to discuss a security 'take me home' service." Sato raised his eyebrows in support. Chris and Jeff looked a little perplexed but knew it would be a good idea and they would hear the details when Danny was ready.

"That wraps it up for today, guys. Have a great weekend and let's keep the machine rolling." Danny glanced at Fred, who signalled no charge.

Danny stayed behind when the others left. He needed some downtime. Although he was in total control of the crew's business affairs, his personal affairs were a different matter. Janice had moved closer, and Miss Whittleston was due in school on Thursday. Janice could be handled, but Miss Whittleston was an unknown. The spark of electricity between them at the governors' meeting concerned him. It seemed beyond his control.

"Everything okay, Danny?" asked Fred.

"Sure, Fred, but lots happening now."

"No probs. Will Sato be popping in tomorrow? I have a small donation."

Danny smiled. He had a soft spot for Fred, and it warmed his heart to see him happy and content. There was a connection between them — and long may it last, he thought.

"He sure will."

CHAPTER 37

DANNY REELS IN THE BANK

"EXCUSE ME, IS MR WILSON AVAILABLE FOR A BRIEF WORD?" Danny smiled at the bank receptionist.

"He's in his office, but he doesn't see people unless they have an appointment."

"Okay, thank you." Danny backed away and joined the queue for Helen Walker's window.

"Hi, Helen, it's Danny. We met briefly when Mr Wilson was behind you, last Thursday. Could you ring through and say Danny Carver would like a quick word."

Helen froze. What did he mean when Mr Wilson was behind her? Bank training and instinct told her to make the call and resolve the situation.

"Excuse me, sir, I have Danny Carver outside. He would like a quick word with you."

Helen put the phone down and Wilson's door opened.

"Come through, Danny, good to see you. I have a few minutes

until my next appointment. You may know him — a Mr Foster from the school?"

"Of course, I do, and so do you, sir. He was at The Griffin the other night. I suggested he come to see you. He's not happy with his current bank."

Wilson's forehead became slightly pinker and he stuttered "Not my finest hour, Danny."

"Not a problem, sir. A drink too many in charming company can do that. Put it behind you. The people at The Griffin are friends of mine. No damage done. In fact, they are incredibly happy with the banking terms you have offered them. Looks like you will acquire a sizeable account — and possibly Mr Foster's too. Please mention my name to John."

Wilson raised his eyebrows at the informality of John but relaxed knowing his reputation was still intact.

"I just wanted to say there will be considerably more activity in the Always Tomorrow account as we are using it for donations made to the school Sports Day program. My colleagues Chris and Jeff are selling advertising space in it. Would you be interested?"

"Be pleased to consider it, Danny."

"Good to hear. Thank you for your time." Danny rose and made for the door, but as he turned to shake Wilson's hand he reminded him of the term deposit rate.

"I'll see what I can do, Danny." Only then did Danny let go of his hand.

Sauntering towards the exit, Danny winked at Helen and frowned at the receptionist. Although not an avid reader, Danny did like a comment he'd seen in a sports magazine, "Winning is in the detail." It sure is, he thought, as he headed off to Fred's to gather his thoughts. Carol Whittleston was due soon and it would be hard to ignore her. He had to avoid being with her and Janice at the same time.

Fred was at the wholesalers. Doreen was in charge, but the

morning coffee run was over, so she edged towards Danny, half expecting one of his curt rebuffs. Instead he congratulated her warmly on her performance at The Griffin.

"I'm assuming there was nothing untoward in Wilson's fall from grace? I'm also assuming John Foster is about to become a new client?" Danny pursued the business line.

Doreen replied confidently "Correct on both counts, Danny. John is ringing me tonight, and I'm popping into the bank when Fred gets back. I have some money to deposit and need to check on Arthur's wellbeing. By the way, Leslie tells me The Griffin's owners are due in from America next week. Two middle-aged men from Bible country, checking on their investment.

Ever the businessman, Danny noticed the owners were from overseas and kept up the pressure on Doreen.

He was happy with the way his crew had dovetailed and were on top of their project responsibilities. He considered his own role and how he acted almost as a Mafia don. His generals were in place. Did he need to add to their numbers and/or increase their responsibilities? The latter carried the lesser risk. He also liked the fact that he had private connections too. His crew just knew what they needed to know.

There were still several commercial opportunities to be developed at school. Priority had to be a meeting with Janice and Sanjira, not only to thank them for the coffee maker but to see what issues the girls had, especially as there were over 150 of them.

Potter remained a thorn in Danny's side, but a plan was fermenting, and Oliver Little the chemist's son might have the answer ... he needed a nudge.

Danny rose to leave, and Doreen waved away the bill.

"Get back to me when you know what date the Americans arrive, will you?" Doreen nodded and Danny left.

Chapter 38

A Delicate Meeting

JORDAN DELIVERED A SHORT MESSAGE TO JANICE AND Sanjira — well, more a direct invitation to meet for coffee in Danny's office at 12.30. Both girls considered a hidden agenda, but only briefly as they knew he would wriggle something into a thank you for the coffee maker.

Danny answered the polite knock on his door with an equally polite "come in." He knew it was the girls, but didn't expect a wicker chair to be first through the door.

"Did you expect one of us to sit on the floor, Danny?" Janice served first: 15-love.

For all his guile and rat-like instincts Danny was immediately on the back foot.

"I've also brought three coffee mugs," said Sanjira. "I hope you like the colour."

"There's a capsule in each." Janice prolonged the torture. Both girls sat down, having first gestured towards the coffee machine.

Danny cringed. He hadn't even read the instructions. The girls burst out laughing.

"Here, we'll do it. We don't want a mess on the carpet." Janice eased the pressure.

However, like all the great commanders in history, Danny bounced back immediately.

"How can I, in my position as school captain, help the girls in our school?" Danny returned serve: 15 all.

"Don't you mean you and your underworld organisation?" Janice asked.

"I do. I thought you would take that as read, Jan." Danny lobbed in a bit of informality. Janice lobbed it straight back. "Janice, please."

Sanjira shuffled in her seat, suspecting the meeting might become too personal.

"The Asian girls have a problem, Danny. On our way home from early evening school functions we are often subject to taunts from younger boys. This can go on for some time if we have a long walk home. The jeers often refer to our traditional dress." Sanjira had chosen the moment carefully. Janice passed the coffees around and Danny felt better. He could now direct the course of the meeting.

"What would make the girls feel more comfortable, Sanjira?" he asked.

"We don't feel physically vulnerable, so we don't need to spend money on taxis or Ubers, but sometimes the boys insulting us get very close."

"Can you identify any of them?" Danny closed in on the specifics.

'No, because there are different ones for each group of girls on any one occasion, and they sometimes keep at a distance."

"It's almost as though we need an escort service, Danny. Someone who could not only offer support but also identify the people responsible and exact some retribution afterwards." Janice glared at Danny, knowing full well Jordan Smith was his henchman. She knew about Danny's connections.

"Could work, but there may be a cost involved if people have to give up their spare time to act as escorts." Danny began searching for a financial angle.

"I'm sure the girls could make a contribution; money is not the issue."

Sanjira' s comments were music to Danny's ears. He slipped into his slow extraction mode, knowing full well that Janice was taking in every word.

"Do you think we could form a walk home escort club? Then on any after-school event night they could log into an app and book a walk home. A member of the senior school would escort them and identify any abusive young offenders. Once recognised, we could frighten them away." Danny relaxed, and there was no mention of money or violence, but Janice had raised her eyebrows when he said frighten.

Sanjira kept batting for Danny. "Do you have someone who could set up the app," Danny?"

"Yes, you know Sato in Year 12? We're good friends. Would you like me to sound him out? Or maybe you'd like to talk to him?"

"No, it would be better coming from you," Janice interrupted. "Not the sort of thing girls should be directly involved in." Sanjira nodded, and Danny went on "Okay, I'll speak to Sato. I'll get a message to you in a couple of days."

He got up. "And finally I'm presuming, no, hoping, you'll be leaving the wicker chair and coffee mugs behind?" His mocking smile and twinkle got an immediate affirmation.

"You buy the capsules though. Do you think you can manage that?" Janice fired one last volley as Danny opened the door. She knew he was a rogue but loved the challenge.

Danny sat back, knowing full well that Sato's proposal would include a financial element. Now where was Sato? Danny checked the timetable and Sato was free in period 4. He wrote out a 'meet me' note and put it in Sato's pigeonhole.

He then texted Jordan Smith. "There's a message in Sato's pigeonhole. Please see he gets it immediately?"

Sato opened the message, and a tinge of excitement raised a smile. Danny had a plan.

"Hi, Sato, thanks for coming round. The meeting with Janice and Sanjira went well. Sanjira suggested setting up an escort walk home club whereby the girls sign up on a term basis, and when they go to an after-school function they can click on an app and book a walk home. What do you think?"

"Did Sanjira really think of that or did you nudge her in that direction?" Sato asked, but he knew the answer.

"Can it be done?"

"Easily, but who do you have in mind to do the escorting?" Sato's look suggested he was out of the running.

Danny smiled and said "Jordan can put a team together. We'll insist on a code of behaviour and dress. The offenders won't do it twice if Jordan gets hold of them. Can you design an app? And work out how we gain financially?"

Sato sat in the new wicker chair and let the strategy flow ...

"Firstly, the app is not a problem. It is one transaction and one contact response. Financially, the girls must pay a nominal term-by-term membership amount, say $20 each. This gives them access to the app via a sign-in code. Then they can text for an escort, stating time and pickup point. The escort walks the girls home, to separate addresses if need be. He also makes a note of any abusers along the way. The girls pay a minimum of $5 each to the escort. A girl on her own pays $10. We keep all the membership money. Jordan pays a nominal amount each term for exclusivity of role, or do you want to leave Jordan out of it? Might that be for the best?"

Danny reflected for a moment. "Jordan can't operate without our coded access to the app and changing the code would eliminate him, so let's play safe and allow him to take the walk-home money. If he charges too much, we switch him off. He's a thug, but he's not a dumb thug. I reckon he'll go for it."

'I agree. I can have this up and running over the weekend. When are you seeing the girls again?" Sato asked.

"I was thinking Tuesday lunchtime. Can you make the presentation to them then? Better coming from you, I think."

"Smart move, Danny. If Sanjira is on board, we have all the Asian girls. Janice will get the rest, if only to keep in with you."

Danny smiled. But even so, he knew he had a problem allowing Janice closer.

"I'll get a message out to meet here Tuesday lunchtime. We can speak to Jordan afterwards. He doesn't have to know just yet. Let's grab some lunch."

CHAPTER 39

DOREEN LOCKS IN THE CATCH

DOREEN SMILED AT HELEN AS SHE SAT DOWN OUTSIDE Arthur Wilson's office. Helen saw it as a very deliberate hands-off smile. Why are people suddenly becoming interested in me, she wondered? First Danny and now Doreen. Surely, they can't think I'm interested in Wilson. He's a sleaze.

Arthur Wilson reflected for a moment before leaving his desk and going towards the door. He dwelt for a moment on Danny's friendly comments of no harm done and thought a professional welcome to Doreen in front of bank staff would have the necessary effect.

Two deep breaths and Arthur opened the door.

"Good morning, Doreen. Please come through." Said a little louder than usual so staff could hear.

"Very professional, Mr Wilson." Doreen mimicked. "Shall I sit here, or would you prefer me in your seat?"

Arthur Wilson was already in deep water, very deep. In all his years in banking, he had been the one in the driving seat. Today he was in trouble — Doreen was in the driving seat with her foot on the accelerator.

Arthur wondered about seat, but then realised it was a quip and sat down.

"Now before we talk business, how do you feel, Arthur, any repercussions? That was a nasty fall."

"No, just a tinge of embarrassment about my behaviour." Arthur took the humble route.

"My only concern was your welfare, Arthur. No apology needed. In fact, The Griffin have offered us dinner, you and me, on Thursday, compliments of the house, wine included. Unfortunately, no gin! I have accepted on our behalf."

Arthur was about to launch into a mild apology and refusal, but Doreen carried on at pace.

"Arthur, I'm sure you will be delighted to hear that I have moved all my accounts to your branch."

He glanced at his computer screen quickly, pressed a key, and sure enough there was a sizeable deposit into both a current and a term deposit account.

"Such a nice girl, Helen Walker. She handled the transfer with great dexterity." Doreen wondered where the word dexterity had come from but felt confident it had hit the spot.

Arthur was wrong-footed and Doreen carried on.

"I spoke to Leslie at The Griffin this morning and he has received confirmation from The Griffin's owners that he can transfer The Griffin's accounts to your branch. By the way, The Griffin is owned by two very wealthy Americans, very Christian from the Bible belt, and they arrive in two weeks for a short stay. Should I arrange a meeting? Maybe you and Helen can see them socially to welcome them to the Central Bank?"

Arthur's training kept him seated, but he wanted to leap out of his seat and do back somersaults. Head office would be over the moon. Wealthy Americans with a Christian background? A safe bet for sure. Where might all this lead?

"Now, I just need to confirm our dinner date on Thursday with Leslie and suggest a time for you and Helen to meet the Americans. What suits you, Arthur?" Doreen glanced at the open diary.

Arthur was getting sucked deeper and deeper into the whirlpool. A few minutes ago, he had been in control. Now he was out of control, but this was the best business day of his banking career. There was no downside and Helen Walker was a necessary participant. All he had to do was confirm dinner with Doreen and a date for the Americans.

He leant forward and pencilled in Thursday 23rd, 7pm.

"Can't put our personal dinner date in the book, Doreen, but please let Leslie know I accept his kind offer for dinner with wine this coming Thursday. Shall we say 7pm?"

"We shall, Arthur. You are a very professional man. Do you have an email address for your regional manager?"

Arthur was so immersed in glory he immediately handed over the details.

Doreen swept the note off the desk and made for the door. Before opening it she turned and winked at Arthur.

"See you Thursday, darling"

The door shut and Arthur fell back into his seat.

This wasn't Wall Street, but it sure as hell felt like it.

Should he promote Helen?

CHAPTER 40

THE POTTER PLAN

DANNY HAD RECEIVED A TEXT OVER THE WEEKEND FROM Jordan Smith saying Oliver Little, the chemist's son, had some information he would like to share with him.

Bartholomew had called an early staff meeting at 7.30am on Monday, so the coast would be clear for a discreet meeting with Oliver, and Danny texted Jordan back "Please bring Oliver to my office at 7.45am Monday."

Danny began to read up on the use and effects of medicinal cannabis. He couldn't trust Oliver 100% so needed some of his own data.

Promptly at 7.45 am Monday Jordan's knurled face half-appeared as he pushed Oliver in.

"Be about half an hour, Jordan," Danny said.

"Morning, Oliver, thanks for getting back to me so soon. I'm assuming you didn't have any trouble?"

"Everything was fine. I told Dad I was working on a school

project with some other boys, so he was only too keen to supply the basic information. I've listed the key points for you." Oliver handed over a plain folder containing his notes.

"Do you mind if I work my way through each of the points? Then if I have a query you may be able to answer it."

Oliver's confidence grew, as Danny had known it would. After all, Danny was sure to need him again.

Danny worked slowly and diligently through Oliver's list.

1) Cannabis, a drug often referred to as pot, weed, marijuana, hash comes from a herb plant.
2) Takes between 3-5 months to grow.
3) You can buy seeds online.
4) Can be taken in the form of a pill and even made into tea. (Danny smiled at the prospect of serving cups of cannabis.)
5) When taken the effects may start straight away and last 3-4 hours.
6) Can make you feel tired, drunk, dizzy or high.

Danny eased back in his wicker chair and looked hard at Oliver. "Good work. Just the information I need. Tell me, does your father stock any seeds for medicinal uses?"

"He has a number of boxes, but seldom uses them. The representatives from the drug companies leave them as free samples. I can get you a box if you wish. There are a minimum of 50 seeds in each."

"That would be perfect. Could I ask you to wrap the box in brown paper, mark it for my attention and leave it with Fred at Fred's Café? Do you know it? It's the one just off the precinct?"

"Yes, I pass it every morning. I'll drop a box in tomorrow," Oliver agreed.

Danny rose to his feet as Jordan knocked and opened the door.

"One more thing, Oliver, what are your weak subjects?"

"Music and art. I'm a scientist really." Oliver left and Danny nodded at Jordan, then picked up his mobile and texted Sato "Please upgrade Oliver Little in music and art."

The Potter plan was falling into place nicely. He looked at the school calendar and noted there would be a Governors' Tour in February, four months hence. Now Danny needed access to Potter's back labs, the one where students grew herbs. He had to either replace what was already planted or ensure his seeds were sown first.

The thought of Potter nurturing cannabis plants on the students' behalf appealed greatly, but he still needed a way into the potting labs. Maybe the girls could help. Or a fire alarm and a quick planting job?

Food for thought.

Bartholomew knocked and popped his head round the door.

"All quiet on the Western Front, Danny?" Bartholomew loved a historical quote now and again, but it made the staff squirm.

Danny responded with "Full steam ahead, General."

Bartholomew smiled. "Oh, one thing before I go. I had a visit from Jeff and Chris. Two of your closer colleagues, I think?" Danny remained silent and deadpan.

"Their ideas for Sports Day are excellent. They already have several sponsors for a program. We've never had one before, and I like the idea of selling it for a nominal amount at the entrance. They've even listed all the competitors in each race, boys, and girls. Very impressive."

"Maybe you should invite some dignitaries, sir, to present the trophies? Lord and Lady Mayor? Governors? Drinks afterwards in the staffroom? I'm sure one of our sponsors could produce a light buffet, and of course Colin Punter could take photographs for *The Advertiser*?" Danny embroidered the discussion.

"Good idea, Danny. When you next see Chris and Jeff, ask them to come in to see me, will you?"

"Yes sir, General." Danny was cringing, but Bartholomew saw the funny side and left.

The week had started well.

A beep on Danny's mobile and a text that read "upgrades complete in music and art." Danny smiled and erased the message.

He then texted Chris and Jeff "Well done. Bartholomew is impressed with your work. Call in and see him later this week. He has some additional ideas."

Such was the importance of the school captain's role, Danny was able to avoid certain lessons. Then he had a brainwave: He would ask Sato to check if Potter would be out of school at a conference at any time during the next two weeks. If not, they would find something for him to attend. If he were out of the way, sowing the seeds would be much easier.

Text to Sato: "We need Potter out of school in the next two weeks for at least half a day. Can you check if there is anything happening locally he could attend?"

Sato texted back immediately "I have just the thing but need to talk to Bartholomew. I'll have the answer by tomorrow."

Wow, even for Sato that was quick!

CHAPTER 41

WALK HOME SERVICE LAUNCHED

JANICE AND SANJIRA WERE DUE AT 12.30, SO DANNY AND Sato met 15 minutes earlier.

"Priority number 1," said Danny, "is to get this bloody coffee machine working."

Sato smiled. He knew that Danny could cope with all the pressure in the world, but the little issues really got under his skin. "How about a test run?"

Danny fiddled about with a capsule and pressed a silver button. Low and behold, it worked.

"There you are," said Sato, "you are now a barista."

There was a light tap on the door. Sato opened it and welcomed the girls in. Fortunately, Danny had borrowed another chair from the canteen, and Janice smiled approvingly as Sato took his place at Danny's side.

"Sato has put together a plan which we both think may solve your problem of uncomfortable walks home." Danny introduced

Sato, and Sato explained the Walk Home plan, outlining clearly how it would work, and the costs involved.

Sanjira liked the idea of a small sum to be handed over at the end of the walk home. The girls would not want to be carrying too much money. Danny nodded in approval. Janice asked how the term membership would be collected and Sato suggested monies could be handed directly to him in the first week of term. He would give the girls a receipt and a code to access the app.

"Is the app ready now?" Sanjira asked.

"Yes, it is. Would you like to test it?" Sato handed over his phone and sure enough there was an app named, 'Walk Home Service'. "If you pass me your phone, Sanjira, I'll give you access and a coded number."

Sanjira handed over her phone and after a few seconds Sato gave it back with both a receipt and a coded number.

"All you need to do now is punch in the coded number on the app and you'll then be able to type in your pickup and drop off points. Within seconds you'll receive a cost and pickup time."

"That's very clever," said Janice. "When will it be available?"

Danny stepped in. "We'll trial it over the next couple of days. When do you think you can get the Year 11 and 12 girls together, Sanjira, to explain the system? Sato will need to be there of course, to accept any immediate term memberships."

"We have a prefects' meeting on Thursday to introduce all the new girl prefects. That would be a good time," Sanjira said.

"Perfect," said Danny. "We'll be up and running by then, I'm sure."

Janice was first to leave. She thanked Sato for his work and, turning to Danny, suggested it would have been nice to have had a coffee, but maybe next time ...

Danny shrank in stature physically and mentally. He uttered a pathetic "Oops, forgot."

Janice fired one last shot "Hope you won't forget to pick the girls up."

Sanjira laughed and they both left.

"Phew, I'm glad that's over. I'll text Jordan and get him to meet me at Fred's tonight after school." Danny had survived another female round of torment.

Sato said he was all right with the timing and would see if he could grab a few minutes with Bartholomew to discuss using Mr Potter. Danny nodded approvingly.

"I'll pop back in afterwards. Will only take a few minutes." Sato left and Danny began a text to Jordan.

Sato's brilliance and flexibility had reassured Danny that the size of his crew could remain the same. Chris and Jeff were a good team, and Chris could ensure Jeff stayed away from any prohibited substances. Janice and Sanjira were opening commercial possibilities within the Year 11 and 12 girls and Danny was satisfied that more opportunities would arise. He just hadn't thought of them yet.

Maybe I'll try this coffee machine, he thought.

A text from Jordan pinged through. "Yes, 4pm." A man of few words.

Sato reappeared just as Danny failed to get the cup under the flow of milk in time, and his trousers were pebble-dashed. He gave a rueful smile, which lightened the moment, and Danny brushed himself down and took a seat. He gestured to Sato to begin.

"Very simple really, Danny. My father is hosting a meeting on climate change for business acquaintances at the local library next Wednesday morning at 10am. It should last about an hour and Father asked if I could find a guest speaker. I just have. Potter is free that morning, so Bartholomew thought it was a wonderful idea to send him to forge stronger links with the local business community.

Danny smiled in appreciation. He knew Potter would search for some connection, but the seeds could be sown in his absence. Danny took out the school timetable and noted the Year 11 girls would be in Potter's labs that morning. Potter would have a replacement teacher in there to cover his absence and he would leave work for the girls to do. Danny would replace that with his own seeding program. Sanjira could help, he thought. Should be a straightforward case of replacing seeds or sowing new ones. They would use the back labs, the ones Potter seldom checked, and would need some new herb labels as well.

Should he let Sanjira in on the plan or just change the work program, Danny mused, then decided the fewer people who knew the better.

Sato sat there expecting more, and when nothing happened he told Danny that Foster had been making sizeable deposits in the Always Tomorrow account. Betting on the school races was going well.

Danny said "Chris and Jeff have got a good number of adverts from local businesses. Bartholomew was really pleased."

"Do you think we need some sort of security on the gate, Danny? We need a narrow entrance so people can queue to get in and pay for a program." Sato was into detail. "If we get a good crowd, we don't want anyone to miss the first race."

"I'll mention it to Jordan tonight." Danny thanked Sato for his diligence and reached across to shake his hand for the first time since they had met in Year 11.

When Sato left, Danny sat back to think about all the activities Always Tomorrow was involved in. As a rule he kept all plans to verbal instructions, but such was the present speed and variation of expansion he wanted to create a flow chart of activity so that at any one moment he could know exactly where each project was. Once he was satisfied, he took a photograph and transferred it to his laptop. He opened a folder and named it 'Apocalypse', and in went the photograph.

CHAPTER 42

JORDAN, AT FRED'S CAFE

JORDAN SMITH WAS A WEIRD BOY. MOST TEACHERS QUITE simply ignored him. He sat at the back of the class immersed in his phone. School was a resting place for Jordan; it had no real significance. Since his involvement with Danny he had become less of a problem for teachers, but more of a problem for misbehaving pupils. Plus, the random amounts of money he received from Danny ensured he played the game. Bartholomew noticed the change and suspected Danny's involvement, but chose not to interfere. Why rock the boat when there was no need? Jordan figured less and less in staff meeting discussions.

Fred wandered over to Danny who was in his usual corner seat.

"A lad left this parcel for you this morning, Danny. Wouldn't give his name. Hope it's not a bomb?"

"Thanks, Fred. No, it's personal, hence the brown paper. Your café's safe with me." The parcel was small enough to take into school without being noticed.

Fred was just about to eject a scruffy youth, when he gestured at Danny who stood up to shake hands with Jordan.

"Coke, Jordan ... can?"

Jordan nodded and Danny walked across to the cooler for a can of Coke.

Jordan listened to both plans, firstly for the Walk Home escort service and secondly for security on Sports Day.

"What are your thoughts on the Walk Home escort service first, Jordan?" Danny needed Jordan's input and understanding.

"Well, it's a cash earner which is good, and it's paid at the time, which is good. Not sure I can get my guys to dress smartly though." Will Sato explain how the app works?

"He sure will. If you go to a posh café for a meal, the smart, polite waiters get the most tips. The girls you will be escorting home are from extraordinarily rich families. Money will not be a problem. What you need is for the girls to be happy with your service, and it may lead to other work."

Danny cut Jordan some rope.

"Okay, but maybe you could meet the guys I'm going to use and give them some help," Jordan said.

Danny leapt at the suggestion. "Let's meet here on Wednesday after Fred closes at 6pm. He'll re-open for us. I'll get Sato to come. How many are you thinking of bringing?

"Four to start with. Just to be sure I get all the cash and pay my blokes. Is that all right?" Jordan asked.

"Spot on. You charge more if it's a longer walk. If you have any non-payers, your guys walk away and Sanjira and I get the money for you. Is that understood?" We don't want any confrontations. Some of the girls have boyfriends who might resent the service and be a bit arrogant."

"Now what about Sports Day security? Can you supply some guys to man the entrance?" Danny knew the answer.

"Definitely. I saw Foster taking a bet off the German teacher, so

I've placed a couple myself!"

"Let's hope they win," said Danny.

"They will," said Jordan

He stood up to go, held out his hand and stared at Danny as he shook his hand firmly.

"See you at 6."

"You will, Jordan. Thanks for coming."

As Jordan left, Danny texted John Foster "Who has Jordan Smith bet on and in which races?"

Ping! Boys, 200 and 400. Jenkinson in the 200 and Philpott in the 400; 8 to 1 and 6 to 1 respectively.

"Put 20 on each for me, and pop into my office tomorrow morning. I'll have the money for you."

Ping! "Done, see you tomorrow."

Fred looked at Danny hoping for an explanation, but all he got was "Can you re-open at 6pm on Wednesday? I have a meeting with a few blokes."

Fred laughed. "Sure," he said. He knew Danny only wanted him to know what he wanted him to know.

CHAPTER 43

A BUSY WEEK

MUCH WAS HAPPENING IN THE WORLD OF DANNY CARVER and, although he didn't usually have time for sentiment, Danny did occasionally reflect on his status in this his final school year. He wasn't really concerned about life after school as he suspected several of his current projects would determine his future course, but one thing he was sure about was adrenalin. He needed it, and the more he had the more he wanted. The prospect of the Americans' arrival had ignited a spark in his brain, and although their visit was two weeks away, he had started to consider possible outcomes. Owning property in another country had to be difficult to control. Misdemeanours could go unnoticed. Government regulations could alter ownership rights. Visas could be revoked. The Griffin was beginning to fulfil most of the criteria for a high-risk establishment. One thing Danny had to ensure was that the Americans had no idea of Doreen's activities. The Griffin had to be a motel, not a bordello ... for now.

The Always Tomorrow bank account was growing nicely. The videos and Doreen's commissions provided a steady flow of income, and it was now possible with the advertising and betting commissions to make larger deposits in the term deposit account, which was getting a higher rate of interest. Doreen's control of Wilson and Danny's control of Doreen ensured no regulatory interference. However, Danny would keep pressing for better terms or a more widespread savings portfolio. Banks always saw property as a safe bet when it came to lending money, and Danny felt a certain leaning in that direction. The Americans might hold the key.

Danny had arranged to meet Sato at Fred's at 5.45, before looking over Jordan's four escort walkers.

"I think we are looking for presentability, a nice smile, clean appearance, soft accent and politeness. What do you think?" Danny looked at Sato.

"I agree but think it's extremely ambitious considering Jordan's appearance. Anyhow, we'll find out soon enough. They're outside." Sato nodded towards the door.

Fred wandered across before anyone knocked.

Jordan came in first, and Fred stood back as what could only be described as a motley crew filed in behind him. Possibly under instruction, they stood in line in front of the counter.

Fred didn't move. Jordan's escort team looked like they had just finished commando training on the nearby moor, with little sleep and no food. Each of them looked straight ahead as though waiting to be interrogated.

Fred closed his mouth, Sato looked at the tabletop and Danny stared at Jordan, hoping for an introduction. None was forthcoming.

Danny took a positive line and kept his comments simple and straightforward.

"Well done, guys. Congratulations on becoming our first escort walkers. Sato and I have produced a short checklist which will help you get lots of walks and earn more money. I'll go through each item with you. The first one is presentability. First impressions count. Which basically means, what the girls think when they first set eyes on you. For instance, when you came through the door, I noticed that Number 3, sorry, I don't know your name, had his shirt buttons fastened wrongly. The second button was in the third button-hole, so the shirt was pulled towards his right shoulder and the shirt flap pulled out from the top of his trousers. (Number 3 began fiddling with his shirt button). Number 4 has blood seeping from a nasty looking graze on his right knee. Possibly from a skateboard fall? Always wise to wear long trousers when you arrive for a Walk Home escort. No one is smiling. I like the discipline, but this is not a meeting with a Mafia Don. As the advert says, smile please! I see Number 4 has a front tooth missing, so maybe just a half smile. Hopefully, your earnings will enable you to get a replacement tooth."

Jordan sensed his team were beginning to relax and said "At ease."

Fred was on the verge of mild hysteria, but a glare from Danny prevented an outburst.

"Any thoughts, Sato?" Danny needed some support.

"Maybe we should give them an introductory phrase. One they can use when they first meet the girls?"

Danny nodded. "Good idea," and glanced at Jordan, who half-smiled in agreement.

"How about 'Good evening, girls, I'm John, your Walk Home escort,' said with a smile," suggested Danny.

There was no response, so Danny asked Jordan to take his team out of the café and come in again one by one and introduce themselves. Jordan nodded in agreement, and Fred unlocked the door and let them all out. When he closed the door behind them a stony silence descended on the room.

Danny peered through the window to see what was happening. Shirts were being re-buttoned, bloody knees wiped, half-smiles practised and Number 3 tried an exaggerated wink.

After what seemed like an eternity, Number 1 walked in ...

"I'm John, your Walk Home escort," he said.

"Is John your real name?" asked Danny.

"No, it's Clive."

"Okay, so go back out and come in using your real name."

Number 2 walked in confidently with a beaming smile. Sato and Fred nodded approvingly. Then ...

"Who's ordered a bloody Walk Home?" This time Fred did have hysterics and had to disappear into the storeroom.

Jordan ushered Number 2 out and in came Number 3, now smartly turned out with buttons and holes aligned.

"Good evening, girls, I'm Wilbur your Walk Home escort." Danny and Sato applauded in appreciation. Jordan managed a half-smile.

"Just one thing," said Danny, "is Wilbur your real name?"

"No, it's Fortescue, but I prefer Wilbur."

"Okay, let's stick with Wilbur."

Last to enter was Number 4, the toothless one.

"Why's he contorting his face?" asked Sato.

"He's the one with the missing tooth," said Danny, "but he's got the intro right."

"Okay, let's get everyone back in for a final briefing." Danny looked at Jordan who went to get them.

Fred had calmed down enough to come back and Danny was keen to finish on a positive note.

"Well done, everyone. You have two days before we go live. If Jordan's app requests a Walk Home escort, he will contact the nearest one. You must practise your contact script, get that right and dress appropriately. Everyone understand?"

"Finally, and most importantly. Do not become involved in any fighting if a young lout appears. Make a note of who the boy is and let Jordan know. He will exact the necessary retribution, and you may be involved in that. Also ask the girls for payment politely if anyone forgets. They will all be told by Sanjira in Year 12, that they should give the escort cash on arrival at their destination. Any questions?"

Fred asked "Free Cokes, lads?" and opened the cooler door.

Sato checked Jordan's mobile phone app and wished him good luck once he was sure Jordan was connected and understood how to answer a call. Jordan gathered up his Coke-swigging team and made for the door, turning only to glance and nod to Danny.

"Well, that was a bit of a struggle, but it's up and running now, Sato."

Sato said he was happy that they were only involved in taking membership monies. A lump sum at the start of each term meant less administrative work. If we get a 50% take up from the girls, that's a sizeable day's work.

Danny agreed. "I feel sure Jordan will improve the service when he realises how much money he can make."

Danny and Jordan left Fred's and headed home, stopping to look at the posters on lamp posts and in windows advertising Sports Day. The glossy posters highlighted the community aspect, the races, the barbecue, the raffle prizes, and there was a phone number for more details on the runners.

"Who do you get through to if you ring that number, Sato?" Danny asked.

"Jeff."

"Then what happens?"

"Jeff finds out if they're interested in placing a bet. If they are, he gives them another number."

"John Foster's, I presume?"

"Correct. We have no direct contact with the money until after Sports Day, when John balances the books. Since his career is at risk and in our hands, he will honour our agreement. When we bank the money, it will be as donations towards a charity we support. Therefore, no problem," Sato explained.

"Good work. Chris and Jeff have done well. I'm assuming they will explain it all at Fred's next week?"

"They will, Danny."

Danny thought for a moment, recognising that if he wanted to develop his crew's confidence, he had to allow them freedom to implement strategies, but as Commander-in-Chief, he had to provide the vision to stimulate and motivate them. The bigger picture had to be considered since this was their final year at school.

"As for the charity, how about the Always Tomorrow charity?"

Sato raised an eyebrow, before suggesting it would need premises.

"I have somewhere in mind," Danny assured him. Sato knew not to ask but would have placed a bet with John Foster that it would be The Griffin.

CHAPTER 44

THE GIRLS

SATO MET SANJIRA 15 MINUTES BEFORE SEEING THE YEAR 11 and 12 girls, to discuss how to present the Walk Home Escort Program. Sanjira agreed to introduce it, and Sato would assure the girls that he and the school captain had vetted the escorts. He would explain how the system worked and ask a girl to join him to help with the demonstration.

Kate, a Year 12 girl, stepped forward.

"Please text this number with your pickup point, delivery point and the time you would like the escort to arrive." Sato handed the number to Kate.

She hesitated, and then texted the number with her current position — the school yard, her drop off point and a time 10 minutes from then.

The room went deathly quiet, and then there was a ping on Kate's phone.

Kate read the text message.

"Hi Kate, my name is John. I'm your Walk Home escort. I will be with you in 10 minutes. Please quote the following code to me on arrival to confirm authenticity: J123. Cost to be paid in cash on completion of walk $10." Kate beamed and the girls applauded.

Sanjira stepped forward to congratulate Sato and address the girls.

"To benefit from our new Walk Home program, each of you has to pay a once-only term membership cost of $15. I have some membership forms here, and Sato will sign them and take your money and a photograph of you holding your form. Just a headshot. May I suggest you line up at the end of the desk? Those who need to get cash can do so as Sato will be here for a while. If you want to pay tomorrow, you can sign up today and your membership will be validated tomorrow when you give the money to Sato."

Sanjira stepped back and Kate came forward first. She took a form and began to fill it in. Soon everyone was filling in forms. Sato took Kate's photo and placed her $15 in a waistband pouch.

Unbeknown to Sato and Sanjira, Danny had been listening outside. He came in and shook hands with Kate and thanked her earnestly. This was not lost on Janice who was about eighth in the queue. Danny smiled at her and mouthed "Coffee afterwards?"

Janice appreciated the gesture, smarmy as it was, and nodded.

Danny quickly made a mental note of the sign-ups, thanked Sanjira and left, thinking she should make a presentation to Bartholomew. He needed to know, and it would be heart-warming for him to know, that the girls were involved and being taken care of. There was no need for publicity, but Danny anticipated a knock on his door in the next few days.

CHAPTER 45

DANNY AND CAROL

DESPITE THE SUCCESS OF DANNY'S NEW COORDINATED approach, he had to deal with Carol Whittleston alone. What bugged him was the electricity between them at the governors' meeting. He had never experienced anything like that before.

He admitted to a personal connection with Janice and felt a certain amount of control. He could keep her at arm's length most of the time, but Carol was quite different.

He was scheduled to meet her at 3pm in an annexe off the library. The room had no windows and the library was often empty. For all Danny's streetwise maturity, he was wrestling with what to wear. White T-shirt and denims seemed too obvious, yet was the alternative school dress too young?

After much soul-searching, he compromised on denims and a school shirt, though even that made him feel uncomfortable. Plus, who might see him as he crossed the yard to the library building?

Danny was Carol's last interview for the day. What to wear had also preoccupied her. The red top, tight black skirt and high heels had been replaced by a more formal grey trouser suit with a navy-blue roll neck top. She squeezed on low-heeled shoes from the back of the cupboard, looked at herself in the mirror and shook her head in disbelief. This was simply not her!

Everything was a consideration for them both.

Danny wondered, do I knock on the door or just walk in?

Carol wondered, do I sit behind the desk or stand up?

Danny wondered, do I move forward to shake hands?

Carol wondered, do I lean across the desk to shake hands?

She was standing behind the desk when Danny walked in. Their eyes met and Carol stepped forward. They both reached out to shake hands, but neither let go and they kissed passionately. When it was eventually over, neither backed away and they couldn't take their eyes off each other.

The internal phone rang, breaking the ice. Carol picked up the phone and Danny could hear Bartholomew's voice.

"Yes, I'll pass the message on Headmaster." Carol put the phone back and sat down.

"Can you pop in to see the headmaster before you leave?"

Danny searched for something of relevance to say, but settled for "Sure."

He pulled up a chair and sat down, but the laser look continued and they stood up simultaneously and embraced passionately again. Neither of them had ever experienced anything like this before. Neither could stop, and neither wanted to. The passion affected Danny's balance, and he felt himself moving backwards until he was leaning against the wall. Carol pressed Danny hard against the wall and an inevitable outcome became apparent. He twisted her around, so she had her back to the wall, and for a moment she wished she had her black skirt on. Fumbling, out of control and passionate, both partners were in unison, and location, time and unlocked doors of no consequence.

Danny and Carol became one. They gripped each other in raw ecstasy. Horizontal, the moment would have continued, but vertically against the wall there were safety considerations, and they wanted to get dressed quickly, but they were both giggling as they zipped up.

Back in a sitting position all they could do was smile, giggle and shuffle until Carol said "Well, thank you, Danny. I think you've made a good choice, career wise that is."

"Thank you," said Danny, do you think I could contact you again to clarify some of the details?"

Carol smiled and flicked her business card across the table and Danny caught it as he rose to leave.

"How do I look? he asked as he straightened his clothes and hair.

Carol laughed and sighed. "Just fine, just fine."

Danny almost floated across the school yard on his way to Bartholomew's office. Anyone might have thought he had just won the lottery.

Bartholomew didn't though. He put two and two together very quickly and began to make fun of him.

"Are you okay, Danny? You look a little flushed." Bartholomew smiled. Wisdom beats streetwise every time, he thought.

"Might be coming down with something, sir." Danny shuffled in his seat.

Bartholomew continued to tease him. "What's that on your shirt collar? Looks like a soft powder — pinkish."

Danny stood up to look in the mirror. He knew what it was. "Not sure, sir. I'll put it in the wash when I get home. Now what do you want me for, sir?"

"Sanjira came to see me today with details of the new Walk Home escort service. It's a wonderful initiative and I suspect you are behind it, Danny? However, let's keep it low profile for now."

"Makes life easier for the girls, sir. That's the main thing." Danny stood up to leave.

"Indeed it does, Danny. One last thing, make sure you wash that powder off your shirt when you get home." Bartholomew knew of course just what had happened, but since Danny's appointment his job had become far less confrontational and in fact he was quite enjoying his role. He would look forward to seeing Miss Whittleston before she left though. He mused over mentioning the powder, then decided out of devilment he would.

Danny melted into the corridor, but headed for the toilet first to address the powder.

As he left the toilet, a lady in a grey trouser suit disappeared into Bartholomew's office.

"Have a seat, Carol. How would you describe your day? I see Danny Carver, our school captain, was your last interview." Bartholomew was loving this.

Carol fought hard to avoid blushing, but Bartholomew was lasering her and, just as she was about to answer, he struck.

"What's that pinkish powder on your sweater, Carol?" Bartholomew stared earnestly at her.

Carol was about to answer when he struck again.

"Our school captain had the same powder on his shirt. Do you think we have a problem, Carol?"

Carol stood up immediately and, in a clumsy attempt to relieve the situation, walked over to the mirror and began brushing the powder off.

"Certainly not, Headmaster. I think the red chalk Danny and I used has drifted onto our clothing."

Good answer.

"What's your opinion of Danny Carver. Can he be trusted?"

"Not sure, sir. He's a very calculating young man, very mature for his age and, if I may say so, very streetwise." Carol stayed poker-faced.

"Hmm, he is. I've given him a long leash and it's proved a good move. There seems to be less hassle with pupils — and staff for that matter. Be careful with him, Carol, though. He can be addictive because he is success-based. Don't let him get too close. Oh and use different coloured chalks."

"I'll make a point of that, Headmaster." Carol leant forward to shake the headmaster's hand, then quickly looked away. Outside she took a deep breath and headed for the car park. Mentally she wanted to move on. Emotionally she needed to see Danny. She didn't know why, but she craved his touch. What was he thinking? Where was he? What happens next? What do I do next?

Sitting in the car, Carol searched for answers, but she was helplessly locked in.

Danny stretched out behind his desk, trying to come to terms with what had just happened. The young man who had an answer for everything was floundering. I can deal with anything and find a practical and a theoretical solution, so why am I wrestling with this issue, he wondered? He allowed himself a wry smile as he thought back to Bartholomew's cross-examination. Danny knew the wise old headmaster was fully aware of what had happened in the library annexe. The fact Bartholomew had not mentioned anything confirmed Danny's value to him. The headmaster could cruise through to an early retirement knowing Danny Carver would control the school and some of the staff.

He glanced down at Carol's contact details and sighed heavily. Then there was a light knock on the door, followed by "Coffee time," and in walked Janice.

CHAPTER 46

UPDATE MEETING AT FRED'S

"I THINK YOUR CREW ARE BETTER THAN JORDAN'S, DANNY," Fred shouted from behind the counter. "At least they can dress themselves." He burst out laughing while Danny and Sato smiled and Chris and Jeff looked bemused. Sato explained, and Danny began the meeting.

"Firstly, well done you two. The posters placed around the town are brilliant. Can you update us on Sports Day arrangements? There are seven days to go."

Chris took out a sheet of paper and began. "I'll give you this at the end of the meeting," he said to Sato.

Danny looked impressed, especially as the paper was A4 size, and appeared to have writing on both sides.

Chris continued, "I'll work through and ask for your thoughts after each step, Danny." Danny nodded. "And you, Sato."

"Firstly, Sam Johnson has agreed to be the MC. He will have four cars parked around the field and one just outside so people queuing can see it. He has also donated a raffle prize: a 10-year-old BMW 3 series. He suggests, and we need to confirm, he use some of his sales force to sell the tickets and we split the profit once the value of the car, which is $4,500, has been reached. Tickets are $25 each, or five for $100. Sales are going really well."

"I thought you said we had to confirm?" interrupted Danny.

Jeff stepped in. "Too good an offer to turn down, Danny, so we confirmed. All the tickets are numbered and coded, and we already have 1,000 stubs. Sam's sales force is unbelievable."

Danny felt like cheering, but just said "Outstanding work, lads. Well done."

"The school PE department has a loudspeaker system we can use. Sam collected it the other day," Chris added.

"Colin Punter has agreed to be the official photographer for all the races. He will also set up a photography station where family and group photographs can be taken. We get 50% of all takings."

Danny nodded in approval. "What about the Punter's wife?" he asked.

"Sausage barbecue. She will bring the barbecue and set it up. Sausage sandwiches at $5. We reminded her that she may need a backup supply of sausages and rolls due to the numbers attending. We get $1 for each sausage sold."

"Fred's coffee stall. Hot fresh coffee sold from the back of his van close to Mildred's barbecue. We get $1 per cup."

Danny asked "How do we know how many coffees Fred sells?"

"We have supplied and numbered the paper cups," Chris explained. "Oh, and Fred wants to call his stall 'Nudge, Nudge'."

"Doreen's fortune tent." Chris waited for questions. None came, but Sato was holding back his tears. "Doreen is charging $25 to read fortunes. Two blokes, Roger, and Leslie, will put up her tent. We get $5 for every fortune told."

Chris paused for a reaction. "I like this," said Danny, "because she'll be sure to offer her other services and there is no direct link to us. Roger and Leslie need a table with Griffin brochures available. I'll get them to do that, Chris. Leave it to me."

Chris turned over his sheet of paper.

"Bouncy Castle. The girls would like to run that, Danny, and they think it should be free. They will man it, so it will give mums free time to wander round the other stalls. Sanjira has an uncle who will provide the bouncy castle, and he's donated $100 to the Always Tomorrow charity. Here's the cheque." Chris handed it over to Danny, who passed it on to Sato.

"Oh, one other thing. Kate and Janice say they will look after the governors. They suggest putting some seats on the grass bank opposite the finish line where they can rope an area off and provide drinks and sandwiches. Gerald Trapper has agreed to present medals to the winners. Gold, silver and bronze. Bartholomew has asked the metalwork department to make them."

"That's excellent, Chris. Janice and Kate are into detail, I can assure you," Danny smiled.

"Bartholomew will make a short speech and open the games officially. I'll speak to him — no, you can, Chris and Jeff. He'll like that. I've no doubt he'll drop into my office next week."

"Video. Henry Legend, the science teacher, wants to video all the races. He's in the parents' support group and wants to sell them. The money goes directly into school funds. Jeff and I think we ought to agree to this. Bartholomew will love it."

Chris waited for approval, and Sato said "I think we have the balance right, Danny. The school has to benefit financially."

"We could also use the filming to check any betting disputes," said Danny.

"We felt it would be a good idea to have Jordan's crew dressed in fluorescent tops as Sports Day stewards organising the queues and seating, and ensuring the runners are ready for each race."

Danny asked how Mr Foster was getting on with the online betting.

"He's getting lots of bets, Danny — amazingly from members of staff, some paying cash direct. Phil the drunk from Fred's has opened a Friday afternoon betting table at Fred's. Fred takes a percentage of each bet placed. We felt it wise to keep out of this one, Danny. Phil has a loose tongue and the less he knows the better."

"Agreed," said Danny, and Sato nodded in approval.

"Bartholomew has invited all the governors, and they're meeting in the staffroom for drinks an hour before the first race. Maybe you should go too?" Chris waited for a response.

"Sure, I'll be there in good time." Then he realised it would be the first time he would see Carol since the library annexe. Should he contact her first?

Chris brought Danny down to earth again. "That's all from Jeff and me. All that remains is to hand over this bag of cash to Sato." Sato looked up as Jeff reached into his rucksack and struggled to lift out a fabric bag containing notes and coins.

"This contains the entry ticket, raffle ticket and advertising sales money."

Danny smiled as Sato dragged the bag across the table to count it.

"That's great work, lads. May I suggest you go back over each of the areas you've covered and keep driving the numbers? Now we have momentum, we must keep it going. I'll deal with the political and diplomatic issues. Let's meet here after school next Wednesday to finalise our plans." Danny stood up and shook hands with Chris and Jeff. So did Sato, and then he sat down again and began to separate notes from coins. "What an outstanding effort, Danny," he said as Chris and Jeff left.

"Now it's my turn to take it to another level," Danny said. "When you've counted that lot, can you bank it? I'm off to make a few phone calls."

Danny waved at Fred to meet him outside, and Fred glanced round the café then had a quick word with Doreen who was in the storeroom.

"Can you ask Phil discreetly how much money he's received in bets and on which races?" Fred knew when to play a straight bat. "Will do. He'll be in on Friday."

Danny thanked him and went off to find a quiet seat in the park to make some private phone calls.

"Hi, John, it's Danny. Just a quick call to thank you for your money-raising efforts. I hear from Chris and Jeff that lots of people, including members of staff, are placing bets."

"It's incredible, Danny, and Friday is staff salary day so I'm expecting a late surge of betting."

"That's great, sir. Might be a good idea to close the books the day before the races to ensure you're not exposed?"

"Good idea, Danny. I'll need some time to update the accounts."

"One other thing, sir. Have there been any interesting bets or large amounts?" Danny was fishing for the answer he wanted.

"Well, one of your colleagues — Jordan Smith — has placed a substantial amount on two races: the 200 and 400 metres. Interestingly, these races have firm favourites in Jenkinson and Philpott, and Jordan has backed them both to come second."

"What are the odds on that happening, sir?"

"Both runners are odds on to win and the double is very popular, so we've had lots of bets," Foster said.

"What are the odds on both finishing second, sir?"

"100 to 1, Danny."

"Might be worth a few dollars," Danny laughed. "Speak soon." He clicked off. He knew that if Jordan were backing both runners to come second, he was having them nobbled. Danny wasn't going to miss this opportunity. He just needed someone to place the bet.

He had two options. One was to get an outsider to place a bet with Phil the drunk on Friday afternoon, the second was to do it with John Foster. Danny knew one answer but was searching for the narrative. Then he pressed the accelerator.

CHAPTER 47

DANNY AND CAROL: TAKE 2

"HI, CAROL, IT'S DANNY."

There was a pause as Carol held her breath. This was the call she craved.

"Hi, Danny, good to hear from you." Carol flopped back onto her sofa and cuddled a cushion. "What's happening?"

"Couldn't hold on any longer — had to speak to you. Do you think we could meet for coffee somewhere?" Danny held his breath.

Carol's immediate response stunned him.

"Red wine would be better. Come around now. I'll text my address." The phone went dead. Danny stood staring at it. Carol rolled around like a schoolgirl on the sofa, then composed herself and texted the address.

Danny responded immediately, moving before he had even finished the text. Only a 15-minute walk or three-minute Uber. No planning needed. He was going to play this purely on instinct.

Carol's apartment was in a small block at the end of a quiet street lined with fig trees and jacarandas. He pressed number 3 and waited.

"Hi, Danny, come up. Second floor. Come straight in, it's open now." Carol pressed the unlock button and Danny walked through. He almost sprinted up the stairs. Carol was putting her glass of red down as he entered. Neither spoke. Neither moved. But the emotion was overwhelming, and then Danny responded instinctively both mentally and physically. In a fumbling connection they both crashed onto the sofa. Garments off, fumbling replaced with calm and sensitivity. Then the crescendo, loud and mutual.

"Do you like red wine, Danny?"

Danny leant back and laughed. "Usually before," he smirked.

"I've more in the cupboard," she smiled.

"I'm sure you have, and I intend to work my way through it," he assured her.

Carol laughed and a gentle uncoupling took place. They still hadn't made it to the bedroom.

"Let's go somewhere for a week at half-term, Danny." Carol fired the first shot, and solved Danny's problem of who could place his first bet.

"Great idea, but a little costly. I'm school captain not purser."

Carol laughed. "I'm sure you'll come up with an answer before you leave." This made it a little more difficult for Danny, but it did allow him to say "I see you're coming to Sports Day."

She ran her fingers through Danny's hair and then reached for her drink.

"I am. Are you seeing the governors beforehand, darling?"

This new personal reference reassured Carol. She was totally committed, and Danny moved in to close the deal.

"I've just thought of a way to finance our half-term trip," he said. "Can you keep a secret?

"Of course."

"I've heard that John Foster is taking bets on who'll win the races. Lots of members of staff are betting. For instance, in the boys 200- and 400-metre races, Jenkinson and Philpott are hot favourites at 2 to 1."

"That sounds like an easy win, Danny. Are you suggesting we should have a bet with Mr Foster?"

"No, as school captain I'm not allowed to bet. I'm sure Bartholomew would frown on it. But it would be a good way of raising money for our trip." Danny left it there, but Carol was ahead of him.

"I could put the bet on. How do I do it?"

"You ring Foster and tell him the amount you want to bet and give him your credit card details. He texts you a confirmation of odds."

"Give me his number. It must be on your phone." Carol winked. She knew he was manipulating the situation, but she loved being part of it.

"Slow down, we would have to put a lot of money on when the odds are so short."

"What do you suggest?" Carol knew Danny had it all worked out but was enjoying the game.

"Why don't you ask Foster for the odds on both favourites coming second?" Danny suggested.

"Okay, give me his number." Danny scrolled down his phone and handed it over to Carol who transferred the number and began dialling.

"Oh hi, John, it's Carol Whittleston from the Board of Governors." John Foster froze, his career and pension on the line.

"Not a problem, only I heard from a friend that I might be able to place a bet on some of the races next Thursday. I'll be at the Sports Day." Carol held the moment. She knew Foster was wary of a prank.

"What were you thinking of, Carol?"

"Well I would like to place a bet on Jenkinson and Philpott both coming second in their respective races. What are the odds on that happening?" Carol flicked the speaker button on.

"100 to one. Very long odds, I'm afraid," Foster said. How much do you want to bet?

Carol glanced at Danny, who mouthed $100.

"Can I use my credit card and place a bet for $100?"

Foster thought all his birthdays had come at once. This was the easiest money he had ever made.

Calmly he asked for Carol's credit card details, then thanked her and texted through confirmation.

"That means, Danny, that we win $10,000, and should be able to find a nice, private spot for our week away." Carol showed Danny the confirmation.

"I'll start looking," Danny smiled.

"No need, my parents have a stud about four hours' drive from here. I'll check if one of the lodges is available. You'll like the area. The lodges are very private."

Danny had thought Carol was very relaxed about placing the bet with Foster. Now he understood why. And Carol knew that if Danny was betting against firm favourites something had been arranged.

Danny's next call had to be to Sam Johnson. He would have the contacts to quadruple the bet. He hugged Carol and kissed her on the cheek. "See you soon," he whispered.

"You know where I am."

Two minutes later, Sam Johnson's phone rang.

"Hi, Sam, Danny Carver here. Can we meet this evening? I have something mutually beneficial I want to discuss with you?"

"Sure. Do you know The Griffin on the edge of town?"

"Yes, I think so. Is it the one just off the main road?"

"It is. See you there about 6." Sam rang off.

Danny's brain switched into overdrive, and he phoned firstly The Griffin, then Doreen.

CHAPTER 48

THE STING: TAKE 2

DANNY WENT INTO THE GRIFFIN WITH THE AIR OF A FIRST timer, and Leslie asked "Can I help you, sir?"

"Yes, I'm looking for the lounge area."

"Just to your right, sir. Enjoy yourself." Leslie looked hard into his desktop.

Danny walked slowly into the lounge, trying to ignore Doreen and Roger who were wrestling over the crossword in *The Advertiser*.

"Hi, Danny, over here," called Sam.

Danny smiled, shook hands limply with Sam and made sure he was sitting with his back to Doreen and Roger.

"What can I do for you, Danny? First let me get you a drink. What would you like?"

"Just a Coke, please." Danny eased back in his chair, noticing Doreen crossing her legs, revealing her stocking tops in her reflection in the window just as Sam got to the bar.

"Another beer and a Coke please, barman," Sam said.

Sam was reaching for his wallet when Doreen played an ace card. "Put it on my tab please, Roger," she said demurely. Sam turned, but Doreen just said "No need. Maybe we can talk later?"

Sam couldn't think of anything to say, so he nodded and left.

"That was interesting. That lady at the bar bought these. Maybe I should return the compliment later."

Danny pushed the commercial button. "Could be a BMW lady, Sam?"

"We'll see. Now, what can I do for you?"

"Firstly, thanks for agreeing to be the Sports Day announcer. I'm sure you are aware that John Foster is taking bets on the races." Danny hesitated, but Sam nodded.

"Well, I think there's a betting scam in the 200- and 400-metre races, and I don't know what to do about it."

Sam remained poker-faced and said "Go on."

"A large amount of money has been placed on Jenkinson and Philpott in the 200 and 400 races respectively for both to come second," Danny explained.

Sam reached into his jacket pocket and took out the Sports Day program. "Both are hot favourites, Danny, at 2 to 1. Are you suggesting they've been got at?"

"I know who put the bet on, and he's a dodgy character, Sam. He wouldn't bet against them if he didn't have some control over the outcome."

"By large amount, are we talking hundreds?" Sam asked.

"We are," Danny confirmed.

"What are the odds of both coming second?"

"100 to 1."

"Give me Foster's number please. I know some bookmakers in town. We can make a killing if you're right," Sam said, and then played the card Danny was hoping for: "If this information proves correct, I'll cut you in for 20% of the profits." He leant forward and shook Danny's hand.

Danny smiled and stood up. “Time I left you to join your lady friend.” He winked and headed for the door. Sam got up and walked towards Doreen’s web of desire.

Chapter 49

Sowing the Seeds

DANNY'S ONE OPPORTUNITY TO SOW THE MEDICINAL cannabis seeds in Potter's lab was on the Wednesday morning while Potter was at the library. He decided to ask Sanjira round for a coffee to explain the strategy. This was high risk because Sanjira might not agree to help. All he needed her to do was make sure no one was in the back lab when Chris and Jeff went in. He reckoned it would take about 30 minutes. The girls had to check the seeds weekly as though they were herbs, but they didn't need to know they were cannabis.

Sanjira listened calmly to Danny's plan. When he finished, she stood up, looked him in the eye and said "It will be done." Then she left.

Danny was stunned, and then Janice came in. "What did Sanjira want?" she asked.

"Just some clarification on the escort program," Danny answered.

Janice switched on the coffee machine and sat down in a wicker chair.

"So, Mr Organiser, what's happening in the high-flying world of Danny Carver?" Fortunately for Danny the coffee was ready just then, and Janice stood up to pour, giving him the breathing space he needed to respond.

"Just finalising details for Sports Day. Are you happy with your role? Is Kate good to work with?" Danny reached for his coffee and Janice smiled. "Yes, and we've checked the weather forecast. Cloudy all day. Even so, we'll have a canopy ready to erect if there's a shower. Can I speak to that dodgy friend of yours if we need help putting it up?"

"You mean Jordan? Of course. I'll ask him to contact you. Is that okay?"

"I don't need to meet him, so a phone call's enough. Also, we thought a lucky dip for the governors and guests would be fun. We'll wrap some presents and put them in a box or maybe a cardboard BMW."

"Great idea. Sam Johnson will love that." Danny laughed as he thought of how to spice the dip.

Then Mr Bartholomew poked his head around the door. "Oh, sorry, didn't realise you had company, Danny." And he winked just before Janice turned around.

Danny froze as Bartholomew went on "Many thanks for your note re the governors on Sports Day, Janice. Good to know you and Kate will be looking after us. Don't let Mr Trapper drink too much. He's presenting the trophies."

Janice smiled. "I'll keep my eye on him, sir."

Bartholomew turned back to Danny. "Good, that's all then, Danny. Pleased to see you changed your shirt. Pink is not your colour." One final wink and he left. Danny tried not to blush, but Janice probed. "You don't have a pink shirt, what's he talking about?"

Danny reached into his desk drawer and took out a red chalk marker. "We were using this to outline Sports Day details and some chalk got onto my collar." Bartholomew was listening on the other side of the door, and smiled as he heard Danny wriggle off the hook.

"Everything okay, Headmaster?" Miss Stanger asked as she glided down the corridor.

Bartholomew stood to attention quickly as the head of his Praetorian Guard approached.

"Just admiring how maturely the young people under our care are behaving. So grateful to you for your support, Deputy Headmistress. Danny and Janice are having coffee." Bartholomew was through his office door before she could reply. If he'd peeked outside, he would have seen his deputy listening at Danny's door and almost fall into the room when Janice came out. "Oh sorry, Miss Stanger. Are you all right?" Miss Stanger stumbled forward on all fours like a foal learning to walk. "Yes fine, thank you. Just dropped my pen. Ah, there it is. Must dash. Got a class of naughty Year 8s."

Miss Stanger adjusted her hair and clothing and stumbled down the corridor.

Bartholomew and Danny sat back in their offices. Bartholomew loved the mischief of it all. He knew Danny was in deep water, and while he was swimming strongly the shark-infested currents ahead were treacherous.

At any rate, Danny realised, he could not wind the clock back, and what had happened over the last few days had happened. He knew there would be a day of reckoning, but the priority now was sowing the cannabis seeds in Potter's labs.

On Wednesday morning, Danny handed the small box of seeds over to Chris and Jeff, then watched quietly as Potter drove off to the library. Jordan was acting as lookout just in case Potter returned unexpectedly.

Chris and Jeff smiled at Sanjira, who had arranged for all existing plants to be taken out of the troughs. All Chris and Jeff had to do was sow the seeds and fix the labels on the front of each planter: "Herbs, do not touch. Germination in progress"

"I'll see they're watered regularly," Sanjira said, as Chris and Jeff left the lab. They nodded and were gone in a whisper.

Danny watched as they crossed the yard, then texted Jordan "Thanks, all over now. Pop in Friday morning." Jordan didn't reply, but Danny knew he would be there.

The Wednesday meeting at Fred's focused totally on Sports Day.

"Let's go over your previous report again, Chris, just to make sure we haven't missed anything. Do you need to add anything?"

"Just one thing, Danny. The word on the street is that there may be a big crowd. Best you hand over the takings to date, Jeff."

Jeff struggled to lift a cloth bag full of coins and notes over for Sato.

"If a big crowd's on the cards, Jeff and I think we should inform the police. If the school road gets blocked, where will people park?"

"Good point. Who owns that field adjoining the school playing fields?" Danny asked.

"Phil's dad," said Jeff.

"Perfect." Fred, have you got Phil's number?" Fred wrote the number down and took it over.

"Carry on with the meeting, Sato, I'm just going outside to make a few calls." Danny left the café to solve the potential problem.

Firstly, he called Phil, then Phil's dad, and then Sergeant Philips at the local police station. The outcome was assured. Phil was obliged to help as he was making so much money taking bets at Fred's on Fridays. He spoke to his father, Ronnie, who agreed to charge $5 for parking. Sergeant Philips was on Doreen's play list, so their conversation was short and sweet.

Danny went back inside. "Let's make it happen, guys," he said. Then Sato raised one more point. "What do we do with all the money we collect on the day, Danny? It could be a large sum."

Danny thought for a moment and then dialled the bank.

"You can go, lads. I'll see you at school tomorrow morning."

"Good morning, it's Danny Carver. Could you put me through to the manager please?"

CHAPTER 50

SPORTS DAY

BARTHOLOMEW GAZED OUT OF HIS OFFICE WINDOW AND sensed an atmosphere like no other in his 20 years at Merryvale High. Both staff and pupils appeared to be moving faster than normal. There was a buzz of excitement in the air. Maybe he should just pop down the corridor and check everything was in order before he addressed the staff. He knocked quietly on the Danny's door and slipped in. Danny was fiddling with the coffee machine. "Ah Mr Bartholomew, would you like a coffee? I think I've got the hang of this machine now?"

"Just a quick short black." Bartholomew knew how to rock Danny's boat.

Danny smiled, then pressed a few buttons and stood back confidently. "Voilà!" He handed the coffee to Bartholomew. "Please sit down, sir."

"I'm assuming the atmosphere of excitement and expectation currently pervading the school concerns Sports Day?"

"Correct, sir. Sport is such a unifying medium. Do you have your opening remarks prepared?"

"I certainly do. I'm thinking of an Ancient Roman theme. What do you think?"

"Gladiatorial works for me, sir. Very appropriate. A sort of 'are you not entertained?'"

Bartholomew thought for a moment then recalled the moment from the movie *Gladiator*. Maybe I could experiment at the staff meeting, he thought.

"Are you coming to meet the governors?"

"Sure, wouldn't miss it for the world."

I bet you wouldn't, thought Bartholomew, knowing full well Carol Whittleston would be in attendance.

"Okay, I'll see you later. Have a good morning." Bartholomew left the room no wiser than when he entered. However, Danny's confident demeanour was reassuring. Now he just had to rev up the staff. Or did he?

Usually the end-of-the-week meeting was a dour affair, but not that day. The air of expectation almost bowled the headmaster over as he entered the room. Bartholomew sensed the occasion and threw caution to the wind. If only he had a helmet! As silence descended on the room, he spread his arms and cried "What we do in life echoes in eternity." A stony silence followed, so he carried on "Are you not entertained?" There was an embarrassed shuffling, then Potter and Miss Stanger shouted "Gladiator!" and the staffroom came alive. Bartholomew's self-esteem began to rise, and he raised his arm for quiet.

Chapter 51

Preparing the Arena

ALL MORNING MERRYVALE HIGH WAS A HIVE OF ACTIVITY. Ropes were pulled, tables carried, entry gates put in place, Sam Johnson experimented with the tannoy, the groundsman checked the line markings, Mildred's barbecue was warming nicely, Mr Woo's noodle urn bubbled away merrily, Roger and Leslie were wrestling with Doreen's fortune tent, The Griffin table was covered with brochures, and Henry Legend roamed here and there, videoing every action and reaction. Punter manipulated his lengthy frame into awkward positions as he took shot after shot with his zoom lens, and finally the bank put up a small marquee and brightly coloured banner, positioned perfectly so people had to pass the entrance and table of brochures. Danny smiled as he noticed Helen Walker laying out brochures and pens.

He stood on the bank opposite the finishing line and surveyed the scene, glowing with pride as his battleground came to life, and then he roared with laughter as he saw Jordan's crew trying to wriggle into fluorescent tops. Across to his left there were already a few cars parked neatly in line with their boots open on Ronnie's field, people sipping wine and munching sandwiches. Danny glanced at his phone and saw there were still two hours to the first race. Time now to prepare to meet the governors — and Carol — but first, one of Doreen's brochures.

CHAPTER 52

LET'S GET THE SHOW ON THE ROAD

DANNY STRAIGHTENED HIS TIE, BRUSHED A HAND THROUGH his hair and smiled at himself in the mirror. He picked an envelope up off his desk with a voucher for a free visit to Doreen's fortune tent and left the room.

The staffroom was a buzz of activity and conversation. Kate and Janice had set a table on one side, beautifully decorated with flowers and a wonderful assortment of finger food. There was wine and soft drinks, and a cardboard BMW (thank you, Mr Atkins), full of lucky dip prizes at the far end.

Janice and Kate wore matching aprons in school colours. Danny quietly dropped the envelope into the BMW before congratulating them on their table.

As lessons ended, members of staff arrived and mingled with the governors. Danny could not feel Carol's presence. Trapper arrived and Kate handed him a glass of wine. "Good to get the first one down the gangplank," he muttered. Atkins sidled up to Sam Johnson's girlfriend Tracie, having checked that Sam was out on the field rehearsing.

Danny tried to look relaxed as he moved from group to group. Small talk didn't really interest him, but he had to do something as he waited for Carol to arrive.

"You look edgy, is everything okay?" Janice asked.

"Just pre-match nerves. This is turning out to be a much bigger event than I thought. Better keep mingling. Excuse me." Danny wandered off but Janice was not convinced. Mr Cool was a little flustered, as though some of the red chalk had jumped from shirt collar to cheek. He's up to something, she thought.

Janice managed to give Councillor Trapper a glass of water between glasses of wine, and Joan Webster busied herself with a small flower arrangement, occasionally dragging Mr Bartholomew over for a nod of approval.

"You must let me arrange some flowers in your office, Headmaster." Bartholomew cringed inside, then suggested a week on Thursday when he would be away at a conference.

Not the answer Joan sought, but access had been granted and there would be other occasions.

Tracie was under extreme pressure from Atkins, who was edging ever closer and becoming ever louder. Danny winked at her and stepped between them. "Sorry to interrupt you, Mr Atkins, but Sam needs some moral support with the tannoy. You'd better go out and help him, Tracie." Tracie didn't reply, she just headed for the door.

"Thought I was doing okay," Atkins complained. Danny consoled him with "You were, but this is not the time or the place. Pop in for a coffee next week: we can talk strategy."

The atmosphere returned to normal. Janice and Kate offered the guests sausage rolls, and Councillor Trapper continued to drink — a little too much, Janice thought, so she took his glass and gave him two sausage rolls and a napkin. Danny smiled at Janice, but then the staffroom door opened and Carol came in. Time stood still as Danny and Carol fought to avoid eye contact. A second seemed like a minute, a minute an hour. Atkins pushed a hand forward and welcomed Carol, who came alive, shook his hand firmly and suggested he might get her a drink. "Come with me," he said, "we have red and white." Danny welcomed Atkins' intervention as his frozen reaction was not lost on Janice. "You've got that look again, sort of stiff and pink," she said.

"I'm just worried Atkins may make a fool of himself," Danny wriggled off the hook.

"It's not your business, Danny, is it?"

"No, I just feel very responsible for the entire day."

"As long as it's only for the entire day, then that's okay." Janice glared at Carol, and Danny searched for an exit strategy, but his instinct had deserted him. He just stood rooted to the spot. Bartholomew rescued him. Now was not the time for his champion to fall.

"Lovely buffet, Janice. You and Kate must be incredibly pleased," he said. "Get me a beer please, Danny, will you?"

How do you move slowly when you want to sprint away? How do you stay calm when you are under scrutiny? Danny smiled and sidled away.

"You must be enormously proud of Danny, Janice. The school is a far happier place since he became school captain."

"I am, sir, but something seems to be bothering him."

"Pressure gets to us all at times. He'll be fine when the races begin."

Danny rummaged through an ice bucket until he found the beer he was looking for. Carol was an arm's length away, still entangled in Atkins' scintillating do-it-yourself conversation. Both needed to make contact, but the stakes were high although Bartholomew had eased the pressure. Danny caught Carol's eye briefly.

"There you are, sir, you'll enjoy this. It's from a local brewery, one of our sponsors. We left it out of the brochure for obvious reasons, but gave him the right to supply all the school's soft drinks for the year. Hope that meets with your approval?"

"Yes, it does, Danny. Maybe you would introduce me to the brewery representative during the afternoon?"

"Of course, sir." Danny would have engaged in any conversation, just to alleviate the pressure of Janice's stare. He avoided looking at her in case she could see right through him. The two most important women in his life were within arm's length, but he couldn't speak to either of them. Then, as manna from heaven, Sam Johnson burst into the staffroom and announced through the tannoy "Would all guests and staff members please make their way to the private area under the blue canopy looking down on the finish line."

As they were about to leave, Danny suggested they all come back after the final relay race.

Bartholomew made the first move, and Joan Webster seized the opportunity to take his arm. "I'm with you, Headmaster. Let's go."

Several younger members of staff joined in with "Tally ho!"

Gerald Trapper reached for another glass of wine, but Janice said "Try this white, Mr Trapper. It's noticeably light," and handed him a glass of water.

Carol suggested Mr Atkins might escort her, and Danny breathed a huge sigh of relief. He picked up a brochure and left.

CHAPTER 53

THE MERRYVALE HOARDS

BARTHOLOMEW STOOD TRANSFIXED, STARING AT THE MASS of people in the playing fields. Guests and members of staff gathered silently behind him. Where had they all come from? To the left of the running oval there was an encampment of tents and advertising hoardings. People wandered in and around. Danny saw an elderly couple disappear into Doreen's tent, just as a rotund character bounced off the Bouncy Castle. "I thought it was for kids," he muttered. Mr Woo was busily spooning noodles onto paper trays, alongside Mildred who, in a fetching red bandana, was harpooning barbecued sausages, then ramming them into a bread roll. Sam Johnson was steering the patrons past his collection of BMWs to their hillside positions. Jordan Smith had negotiated a fee with him to ensure no one got into the cars. The field was full of cars and Danny could make out Ronnie, Phil's dad, waving his arms and stumbling about.

The competitors' area was a mass of young athletes writhing

and wrestling with their coloured garments and preparing to run the race of their lives. Chris and Jeff had agreed to act as race stewards, having first deposited a huge sum of money in the bank's security vehicle.

Guests and staff were motionless. Someone had to say something.

Again Sam Johnson came to the rescue and announced "Ladies and gentlemen, would you please put your hands together and welcome our headmaster, Mr Bartholomew, the school governors and guests."

Bartholomew shook off rigor mortis and raised both hands. The crowd raised theirs too, and it was a scene of historical drama. Bartholomew's confidence grew. He became Caesar, or a soccer manager returning with the league trophy. When he moved forward the mob cheered. Sam Johnson upped the tempo. "Remember, everybody, what we do in life echoes in eternity." The mob began to chant "Mew, mew, mew," prompted by Tracie holding up a cue card with MEW on it in bold red capitals.

Bartholomew was saturated in glory. If only he had a chariot and two white horses. He led the guests to the private area, raised both arms for quiet, reached for the tannoy and shouted "Are you not entertained?" The crowd loved it and "mew" reverberated around the Oval.

Danny stepped in and suggested everyone take their seats and "let the games begin!"

Bartholomew handed the tannoy back to Sam, who announced the competitors for Race 1.

Danny noticed many spectators reaching into their pockets and bringing out what appeared to be betting slips. Sam calmed them all down before the starting gun sounded, and a crescendo of noise met the runners as they sped down the track. Cheering and jubilation from some, cheering and despair from others, who threw their losing slips into the air.

Janice marshalled Gerald Trapper to the podium and ensured he gave Gold to the winner, Silver to the second and Bronze to the third. "Well done, Mr Trapper. Would you like another glass of white wine?" Danny was within earshot, and the afternoon continued with great merriment.

Sam Johnson made sure the sponsors and advertisers received plenty of publicity. "May I remind all of you that in the tented area, you can still buy noodles from Mr Woo, and the lady in the red bandana who looks like a serial killer, Mildred, is barbecuing, nay cremating, some sausages. Mildred raised her giant fork in the air and began waving it about. Customers backed off until a sausage had been harpooned, then tentatively offered an open bread roll. Mildred jammed the sausage in, before asking "Who's next for a whopper?"

Danny was a little concerned when the elderly couple who had gone into Doreen's tent came out looking distressed, and asked one of Jordan's crew to run down and tell Doreen that she should only predict good news.

Carol was sitting close to Bartholomew, but couldn't avoid Mr Atkins' leering attentions. Danny thought it wise to slip away and see the goings-on on the ground for himself. He wandered in and around tents and stalls, offering support and generally making people laugh. This was Danny at his best, surfing on a wave of success, communicating in his distinctive style. He loved ordinary people who lived every day as it came — not a hint of pretence, just a contribution in its simplest form. Danny never saw himself as a working-class hero, but he thrived on their happiness and humour ... and it was all for free! He really saw himself as a guide not a manipulator, even though the distinction was a grey area. And he wasn't calculating what the day might generate financially. As for most winners, the process was the main concern. The money would then fall into place. As Danny strolled around, he knew the process was working.

Throughout the heats there was great excitement and support for all the runners. During the short break before the finals everyone could feel the suspense as parents and guests checked their betting slips discreetly.

CHAPTER 54

GOING FOR GOLD

THE 200- AND 400-METRE FINALS WERE THE LAST RACES OF the afternoon. Danny had written the program to ensure maximum crescendo, especially as everyone knew how good Jenkinson and Philpott were. Both had successfully anchored their relay teams to victory earlier.

As far as the crowd were concerned, the entrée was over — bring on the main course.

Sam Johnson raised the tannoy. His voice showed signs of failing but he filled his lungs for one last burst of enthusiasm after glancing first at Danny and then rather slyly at three swarthy, dark-suited Latin types standing just opposite the finish line.

"Now the penultimate race. The one I know you have all been waiting for." There was a deathly silence. Hands reached into pockets. People glanced at their betting slips and shuffled their feet nervously.

"The boys 200-metre final. Over to you, Mr Starter." Sam nodded to the starter and tried not to look at the Latins, now mysteriously two, to his left.

The starter gun was fired and Jenkinson shot out of the blocks. After 50 metres he was the clear leader and as he turned the bend the people who had backed him began to jump and cheer. He was at least five metres in front as he entered the straight, then 10, the win a formality, when suddenly there was a second, louder, shot and he stumbled and fell. He leapt back on his feet, but stumbled again, and when he lunged towards the line he was overtaken in the briefest of moments. A hush descended upon the crowd. The unthinkable had happened. Jenkinson had come second. Betting slips were crushed in tight fists. Spectators shook their heads and sighed. The third Latin re-appeared, and Sam thought it wise to move on quickly.

"Wow, what a finish! But that's sport, ladies and gentlemen. We all live to fight another day. Now we move on to our final race of the afternoon, the boys' 400 metres. As you can see, the boys are down in front of us ready for this one lap finale."

The runners moved around nervously, waiting to be called by the starter. Some took a final sip of water. An olive-skinned character thrust a bottle into Philpott's hand and muttered "Dad said take a drink." Without thinking, Philpott took a big gulp as the starter called them to their marks.

The gun went off and the eight finalists headed for the first turn. Philpott was nicely placed in lane 3 and had a clear view of the five runners on his outside. The crowd analysed the start quickly and came alive as the runners sped down the back straight, Philpott about a metre ahead. Then suddenly his face turned crimson and he slowed as they rounded the final bend, lurched forward and began to vomit. Coughing and spluttering, he tried hard to carry on, but to no avail. The race was over, and a small family group cheered noisily as their son crossed the line.

The crowd were stunned! Their hero had fallen.

Sam seized the moment after glancing at the expressionless Latins who were leaving the arena. "Are you not entertained?" he screeched. "What an afternoon of high drama! Please, ladies and gentlemen, please continue to avail yourself of all the fabulous treats on offer. We still have an hour before we close. Remember, all your contributions go to the School Fund. Let's put our hands together and welcome, once again, our wonderful headmaster Mr Bartholomew."

Sam thrust the tannoy at a startled Bartholomew, who edged nervously forward. Danny stepped in with perfect timing "They are in the palm of your hands, sir. Give them your best."

Bartholomew searched for a historical response and Danny handed him a crumpled sheet of paper. "You dropped this, sir."

"Ladies and gentlemen, We have been royally entertained by the extraordinary pool of talent revealed by our community. You, the people of Redberry, have created an occasion of Olympic proportion. I raise my crown to you ... or should I say mortar board?" Bartholomew smiled at Danny, who nodded politely. Several members of staff cringed, and the mob clapped half-heartedly, not knowing what a mortar board was. One gentleman suggested it was a First World War term.

Bartholomew concluded by promising to contact all parents, sponsors and guests with a final total. "Have a safe journey home, and may your God go with you."

He handed the tannoy back to Sam, who immediately launched into "Three cheers for our headmaster — hip hip hooray, hip hip hooray, hip hip hooray!" Half the crowd joined in, and many people threw crumpled pieces of paper into the waste bins and made for the gate. The winners kept a low profile. Jordan nodded at Danny. Sam placed a winning arm around Tracie and they wandered off. Janice had one arm wrapped around Mr Trapper, who was incoherent and literally legless. She desperately wanted a word with Danny, but first she had to get Trapper back to the staffroom.

Danny mouthed "I'll see you in 20 minutes" and Janice nodded, but who knew what Danny could get up to in 20 minutes? As soon as Janice disappeared, Danny moved across to Carol and slipped a note into her hand.

Back in the staffroom there was great excitement and amazement. Redberry United got smaller crowds. Why did so many people come? And everyone was asking how much do you think we raised? Some thought thousands.

Danny came in and members of staff began to clap. Bartholomew stepped forward to raise his hand. Janice longed to join in, but she had to hold Trapper upright in his armchair. Potter was sulking in the corner. Carver could not be challenged.

Danny circled the room, and fortunately Atkins was still entertaining Carol. Henry Legend said he had more than enough video clips to make an Oscar-winning movie. Mr Foster tried discreetly to let punters know they would receive their winnings the next morning at break. Danny stopped at Janice and Trapper.

"Well now, you are the man, Danny Carver. You have won over the crowd," Janice said, which made Danny laugh out loud.

"Got to keep circulating. Let me know if you want a hand to get Trapper into a taxi," he said.

"Oh, I will for sure. Then I was thinking you might need one?"

"Sounds like a great idea to me." Danny was on fire. At which point Chris, Jeff and Sato came in. Danny immediately split them up.

"Go get some food, guys. I want a quick word with Sato." Chris and Jeff started at opposite ends of the food table. "Meet you in the middle," laughed Chris.

"Thoughts?" asked Danny.

"Could be beyond our expectations. I went over to the bank's security van three times with sacks of money. By the way, Helen Walker sends her regards. All the stalls were busy, so our commissions will be good. Plus the bets you placed. I've made a list of all our agreed and potential income streams. We should go through it when you've time."

"Agreed. I'm seeing Janice tonight, so let's meet at Fred's tomorrow after school. We should have a clearer picture by then. Want some food?"

Sato smiled. This was the Danny he loved. The calm super-achiever, never one to bask in glory, but wanting everyone under his influence and umbrella to realise his talent. He needn't worry — they did!

"Oh, one other thing, Danny. Did you notice those three blokes in dark suits? I saw them talking to Roger and Leslie. I think they're staying at The Griffin. Danny gave his usual non-committal look, but Sato knew he had taken that in.

Chris came over. "The careers lady said congratulations and thanks for the invite. She's leaving now."

Danny suggested to Janice it was time for Trapper's taxi, and Bartholomew stepped in and agreed. "You've done a wonderful job, Janice. Now spend some time with this young man. Let's get Gerald out to a taxi."

Arms were clamped around Trapper and he was raised to his feet. He half-walked, half-stumbled past the smiling staff.

As the taxi pulled away, Bartholomew decided to have some fun with Joan Webster and grabbed a bunch of flowers from the nearest vase. Danny smiled as he saw Bartholomew hand them to her, wondering what he was saying.

"My parents are away tonight, staying at Gran's. Let's grab a takeaway and relax. It's been a long day," Janice said. "Great idea," Danny replied, and she raised her eyebrows. It was never that easy.

Slowly the staffroom emptied, several people moving on to the nearest pub. The winners didn't want to let Mr Foster out of their sight, and Foster's rosy glow suggested he was on the right side of the financial ledger.

Chapter 55

A Cosy Evening

DANNY AND JANICE SPENT A COSY EVENING TOGETHER. HIS willingness to relax surprised her. A glass of wine and Netflix were not usually Danny's scene, however better not to ask any questions, but just go with the flow. Danny had programmed himself, and even suggested Janice choose an appropriate film. He did propose a short list, which included *Gladiator*, but Janice plumped for *The Bridges of Madison County*. Well, at least Clint Eastwood was in it, Danny thought.

An hour and two glasses into the film, Janice pressed the pause button and fired a piece of heavy artillery.

"I take it you'll be staying the night?"

"Only if you're comfortable with that? What's the likelihood of your parents coming back?

Janice recoiled a little. It was never this easy.

"I'll phone Mum around 10 o'clock just to check. It's a two-hour drive, so if they haven't set off by then they'll stay overnight.

But they may leave early as Dad has a hospital appointment."

Danny seized the opportunity. "Great! Because I'm meeting Sam Johnson at 7. He wants to introduce some Italian friends to me before they fly back to Italy. Another top-up?"

Danny filled Janice's glass and pressed the continue button, before putting an arm around her shoulder, and they both sank back into the settee as Clint and Meryl continued their middle-aged romance.

The morning sunlight was just beginning to seep through the bedroom curtains when Danny cast a one-eyed glance at the bedside clock. Slowly he began to disentangle himself from Janice's arms and legs — almost free, and then Janice re-wrapped!

"Got to go, I'll see you at school. Coffee in my office at break?" Danny, in a move Houdini would have been proud of, extricated himself from Janice's tentacles.

"Okay, see you then," Janice went back to sleep.

Danny thought about a shower, but decided it was wiser to leave the battlefield quickly. He did smile though as he went through the lounge. "Thanks, Clint," he muttered, "great night."

The Uber was 10 minutes away, and it was about a 10-minute ride to Carol's. Danny couldn't believe his luck — the driver was his old friend Mohammed.

"Big night eh, Danny?"

"Huge, Mohammed."

"Big morning eh, Danny?"

"Mum's the word, Mohammed."

"Sure is, Danny. I see you're not going home."

"Life's a challenge. See you next time. I'll give you a tip." Danny tapped Mohammed on the shoulder and got out of the car two doors away from Carol's apartment. The curtains were slightly open as Danny went up the stairs, and the front door was ajar.

"I'm in here." Danny knew Carol was in the bedroom, even though he'd never been there. Their mutual passion hadn't taken them further than the lounge carpet or settee.

'I'll make you breakfast afterwards. I assume you'll be dashing off?"

He undressed quickly and slipped between the sheets ...

"Tea or coffee?"

Danny pushed apart the shower doors and shouted "What?"

"Tea or coffee?"

"Coffee, please." He closed the doors and soaked up the hot water, shampoo and shower gel.

Carol smiled to herself as she poured the coffee. Danny was her Top Gun, her Tom Cruise. Of course, she knew there was no future in the relationship. She had tried before and to no avail. This was pure lust, raw and fulfilling. Why rock the boat? She wrapped her dressing gown tightly around her waist and put two mugs on the table. Danny walked into the kitchen, still drying his hair.

"Here, sit down and have your coffee." Carol realised that telling Danny to do anything was high risk. Best you could hope for was to steer him in the right direction. He might or might not respond.

"You'll be the school hero today. You know that don't you? But then again, it's the process that satisfies you not necessarily the outcome. Am I right?"

Danny smiled and whispered "You're not wrong."

"So, what's your next challenge?"

"When are you in again for a Careers Day? Book me in for the final one of the day, and I'll bounce a few ideas off you then."

Carol knew Danny had no plans to bounce any ideas off her, he was just getting ready to leave.

"Right, got to dash." He leapt to his feet, took a final swig of coffee, kissed Carol on the cheek and headed for the door.

"What about your hair?"

"It'll dry on the way to school. See you soon." And he was gone.

Carol wrapped both hands around her coffee mug, raised her eyebrows and smiled, wondering how on earth she had got herself in this position.

Chapter 56

Some Pressure

TWO STREETS FROM THE SCHOOL ENTRANCE DANNY COULD feel the buzz in the air. As he walked through the gates, several younger boys stopped footy to say "Hi Danny!"

His crew were idling in their usual spot and Jordan was admonishing a lad from Year 9 but stopped as Danny passed to nod approval.

"Pop in at lunchtime, okay?"

Jordan nodded and carried on twisting the Year 9's ear.

Danny laughed. "Fred's after school, lads?"

He headed for the staffroom, but as he approached the door, he sensed the quiet. Usually you could pick up small groups chatting away. He decided against going in and that a few minutes in his office might be the smarter move, but before he reached his door, the headmaster's door opened and two smartly dressed men in their 30s came out. Danny let them past, and a few seconds later Bartholomew knocked and came in.

"Morning, Danny, did you have a good night's rest? You certainly earned it!"

"Tossed and turned a little, sir. Hard to curb the adrenalin. I'm sure it will wear off." Danny was comforted by Bartholomew's approach, but even so he suspected a problem.

"Those two men who just left are from the Police Department. CID. It seems they are investigating a money-laundering scheme, possibly initiated from overseas. An event such as our Sports Day, which generated huge numbers, could be a target. What makes it more likely is that there are rumours circulating that a betting ring might have been operating." Bartholomew took deep breath and waited for Danny to say something.

"Do they have any firm leads, sir?"

"No, although they are suspicious of a group of three Italians who are staying at The Griffin."

Danny raised his eyebrows and Bartholomew continued.

"The motel on the outskirts of town."

"I know the one, sir. Never been there, mind you."

"Keep your eyes and ears open will you, Danny, and let me know if you find out anything. We made more than $10,000 yesterday. The most the school has ever earned from one event, and there is still more to come in. Well done. I hope you and Janice had a pleasant evening."

Danny forced a shy blush. "We watched *The Bridges of Madison County*, sir."

"I'll bet you did ... for a while," Bartholomew winked and left the room.

Danny sat behind his desk and realised how important it had been that he made all his fundraisers act independently. The three Italians concerned him, and he suspected Sam Johnson might be involved. A case of BMW money meets pizza money! No need to investigate it at this stage though. Sam had promised to cut Danny in for 20% of any profits. Danny went over all the financial revenue streams and satisfied himself that although he knew about them he was not directly involved.

Then a tap on the door, and a bunch of flowers preceded Janice's entrance. "Thought these might freshen up your office. Pass me the vase, please. Here, put the old ones in your bin. The cleaner will take them after school." Janice smiled and left.

The day went by slowly. Danny passed Mr Foster in the corridor and winked. Foster's broad smile showed all was well and he had turned a profit.

Mr Atkins shouted from his window "Don't forget our strategy meeting, Danny."

"Not a chance, sir. Just let me clear my head from yesterday. Maybe meet Monday lunch, say 12.30, my office?

Atkins called "Perfect!' and closed the window.

Chapter 57

Onwards and Upwards

FRED'S CAFÉ RESEMBLED A BATTLEFIELD THE DAY AFTER the battle. Tables were covered in used cups, mugs and plates. Phil the drunk was dozing in the corner. Fred and Doreen were nowhere to be seen. Danny and his crew stood there, surveying the scene. Where to sit was the number one priority.

When the storeroom door opened, Fred and Doreen emerged, Doreen straightening her dress and Fred with a stupid grin.

"What the hell's happened here, Fred?" Chris asked.

Doreen jumped in. "We've been swamped for five hours non-stop, cooking and serving."

"The best day in the café's history, boys," Fred smiled. All down to you, Danny. Everyone has been talking about the Sports Day carnival."

Danny laughed and got everyone back on track. "Do you think you could clear that table in the corner for us?"

"The usual, boys?" asked Doreen.

They sat down just as Phil wobbled and fell flat on the floor.

"Better give him a long black and send him on his way," Danny suggested.

Drinks arrived and Sato handed everyone an A4 sheet. "I want these back before you leave. They're only rough drafts." He glanced at Danny, who nodded approvingly.

They studied the numbers silently. Chris and Jeff were in awe of the amounts, Danny more circumspect. Sato waited for their comments.

"As I see it, $15,325 went into our account this morning?" Chris and Jeff stared at Danny in disbelief.

"Yes, and I checked with the bank to confirm that figure at lunchtime. By the way, Mr Wilson would like you to pop in and say hello," Sato said.

"What's the list of names at the bottom?" Jeff asked.

"They are the people or organisations that still owe us money. Most of this will be cash. Not sure what your arrangement with Sam Johnson was Danny?"

"20% of his winnings, probably cash, and we will have to trust him with the correct figure," Danny answered.

Sato pushed ahead. "I saw him talking discreetly to those three tanned-looking guys. Do you think they were involved, Danny?"

"I do, but we won't know until I speak to Sam — hopefully over the weekend. All the other people we can trust, and they'll pay over the next few days. As I said right at the outset, the less we're involved the better. The more winners, the safer we are. Now, the list:"

1) Sam and the Italians
2) Mr Woo
3) Mildred, the butcher
4) The Griffin Motel
5) Bank
6) Doreen's fortune tent
7) Legends video (donate to school)

8) Punter's weekly rag
9) Foster's betting
10) Escort walking.

They worked through the list, occasionally stopping to ask Fred not to sing or clatter the crockery.

Doreen finished the washing up and signalled to Danny. She put a roll of notes into his hand and thanked him.

"My pleasure. By the way, do you remember Alan Atkins from school?"

"Yes, I do. A bit arrogant, I thought, but generally okay," she said.

"Well, I'm seeing him on Monday for a strategy meeting, trying to improve his way with the ladies. Could you bear that in mind if you're prepared to see him again?"

"Ha! Not a problem. He has my number."

Danny went back to the table and handed the money over to Sato.

The commission will come in over the next couple of weeks, so no need to panic. By the way, Bartholomew had a visit from two policemen this morning. CID. They were talking to him about a money-laundering scheme and a possible gambling racket. They're aware of the three Italians staying out at The Griffin. This is no threat to our operations, but mum's the word if you're questioned. The same applies to the gambling ring run by Foster. Foster knows the score. If he goes down, he goes down alone. He won't involve us. So, a low profile for the next few weeks. Then we turn our attention to Potter and the marijuana plants.

Chris said "I sneaked into the lab last Tuesday. The plants have really grown, and they smell strange."

"I looked at the school calendar and the governors' annual tour of the school is in four weeks' time," Danny added.

"The plants will be twice the size by then. I'll double check with Sanjira that the labels are in place," Chris said.

Danny was just about to close the meeting when he got an SMS. "Meet me at Fred's tonight 7pm", signed Sam.

Danny thought for a moment. "Fred! Can I use the café tonight for a one-on-one meeting at 7pm?"

"No problem. Here, I have a spare key." Fred handed the key over and Danny told the crew he was meeting Sam.

"Smart move," said Sato. "Will you need me?"

"No, but possibly afterwards. Have you got anything planned for tonight?"

"Just doing some work on my computer."

Chris and Jeff raised their eyebrows and smiled.

"Okay, guys, we're done. I'll text you when we can meet again. Remember, low profile and hand any income you get to Sato. Have a great weekend."

Chris jumped to his feet and ran his fingers through his hair. "You bet I will!" And he headed for the door.

"Thanks for the key, Fred. Are you okay with the bill?" And they all laughed.

CHAPTER 58

EUROPE ON THE HORIZON

DANNY HAD LEARNT FROM HIS PREVIOUS MEETING WITH Sam, not to force an issue. If Sam had a future within or as an attachment to Danny's organisation, he had to prove his integrity and tonight at Fred's was the start point. If Sam hesitated or wavered on the financial outcome, that would be it.

Fred had left a light on in the café and a coffee pot bubbling away on a hot plate. Nice touch, Danny thought.

When Sam came through the door, Danny glanced at the time. "Coffee?"

"Please. Just one sugar." Sam looked around the room and sat down at a table away from the window. Danny noticed a bulge in his jacket pocket.

"Thanks. Let's get straight to the point. You're a smart lad, Danny. Here's your 20%." Sam slid him a bulging envelope under the table.

Danny reached out and took the envelope. He stared at Sam, inviting a comment.

"$5,600," Sam whispered.

Danny remained silent. Sam had ticked the first box.

"I can go through the figures if you want, Danny?"

"No need. I'm more interested in your three Italian contacts, and by the way so are the CID. They were in Bartholomew's office this morning."

Now Sam was extremely impressed, as Danny had ticked his first box.

"No need to worry, Danny. I have been dealing with Simone and friends for a few years now. I occasionally send over a car and they sell it on their car lot. They can't get a BMW sales agreement, so a car from me adds a bit of glamour to their range. They're over here looking at my stock. Being Italians, they like to look the part, swarthy and mysterious and always in black.

When I mentioned the two races and the odds, they were extremely interested and placed a considerable cash bet with me. Like you, they have been paid, and they go back to Italy on Sunday. They would like to meet you. I explained you were the architect of the games. Why don't we have dinner with them tomorrow night at The Griffin? Just a get-to-know-you meeting. I'll shout the meal. By the way, that lady you introduced me to — wow, she was a bit direct! She and Simone have been getting on really well."

Danny warmed to the news of Doreen's relationship with Simone. Finding a rival's weak spot was a vital part of understanding how to proceed professionally.

"Sounds good. What time do you want to meet?"

"Let's do drinks at 6.30 in the lounge?" Sam suggested.

Danny stood up and shook hands with Sam. "Thanks for the cash, see you tomorrow night."

Danny stayed behind for a few minutes just to clear his head, and then sent a cheeky SMS to Doreen: "Ciao Doreen, come stai?" He smiled, turned the hot plate off, tapped the side of his rucksack and made for the door.

The plan Sato knew was in Danny's head was beginning to take shape.

"Hi, Sato, I'll be passing your place in half an hour. Can I leave an envelope with you?"

"Text me when you're outside. I'll come down and collect."

Danny walked purposefully towards Sato's. Where was he vulnerable, he wondered? He had to stay at school until the end of the school year and leave on a solid footing. After all, his post-school plans meant he would be staying in the area. His community of support, all the local businesses he had helped, would still provide revenue for him and, who knew, maybe he would be invited onto the school's Board of Governors. He smiled at the thought. He could see Carol's face as he broke the news! Janice however might not be so pleased. Thinking of Janice, it was 8pm. Would she be there? Or should he ring Carol? She most definitely would be. Or did he need a good night's sleep?

Danny's mobile beeped and a text came through. "Sto bene, Danny." Danny burst into laughter and checked the meaning before texting back. "I'm having dinner with Simone and friends tomorrow at 6.30. Play it cool."

"Si, capito," the reply came back. Danny guessed the relationship with Simone had progressed to another level away from the bar.

What a day! Sato took the envelope and said he would bank it in the morning.

"See you Monday." Danny turned to walk away as an Asian face disappeared behind a curtain. His crew were on fire. He was a happy man.

Chapter 59

Dinner at The Griffin

IT WAS HARDLY 6PM AND THERE WAS DOREEN, QUEEN OF The Griffin, with three Italians hanging on her every word. Simone was intoxicated by her and had taken a special room at Doreen's invitation where she had cemented their relationship, and obtained a significant number of euros. She continued to rotate on her bar stool, first exposing her right inner thigh stocking top, then the left.

Meanwhile Roger and Filippo were exchanging eye contact, firstly in response to Simone and Doreen's antics, but one glance lasted a little longer and the connection was made. Roger eased along the bar and put an extra straw into Filippo's cocktail. Filippo picked out one of the straws and flicked its contents over Roger, who squirmed with pleasure.

Massimo looked for some personal comfort, but only Leslie in reception was close by and he couldn't join the party.

Sam Johnson walked into the early evening debauchery and cast a questioning eye in Doreen's direction.

"Your friends are such fun, Sam. Come and get a drink. Roger, pour Sam a scotch."

"Will it be a double, sir?"

"It better be." Sam moved towards a nearby table and sat down, and Roger placed a double scotch in front of him.

Danny arrived and looked hard at Doreen, who understood immediately. She pushed Simone, who was drooling, away and said "Go sit with Sam, we'll talk later."

Sam took Danny across and the Italians followed, but not before Filippo had blown Roger a goodbye kiss.

Sam created some semblance of order by introducing Danny to each of the Italians. Simone spoke in broken English. "We were very impressed with your Sports Day, Danny."

"Thank you. I assume your journey proved lucrative?"

Sam looked at Simone and said in broken Italian "You made lots of euros."

"Si si," Simone cried. We are incredibly happy. Maybe you can come visit us in Italy, Danny. I have some friends in the south who would like to meet you, I'm sure."

Danny held the moment as he tried to understand Sam's role. It had to be more than just sending across the odd BMW.

"Ciao, Simone. Italy sounds like a fascinating place. I can surely consider it."

Massimo, who had played a minor role in the initial debauchery, took centre stage. "Danny, I have instructed the chefs to make an Italian meal to celebrate our meeting. With my supervision they have made the speciality of our region, a pork risotto. As our guest we would like you to choose the wine." Massimo handed the wine list over to Danny, who calmly opened the pamphlet to a section marked red wine. No 4 on the list was an Italian Barolo. "No 4, please." Danny handed the pamphlet back.

"Perfetto," said Massimo. "Now we can eat and drink. But first I go check the risotto."

Sam gestured to Roger. "Bottle of Barolo, Roger, please."

Filippo stared hard at Roger's bottom as he walked back to the bar. It was not lost on Doreen, who whispered to Roger "I'll shout you a room. Leave it to me." She spun off her stool, pulled her skirt down a couple of inches grabbing the whole table's attention, and sauntered out to reception.

Massimo returned from the kitchen with a steaming bowl of risotto. With Italian gusto he placed it in the middle of the table. One of the kitchen staff laid out the plates as Roger hovered in the background with the Barolo and five glasses.

No people in the world reflect their culture better than Italians at mealtime. Food is the centre of their universe. They command the table, and non-Italians should just sit back and let it happen. It is a work of art.

Roger invited Simone to taste the wine, which he did with calm assurance. No words were needed. Then he signalled to Roger to pour.

Danny appreciated the value of this cultural interaction and relaxed. He asked a few questions about Italy and where the boys were from. He even tried a few Italian phrases which amused and impressed them.

Sam was watching and listening intently. Simone was his entry point into Italy, but the odd car sale was often more trouble than it was worth. Sam was looking for excitement as well as expanding his business. He knew the car trade well but needed another interest to run parallel. Danny had emerged from the most unlikely place. He was smart: a winner who did not dwell on his victories, but constantly looked ahead. In the big wide world, he could be a success story. Sam watched Danny win the Italians' respect.

Doreen came back, winked at Roger and calmly slid a key, No 24, across to him. Roger spun it in his hand, and Filippo acknowledged it with a smile and raised eyebrows.

Danny kept a straight face as the others struggled. He left to ask if Leslie had a room plan of all the rooms. "And do you have the dates the Americans are coming and their names, please?"

"I'll put them all in an envelope before you leave, Danny. If I'm not here it will be in my tray."

Sam was beginning to show signs of frustration as the Italians became more raucous. Simone occasionally left the table to whisper sweet nothings in Doreen's ear.

"Maybe, we should meet privately, Danny, when the boys have gone home?" he suggested.

"Yes, tonight is not the time." Danny stood up to go and they all shook hands.

Doreen winked at Danny and mouthed "Coffee tomorrow morning?"

CHAPTER 60

THE BIG PICTURE

DANNY SAT AT HIS USUAL CORNER TABLE, AND WHEN DOREEN gave him his coffee she whispered "Fred is going to the wholesalers in a few minutes. We can talk then."

Danny had only had one question for Doreen: "How can you expand your business?" He saw real potential in developing his investments, but he needed a home for them. The obvious place was The Griffin. A preliminary look at the plans suggested rooms could be converted into individual business premises, each producing a rent. But how to get the place?

When Fred left, Doreen sat down opposite Danny so she could watch the customers.

"If you had the premises, Doreen, how would you expand your business?"

Doreen froze. She was doing okay on her own.

"Well, I suppose I could employ a couple of escort girls and maybe set up a massage business."

“Could it be done under the guise of a Wellness Centre?” He knew the answers, but wanted Doreen on board.

“Sure, but I haven’t got the cash for premises. Rents are so expensive.”

“You already have the premises.”

“You mean The Griffin?”

“I do.”

“But it’s owned by two Americans, and they’re coming over in two weeks’ time. They could shut the place down.”

“They could, or they could lose the place. Let’s say the police found out The Griffin was being used for ill-gotten gains. They could arrest the owners and freeze their passports. The court process could take months. I know the bank has recently provided a loan for refurbishment. They would want to protect, or more likely call in, their loan.”

“I’m seeing Sergeant Philips tonight. Maybe I could ask him a few questions?”

“Maybe you could, and maybe you could ensure you get the right answers.” Danny raised his eyebrows as the penny dropped. “We don’t have much time to make a plan so I’ll need to speak to you tomorrow morning.”

Doreen hesitated, then said “We’re closed on Sundays, but I’ll be here at 8am if that suits?”

“See you tomorrow at 8. There’s a customer at the counter.”

Doreen made for the counter. She had a lot to think about, but there had been a chemistry between her and Danny since day one, and she had confidence in him.

Danny stood in the precinct thinking about where all this had begun. The path forward was opening out before his eyes. Everything had come together at the presentation evening and Sports Day. What he had to do now was make it all happen.

He had a mental list swimming about in his head. If he could get the premises, he could have:

- A wellness centre (Doreen)
- A TAB betting room (John Foster)
- Mr Atkins from school could handle all the refurbishments
- An Italian restaurant, which Massimo could set up from Italy
- A BMW desk with a car permanently on display outside (Sam Johnson)
- A promotions board for local businesses (Fred's, Mr Woo)
- A bank introduction desk with a direct phone line.
- *The Advertiser's* office (Mr Punter)
- A room for business meetings, birthday parties, etc. (Chris)
- Security (Jordan).

Danny was fully aware that this was everyone's final year at school. Sato had said that he would like to study IT and economics at university. This would suit Danny, and maybe Sato could set up a small computer room at The Griffin for guests?

Jeff was a free spirit and a bit unreliable to say the least. Maturity was some way off and Danny could not see a defined role for him but he was loyal, so decided to see if one presented itself as the year unfolded. The devil in him saw roles for both Carol and Janice, but it was high-risk strategy to have them close to each other.

Danny was a Gemini with a big personality. The Jekyll in him challenged him to take the risk, and then the Hyde pulled him back from the precipice. He admired Donald Trump and Johnny Depp, both Geminis. He was versatile, youthful, curious and fun, but did not suffer fools gladly and could suss them out quickly. He did not like the term 'devious' but had to accept that many people would see him that way. There would always be a tomorrow for Danny, and the sooner the better!

CHAPTER 61

THE AMERICANS

DANNY HAD STARTED TO REALISE HOW IMPORTANT research and planning was in growing a business. Consequently, he was trying to find out the backgrounds of Charles Jackson and Eugene Danner, the owners of The Griffin. Both were from Oklahoma City. Danny skimmed through the historical past and evangelical Protestantism of the state. He wanted to understand the two men.

He noticed that people from that area, in terms of their social and cultural context, had distinct health and educational levels, compared to other parts of the USA. For example, Oklahoma had the lowest levels of educational attainment and the highest rates of obesity, cardiovascular disease, teenage pregnancy, homicide and sexually-transmitted infections in the country. Danny contemplated the significance of these facts in relation to his meeting with Doreen, paused for a moment, then set off confidently.

Chapter 62

The Strategy

DOREEN OPENED THE CAFÉ PROMPTLY AT 8AM.

"Fred never gets up before 11 on a Sunday, Danny. Then he spends at least an hour meandering around the house complaining about his hangover."

Danny smiled. He could just picture Fred. He had a fondness for Fred, but that did not extend to his playing a more permanent role in Danny's future.

"I can't switch the barista machine on, but I can make you a coffee from the kettle if you like?"

Danny wanted to cover things thoroughly, which would take time, so he nodded politely. The Americans were due in two weeks, and time was short.

Doreen sat down opposite him, out of sight of any passers-by.

"Sergeant Philips stayed the night, so we spent most of the evening in the bar. Without going into any detail about your plans, Danny" — Danny raised his eyebrows — "I did ask him what would happen if, as a policemen, he was found to be visiting me." Danny thought this was a good approach. "If he were on duty, he would be severely reprimanded and possibly demoted. If off-duty, he would be reprimanded and advised to stop. By booking a room and staying the night, he was insuring himself. If the police found out that the premises were being used, let us say, as a casual brothel, then they would be closed and the owners charged with obtaining money under illegal pretences using street girls. That would mean a criminal charge and subsequent court appearance before the magistrates, which could take weeks. Passports would have to be surrendered so the offenders could not leave the country." Doreen took a breath and sipped her coffee, knowing full well that her final comment was what Danny had been waiting for.

"You've obviously already worked out, Doreen, that my plan is to buy The Griffin from the Americans. I need some ammunition so I can get the premises quickly and at a greatly reduced price. What about a bank valuation? Can you organise that tomorrow with Leslie?"

"I'll ring him now. In fact, I'll ring Wilson at the bank first thing tomorrow and tee him up. Maybe I can meet him at The Griffin."

Doreen stood up and took out her mobile. It was 8.30am and Danny liked her style. One thing he could not stand was people who dilly-dallied. Doreen had gone over to the far side of the room and was chatting earnestly.

"Done." She sat down and took a sip. "Ugh, need to warm that up. Do you want another, Danny?"

Danny nodded and Doreen went over to the kettle. She would never win an Oscar, but, gee, she could get a job done.

"I'll see Leslie tonight, Danny, and get the okay from him."

Danny continued, convinced Doreen could handle it "I'll need to video the Americans in bed with call girls and have them arrested for using the premises as a brothel. He hesitated for a reaction. Doreen remained impassive; she knew what was coming.

“Two questions. Firstly, for a price can you get two reliable call girls? And how much?”

“Secondly, has Henry Legend been to see you?”

“You mean the teacher from school?” Danny nodded. “Yes, he has.”

“Good. Then I need you to get him to fix up video recording equipment in each of the rooms.”

Doreen thought for a moment before answering Danny’s first question. “I can get two girls for the night at $500 each and free drinks, plus they keep the money from the clients.”

Danny laughed. “All your clients get free drinks.”

Doreen blushed a little and carried on “What did you have in mind for me?

“$2,000 paid in cash up front,” Danny answered.

“I was hoping for three.”

“Can we close the deal at $2,500?” Danny waited.

“Agreed.” Doreen stood up and offered her hand; Danny laughed and shook it.

“We need to speak daily. I’ll pop in with the crew after school tomorrow. When I’ve finished with them, we can chat.”

CHAPTER 63

SCHOOL LIFE CONTINUES

DESPITE ALL THAT PLANNING, AND ALL THAT HAD GONE before, one simple fact remained: Danny and his crew had still to finish Year 12.

Danny met them at their usual spot in the yard. Jordan, for a quick $5, had agreed to keep any younger boys away. A stern look usually did the trick.

"How are all our grades looking, Sato?" Danny knew schoolwork seemed a tedious topic after all that had happened, but better to finish the year on a good note.

"As of last week, you look a certain B and Chris and Jeff C+."

"Okay, upgrade all three of us to B+ and B. We can't do much about the written exam. Maybe try and do some revision beforehand. Unless of course you could access the exam topics from the education website?"

"I'll see what I can do." Sato never said no!

Chris and Jeff said "Phew!"

"We have two major projects to bring to fruition: in two weeks, the owners of the Griffin fly in from America. I am arranging a strategy which will put us in a favourable position to acquire The Griffin for Always Tomorrow." There was a silence, and Chris and Jeff just stared. Sato had suspected as much, and Danny knew it.

"At this stage you do not need to know any details. What I do need is for you two, Danny looked at Chris and Jeff, to keep on driving our current ventures, and visit our, let's say, clients so that when we do acquire The Griffin they can avail themselves of our facilities. I do not want to interfere with any post-school career plans you may have, other than to say The Griffin will offer a few career opportunities of its own. At this time only the four of us need to know though."

This was just what Jeff wanted to hear. Danny had saved his life once, and the security of being under his umbrella was vital in keeping him on the straight and narrow.

Chris envisaged more of a corporate entertainment role and, little did he know, Danny had already pencilled him in.

Sato had to keep developing his commercial skills and go to university. Always Tomorrow would pay his fees and they had to discuss which courses he would take to complement Danny's European plans.

"Our next major project is to remove Potter, and the governors finding out about the 'herbs' growing in his lab." Even Sato smiled at this one.

"Just one slight problem," interrupted Jeff. "The plants have grown really quickly, which is what they do, and they have started to smell."

Danny, Chris and Sato were dumbfounded.

Jeff loved that moment, and waited before he said "I mentioned this to Sanjira, and she came up with the answer, which I have authorised. I've asked her to proceed."

"And what is the answer, Jeff?" Danny asked.

"Indian curry."

The silence was broken by raucous laughter. Tears began to well up in Chris' eyes. Sato laughed uncontrollably, but Danny spoke quickly in support of Jeff. "I'm sure we all understand the value of using curry, but how was the operation set up?"

"Sanjira, being of Indian descent and used to the different smells of Indian curries, quickly picked up on the smell of the 'herbs'. She knew Potter would notice too, so she asked him if she could store some containers of curry there until she could put them into her freezer at home. The curry apparently has to settle before it can be frozen. Potter hadn't got a clue about this, so immediately said yes, so long as Sanjira used the back lab where the herbs were growing. Hence the perfect solution. All Potter can smell if he goes in the lab is Indian curries."

Chris began clapping, as did Sato and finally Danny. "Absolutely brilliant," he said. "Let's get back to class and meet at Fred's after school." Danny slipped Jordan $5 and normal service resumed.

CHAPTER 64

DOREEN'S CREW

DANNY WAITED UNTIL FRED HAD PUT THE DRINKS ON THE table.

"Any questions after this morning's meeting?

Chris said "I have some ideas for my role when we get The Griffin, Danny."

"Great, let's hear them."

"I like entertaining, dressing well, meeting people, so I'd like to be considered for a corporate role, possibly in marketing, attracting business groups, birthday parties, etc. I also think we should advertise overseas. Those three Italians stayed there and loved it. Plus, Doreen's a big attraction."

Jeff and Sato nodded, obviously impressed.

Danny agreed. "Perfect role for you. When the exams are over maybe you could put a more detailed proposal together?"

"Don't you think I should wait until we've got the place?" Three pairs of eyes turned on Chris.

"Okay, okay, I'll do it after the exams," Chris smiled.

"If there's nothing else, you guys can go. I've a meeting with Doreen when Fred closes up."

Sato mouthed "I've altered the grades to come into effect just before the exams."

Not a long meeting, but fruitful, Danny thought.

"I'm away, Danny. Doreen wants me to pick up some package from the Post Office. She'll lock up." Fred sighed as he left.

Doreen had worked her magic again.

The final group of customers left, and Doreen flicked over the open sign to closed. Danny noticed that she didn't lock the door though and sat down so she could see it.

"The Griffin is being valued tomorrow morning, Danny. The figures will be given to Leslie, who knows to make a copy he'll leave on his tray for you. He'll text you when he gets them."

"Great work. Did Wilson suspect anything?"

"No, he was more interested in my right thigh. Apparently he's having a meeting with his regional manager soon and would like to use the lounge at The Griffin. He asked if I could be available as a visual attraction."

Danny smiled as another piece of the jigsaw fell into place. If Doreen could hook the regional manager then approval for any loan would be granted more easily.

"That's good work, Doreen. Could the Federal Treasurer be on your radar?"

Doreen laughed. "There's always a tomorrow, Danny."

At which point the café door opened. Doreen smiled, and Danny turned to see two obvious ladies of the night.

"Come in, don't just stand there," Doreen urged. "Danny, these are Jasmine and Claudette, the two ladies I told you about. They wanted to meet you personally."

Danny was thinking at top speed. He did not really want to meet the girls, but he could see it from their point of view.

"Now which one are you?" he asked.

"I'm Jasmine, this is Claudette."

"Pleased to meet you both. I take it Doreen has explained what we would like you to do and the payment terms. I trust these are acceptable to you?"

Jasmine and Claudette had never been spoken to like that before and looked awkwardly at Doreen.

"Just say yes, girls. I'll take care of you. Danny also needs your assurance that you will not mention who's paying you or that this meeting ever took place, especially as I'll be paying you in cash." Doreen waited until both girls nodded.

"I'm sure you appreciate that this could become regular safe work for you?"

"Jasmine said "It's perfect. Do you want us to sit at the bar in the lounge, Danny?"

"No, you'll only come to The Griffin when Doreen contacts you with details of a client. Doreen will deal with all the bookings and payments from punters. Can you give her some photos? She'll get the best ones copied and they can be used to attract clients. If there's a cost involved, please let her know. All you need to do is be exceptionally good at what you do, and make sure the clients want to come back for more. You know what I mean?"

Claudette asked "Do you want a free trial, Danny?"

"Ha-ha, lovely idea but I've got enough on my plate, thank you. Just keep in touch with Doreen. We do not plan to add any more girls, so it's up to you to make it happen. As a gesture, I'm giving each of you $150 to buy some new clothes. Nothing too tarty — I want you to be classy, understand?"

"We do, Danny, thank you. Can we have the money now?"

Danny laughed. "Of course. Here you are, and you can go now. Doreen will be in touch."

Both girls left and Danny looked at Doreen.

"They'll be fine. I'll make sure they dress appropriately. I've known them both for a while. They tend to work together and look after each other," she assured him.

"Maybe the regional bank manager could be a client for one ... or both," Danny mused.

The simplicity of Danny's thinking and approach to establishing a business was admirable. He was a clear and logical thinker. Each project was carefully thought through step by step. However, in matters of his own heart he was floundering. He was attracted to both Janice and Carol for quite different reasons, and Carol was somewhat older. His relationship with Janice would be tested when they both finished school. Carol had the advantage of her own accommodation, which was a major asset. Danny had no idea what Janice intended to do. He considered broaching the subject with her, then changed his mind. How would she react when she realised he owned The Griffin? Carol could even rent an office there. He decided to let his relationship with both roll along and just react to events.

Then a text arrived. "Come round for dinner, 7pm? Carol." Danny immediately accepted, then turned off his phone. No one could contact him now.

CHAPTER 65

THE MAIN PROJECTS

THE DAYS WENT BY AND DANNY KEPT THE MACHINE rolling. His crew were occasionally seen in the library, and Bartholomew had never known such harmony in the playground. Staff were busily preparing for the Year 12 exams. Reputations would sink or swim on the back of the students' results.

Danny had the valuation for The Griffin, and at first the amount took his breath away, but Doreen entertained Mr Wilson on a couple of occasions, and he provided the strategy Danny needed for the purchase. Sato became familiar with the figures, commercial loans and repayment flexibility. The one thing that Danny and Sato were both convinced of concerned the ownership: there would be a temptation to bring in an outside partner to help with the purchase. However, this should not happen, even if there were severe pressure from the lenders. Always Tomorrow would remain in the hands of Danny and his crew.

Both Danny and Sato knew the key to The Griffin's purchase

lay in Danny's ability to get the current owners to sell at a much-reduced price. Danny met Doreen several times and knew she could give her girls a day's notice. He gave her the arrival dates, and she promised to invite Charles and Eugene for drinks in the lounge on the Saturday evening.

Under the pretext of refurbishing the bedrooms, Doreen had persuaded Henry Legend to install private video equipment in five of them. She had visited him with a G&T at least twice. The visits lasted about 15 minutes. At Doreen's request, Leslie would be the only one able to start filming. He too could lose his job.

Danny thought at least two nights' filming would be necessary. Jeff offered some tablets which could be left strategically in the Americans' bedrooms, and Danny raised his eyebrows but bowed to his street knowledge.

Sergeant Phillips would be informed of what might be going on by text. Doreen would contact him later that day to invite him for drinks and maybe a freebie. She would massage his ego and arouse his interest in the salacious behaviour taking place at The Griffin, so a promotion and local publicity were sure to follow.

"I hope you'll still be interested in me when you're Inspector Phillips," she teased.

After the arrest, Leslie would find the drugs in Eugene and Charles' rooms and contact Sergeant Phillips. Then the noose would tighten slowly to a point where Danny could talk to them about selling The Griffin so they could get their passports back and leave.

Danny called a meeting at Fred's to finalise details for the two major events about to take place. "There may be an overlap so we must be sure not to panic and, more importantly, keep a low profile. The key players outside our group like Doreen and the bank are all incentivised and well-connected."

"When do the Americans arrive, Danny?" Chris asked.

"They land on Thursday and should be at The Griffin by

lunchtime. Doreen will be in the lounge from 6pm as Leslie has organised welcome drinks for them. Her girls will be on call, although Saturday evening may be more likely for the fun and games. If we can begin videoing on Thursday that would be a bonus. I've asked Sam Johnson to drop in on Saturday to meet the Americans, and that will ensure their staying in. Sam will fuel them with drink and Doreen will signal for the girls to arrive and introduce them. She'll take care of Sam herself — seemingly he's good money." They all laughed.

"Are they both straight, Danny?" Jeff asked.

"If one of them isn't, Roger will step in. Doreen has checked ... make that 'threatened'."

"Will you be there, Danny?" Jeff asked.

"No, I don't want the Americans to suspect anything. Leslie will contact me if something goes wrong. I don't expect it will because everyone benefits from its success."

"What are Doreen's girls like, Danny?" Chris asked.

"Dangerous, extremely dangerous. I gave them some money to buy seductive clothing, so they will not fail."

"Maybe we should get Leslie or Roger to take some photographs?"

"That's already been taken care of." Danny left the table to chat with Doreen.

"Right, Doreen will ring Roger to check he can get a camera. Now, our other project, the governors' tour of the school. Any news from the lab, Jeff?"

"Sanjira knows about your plan to expose Potter, Danny. She hates the way he drools over the attractive Asian girls and she suggests encouraging the governors to take 'herb' tea, using the leaves when they tour the science labs. She'll appoint two girls to prepare the tea so it will be hard for the governors to say no. We could use Kate and Janice."

"How will drinking the tea influence the governors, Jeff?" Danny asked, knowing Carol would be in the governors' party.

"Giggling. They will almost all start giggling. Some may wobble about and push and pull the others. Gerald Trapper may have a problem if he falls over."

"How long will this go on for?" Sato asked

"Depends how much they drink, Sato, and everyone is different. Some may need medical attention."

"How do we make sure at least some get medical attention, because that's how we can nail Potter —when the plants are identified as marijuana?"

"Easy, my mother is a school nurse and I've arranged for her to join the governors' party. Bartholomew has already agreed — he said "You never know when we might need her" jokingly. Plus, Mum is looking for more work.

"Can she detect marijuana use, Jeff?"

"She's my mum, Danny — not a problem!"

They all laughed.

"Okay, make sure she does. I'll be going round with the governors too, and Potter will be focusing on me, not the tea drinking. Make sure you keep alert over the next few days. If we nail these two projects, we can leave school on a high with a bright future."

CHAPTER 66

THE AMERICANS ARRIVE

LESLIE WAS THERE TO MEET THE AMERICANS AS THEY squeezed out of the taxi. He arranged for their luggage to be taken inside while both men spent a few minutes looking over the frontage of The Griffin and the car park area.

Leslie was surprised how large both men were as they stretched after the long flight, and he wondered about the beds if anything sexual transpired. Loud and brash was how Leslie's predecessor had described them, and that proved to be right as Charles launched into a tirade of abusive language, firstly about the flight then the size of the taxi. Leslie was his diplomatic self, and suggested a drink in the lounge before they registered.

"Good idea, do you have bourbon?"

"I'm sure we do, sir. This way."

Roger was daydreaming behind the bar when Leslie winked at him and asked "Could you provide our new guests, Charles and Eugene, with a bourbon?"

Years of working together meant immediate understanding. Roger responded "We have a Scottish version, which is a malt whisky. I'm sure that will hit the spot."

"Well, they're renowned for their whisky." Charles bought it and Leslie smiled, somewhat relieved.

"Just come through to reception when you're ready." He slipped away.

Roger contemplated some small talk, but neither guest appealed either physically or intellectually, so he decided to polish some glasses at the other end of the bar.

"Gee, that was great," said Charles.

"Certainly got the old bones warmed up again," Eugene added.

"Okay, let's get some sleep. Check-in through here?"

"Sure is," said Roger.

"We have five rooms available. One of them is a twin; the others are single rooms." Leslie had made sure that all five rooms with video surveillance were available.

"Okay, let's have a look at two of the singles. What's your name again?" Charles didn't even look at Leslie.

"Leslie, sir, as before," said Leslie, tongue in cheek. He would have no problem with switching on the video recorder.

"This is room 39, sir, and it has all the amenities you may need, including a king size bed."

"Excellent, let's give it a try. Charles flopped onto the bed, rolled about, then jacked himself up into a sitting position. "That's fine. Is room 40 the same?"

"Sure is," Leslie headed for the door and Eugene followed him.

"I'll have your luggage sent through, Charles." Leslie ushered Eugene into the corridor and closed the door.

When the luggage was in both rooms, Leslie texted Danny "The monsters from America have arrived and are safely in bed. All good."

Danny smiled as he knew exactly what monsters meant. He too had done his homework.

CHAPTER 67

A CASUAL MEETING

DOREEN WAS ON HER USUAL PERCH AT THE END OF THE bar when Charles waddled in.

"Hey, barman, get me one of those malts you gave me at lunchtime, will you?"

Doreen stepped in. "Roger. His name's Roger, and we like our guests whoever they are to say please."

"You know who I am?" Charles stared at Doreen.

"I do, and the same rules apply. Do unto others as you would have them do unto you." Doreen wriggled about on her seat, carefully crossing her legs and giving a little tug to her hemline, just enough to interest Charles and set both the tone and the agenda.

"I see. And who may you be?" Charles assumed a more diplomatic approach. After all, this lady might be a regular guest.

"My name is Doreen. I am an occasional guest and a regular visitor for drinks and meals in the restaurant. The food is excellent by the way. Let me pay for the malt, Roger."

Doreen slid $20 across the bar. Roger knew full well not to mention a tab.

"That is mighty kind, ma'am. My name is Charles. My colleague, Eugene, who will be joining me directly, and I are joint owners of this fine establishment. Pleased to meet you, and here's to your good health. We're here for a couple of weeks."

Charles raised his glass and Doreen raised hers, but not before she had straightened her back and pushed forward a plunging neckline. Charles took note.

"Now come and sit a little closer to me so I can really get to know you," she winked cheekily.

Charles did not need the wink; he was pushing his stool across before the wink started.

"Not too close now. You are a big boy, Charles. Ah, this must be Eugene."

Charles tried to conceal his disappointment. Still, this was only the first night and he was making good progress, or so he thought.

"Would you like a malt, Eugene? I'm in the chair." Doreen began to feed another fish.

"That's truly kind of you, ma'am. Eugene, from Oklahoma state."

"Bring over a stool. Charles is about to tell me his life story. You might want to add yours? Now before you start, Charles, I only want the juicy bits — some scandal and sharp business practice. You know, what you really like ... What you get up to on your global trips ... Have you been to Asia? I hear lots goes on there — the clubs and hostesses, all beautiful girls and plenty of them."

Doreen giggled and rocked on her seat.

Charles could not wait to start.

"Well, Eugene and I did go to Bangkok last year, and we found a street so full of bars and girls. What was the name of that street, Eugene?"

"The area was called Sukhumvit."

"Don't you just love that word, Doreen?"

"Sure do, big boy." Doreen winked at Charles, who adjusted his sitting position.

Eugene, who had obviously dealt with this situation before, continued "We visited Nana, the red-light district. Nana has the highest concentration of hookers in Bangkok. Charles loved the soapy massage girls."

"Sure did. Gee, you could move those little beauties around in the soapsuds. I almost lost sight of one covered in foam." Charles laughed out loud and the bar began to shake. Roger steadied a few glasses and filled two more for 'our guests'. Doreen gestured, "Another G&T please." Roger nodded and knew to leave out the gin. It was only 6.45.

"And what were you doing, Eugene, while Charles was up to his neck in bubbles?"

"He went upstairs with some Asian girl," Charles interrupted. "He likes those Asian girls, old Eugene."

Eugene blushed a little but did not deny it.

Doreen had now partnered Eugene with Claudette and Jasmine with Charles. And another $100 went on the hourly rate.

"They tell me you can buy a tablet at the start of the evening that helps you relax and have a good time?" Doreen began fishing again and glanced at Roger.

"Sure can, and yeah, they do work. We were firing right through the night, eh Eugene?"

"Trouble is, Doreen, we couldn't remember much next morning," Eugene admitted.

"Not to worry, you're both here now. Maybe you'd like to have a look at a couple of my friends though, privately of course. More drinks please, Roger."

Doreen smiled knowingly at Roger who moved away from the bar and reached for the malt and two small tablets nestling in a tiny saucer. He put the tablets in the glasses and swirled them around so they disappeared.

Doreen rummaged through her bag before taking out a handful of photos.

"You'd better take a big drink before I show you these — and please, no loud noises. There are guests in the restaurant."

Roger slid the two glasses over to Charles and Roger.

"Come on, straight down; let's not dilly-dally." Doreen played her trump card.

As Eugene and Charles downed their drinks in one gulp, she laid six photographs along the bar.

"Quiet please," she whispered.

Roger held his breath and scanned the room.

Both men studied the shots.

Charles shuffled them around like a croupier in a casino.

"These three are mine, the others are yours." Charles slid three across to Eugene.

Charles kept the ones of Jasmine and Eugene had Claudette's.

"You can't keep them, but if you approve maybe I could arrange a meeting with them, say here on Saturday night?" Doreen waited for the drooling to stop. "Boys, are you listening?"

Charles sat upright and looked at Eugene, who nodded.

"You sure can, lovely lady, you sure can. Now what is your name again, Rodney?"

"Roger, sir. Very close, but Roger."

"Drinks all round again, Rodney. Gee, this malt is so smooth. G&T, Doreen?"

"Yes please, big boy. Maybe a double?"

"Great idea. Let's double up, Rodney."

Roger smiled, doubled the tonic and added half a tablet to each of the malts.

Jet lag and alcohol are poor bedfellows!

The next morning, Charles couldn't lift his head off the pillow or see straight. He peered into the slowly clearing mist as a marching band played between his ears. He recognised the experience. He'd been here before. He tried to attach the feeling to some recollection of what had transpired the night before. And what was that long dark thing hanging from the tabletop? The curiosity was too much for him. He raised himself up to a seated position and contemplated the distance between the long black thing and the bed. A minute, maybe two, passed, then with a mighty heave he got to his feet and staggered towards it, and the written note beside it.

"Hi, Tiger, In memory of a lovely evening. See you Saturday with the girls."

Charles ran his fingers along Doreen's stocking and the previous night's picture came into focus. A knock on the door and in walked Eugene, or the ghost of Eugene.

"You look like I feel, man," Charles said.

"I don't feel anything, I'm numb from the neck down and detached above. What's that?"

Charles flicked the stocking and the note across.

"Wow must have been some night. Wish I could remember it." Eugene began to smile as he read the note and the room came into focus.

"Breakfast?"

"Hope they've got some juice."

Charles dressed slowly and carefully. Eugene looked at himself in the mirror and shook his head. Day 2 was about to begin.

CHAPTER 68

A BIG WEEK

BARTHOLOMEW TAPPED ON DANNY'S DOOR AND POPPED his head round. "You free for a minute?"

"Certainly, sir. We need to finalise plans for the governors' tour of the school on Wednesday."

"My thoughts too." Bartholomew sat down opposite Danny.

"Just let me clear these revision notes out of the way, sir."

Bartholomew raised his eyebrows. Danny had not revised in seven years and his B grading was a mystery. Still, all was quiet on the western front, so to speak, and maybe for that reason the B was justified and easy to accept.

"You're joining the governors for the school tour, Danny?" he asked.

"Yes, sir, looking forward to it. I've got to know some of them quite well."

Bartholomew raised his eyebrows again. "I thought we all might meet in my office at 1.30. The staff usually get quite anxious about this visit, especially those with pupil control difficulties, so meeting in the staffroom might only increase the anxiety."

"Why don't you let me have a list of the poorly behaved classes, sir, and I'll make sure they behave."

"I can tell you now." Bartholomew took a crumpled piece of paper out of his pocket and handed it to Danny.

"Ah, 8C, 9D, 10A — that's a surprise, sir — and 12C. Leave it with me. I'll ensure they behave throughout the tour." Danny smiled

"I thought we would visit the classroom block first, then move across to the gymnasium and finish in the science laboratories. Be a little more interesting." Bartholomew waited.

"Good idea, sir. The Asian girls are growing some interesting plants, Sanjira tells me. If you like curry, that is?"

Bartholomew liked the odd curry, usually from Mr Woo's.

"I do, and Indian will make a change from Mr Woo's. I presume it is Indian?"

"Janice tells me the Indians make the best curry, sir, and Sanjira is very reliable."

Bartholomew smiled and wondered what Miss Whittleston might recommend. However, no need to rock the boat now.

"Okay, enjoy the rest of your day revising." Bartholomew paused, inviting a response, but all he got was Danny pushing the pile of revision notes back across the desktop.

"I will indeed, sir. Thanks for popping in."

Danny sent a text to Jordan. Need to speak today. Can you come in around 12.30?

Jordan was never late. He had a money supply train driven by Danny and he trusted him implicitly. On the dot of 12.30 he knocked on Danny's door.

"Come in." Danny had known who it was even before the knock. He thrust the note across the desktop and Jordan looked at it. "I'm on a tour of the school with the governors this Wednesday, and Bartholomew has given me a list of classes where the teachers have little control. Obviously it's a stressful time for those teachers, and in some cases their jobs may be on the line. They are basically good people, so I'd like to help them. I want you to ensure those pupils are well-behaved on the day. You will of course get paid on Friday. $40."

"I'll speak to each class. Can you let the teachers know that, when I come in, they should wait outside until I've spoken to the class?"

"I'll do it now. They'll all be in the staffroom. Thanks, see you Friday."

Jordan left without another word.

Danny followed. He needed to speak to those members of staff before they finished lunch. Jordan would act fast.

"Just a brief word if I may, teachers. I will be joining the governors on Wednesday and I know each of you have hard-to-control classes on that day, so I've arranged for Jordan Smith to pop in and talk to each of them. When he arrives, just introduce him, and leave the room. He will only have a brief word, make his point and leave. Everything should be fine from then on. Any questions?"

There were looks of both relief and gratitude. A couple of the teachers were in their first year and did not look much older than Danny.

"Thanks, Danny. That would be a real help. Will it last?" asked a young female teacher, whom Danny suddenly found quite attractive.

"I think you can make that assumption. If you have any further queries, please don't hesitate to come to see me in my office. You may have other individuals who are troublemakers or disrespectful."

Danny smiled at her and apologised for not knowing her name.

"Alice. Alice Brown."

The bell rang and Danny suggested "Better move quickly. I have a revision class."

They thanked him and left with a collective smile and a bit of chit-chat.

Danny made a mental note of Alice Brown ... and expected a visit.

CHAPTER 69

SATURDAY NIGHT AT THE GRIFFIN

THEY ALL MET AT FRED'S CAFÉ EARLY SATURDAY MORNING, and Fred chatted as he put down their drinks. They had learned to be both polite and interested, and Doreen always beckoned Fred away after a minute or so.

"Let's go over where we are in the scheme of things. Firstly, have you been round our various revenue streams? Is everyone okay?" Danny asked.

Jeff's newfound confidence prompted the first response. "Everyone's still buzzing from the Sports Day, Danny. Some people made money, and everyone lost money on the 200- and 400-metre races. We've collected more commissions. Chris has the money."

Chris pulled a bag of loot from his rucksack and handed it over to Sato.

"There's a note inside with the breakdown of cash and who the money's from," he said.

Sato slid it into his briefcase.

"Great, well done. Tonight The Griffin's owners meet Doreen and the girls. I've invited Sam Johnson over to make up the numbers. He's a client of Doreen's so he'll be comfortable in their presence. Plus, when the girls go back to Charles' and Eugene's rooms, Sam will have Doreen to himself — or vice versa. Seemingly Thursday night was a successful meet and greet. I spoke to Roger who was not too impressed with the Americans, but extremely impressed with the tips they gave ... and the ones he took."

The crew laughed. The excitement was beginning to bubble.

Doreen sensed their mood. "Refills, boys?" she called across the room and at least three male regulars answered "Yes, please."

Danny let them laugh. He had covered all bases, even asking Leslie to text him 'Roll out the barrel' when the videos were running."

"Where will you be, Danny? Can we contact you if anything goes wrong?" Chris asked.

"I'm taking Janice out for dinner at the Italian restaurant down the road from The Griffin. He's a good old Italian bloke and needs the money." Sato raised an eyebrow. "We're eating early — probably be finished before Doreen sees the Americans. Leslie will text me if there's a problem, but I'm confident Doreen can handle it all. I've got the contact details for Jasmine and Claudette if anything should happen to Doreen. All I want to do is meet as usual on Monday morning in the school yard and I'll update you."

Danny stood up and glanced across at Doreen. He needed a quick word.

Sam Johnson closed early on Saturday afternoon. He knew the Americans had arrived and was trying to think up a deal.

"You'll feel better, guys, when you've had your first drink. It's called 'hair of the dog' over here!" Leslie smiled at Charles and Eugene.

"I'm sure it is, but where we come from it's called bourbon," Charles replied.

Eugene puffed out his cheeks in a form of acknowledgement. He'd been here before with Charles, and at 6.45 he knew there was a long night ahead.

"Enjoy your evening. Doreen arrived a few minutes ago and asked me to tell you the first drink's on her. Now, for safety, would you like to leave your keys at reception?"

"Good idea. Will you be here all night, Leslie?" Eugene asked.

"Yes, I will, so don't worry. If necessary, I'll make sure you get to your rooms safely." Leslie smiled. He couldn't wait for the action to start.

Charles strode manfully into the lounge. "Two of those malts, Rodney, please."

"Roger, sir. It's Roger."

"So it is."

"Hi, Doreen. The first ones are on you — great to hear!"

Doreen had gone to town on her make-up and clothes, not so much for the Americans but more for Sam. Under Danny's direction, she was in pursuit of a sponsored BMW with 'Wellbeing' emblazoned on both sides. She had already identified the room she would use at The Griffin. Her dress code could be described as Parisian: ruby red lips, shorter than usual black leather skirt and tight red top with an off-the-shoulder black strap on the left. Black earrings hung hypnotically. It was impossible not to notice her.

Charles searched for an adjective and, after a gulp of malt, came out with "Very alluring, Doreen."

She reached forward and stretched to place a seductive kiss on Charles' cheek. "Thank you, Tiger."

Eugene hoped for similar, but Charles' ebullient personality always stole the day. Eugene played a minor role and had learned to bide his time. In this case he knew two girls were coming, so all he had to do was stay calm and try not to drink too much!

Sam too had wrestled with what to wear. He had had a hot shower and wanted to turn a mundane day into an exciting finale.

He opted for a casual look, then stood sideways — and the mirror did not lie. He could breathe in, but only temporarily. Denims, open shirt and a casual jacket. He shaved and sprinkled on some Louis Vuitton. If that doesn't work nothing will, he decided. Take the car or Uber? Uber. Safety first.

Mohammed dropped him off at the entrance. "Have a good evening, sir. Will I see you later?"

"You may. You may well, but my gut instinct says tomorrow morning."

Mohammed laughed. "Have a great night, sir."

Leslie stopped Sam at the entrance.

"Hi, Mr Johnson, could I have a quick word? Doreen asked me to explain that the two Americans are very brash and loud. She has also arranged for some female company for later in the evening, so relax. She's looking forward to some private personal time alone with you later."

"Thank you, Leslie. Very reassuring."

Doreen was leaning over the bar as Sam went into the lounge, her left stocking top in clear view. The black leather skirt looked more like a wide belt and the two rotund Americans were fighting to keep their hands off her.

"Oh, there you are. Thought you were never going to get here. Let me introduce you to Charles and Eugene, owners of this fine establishment. Give Sam a G&T, Roger, will you? Now, boys, this is Sam. He owns the local BMW dealership. He is a prominent local personality and sits on the school Board of Governors. Now get to know each other. I have a quick phone call to make." Doreen winked at Charles and Eugene and headed to the reception.

"Are the girls on hold, Leslie?"

"Yes, they're five minutes away in the pub at the end of the precinct."

"Good. Give them a call and tell them to get a taxi over here now. Tell them the Griffin will pay for the taxi. Make sure you put the taxi fare on Charles' account."

"Will do." Leslie loved the excitement.

Doreen went back to the lounge. The boys were chatting away merrily, but they stopped as soon as they saw her. She took her time sitting down.

"Now you two, I want you to be on your best behaviour as your guests are about to arrive. Try not to be too loud and brash, Charles. This is The Griffin, not the soapy bar in Bangkok. The night is young so there's plenty of time for you to relax — and in private if you wish.

Sam liked the narrative and grew in confidence when he realised Charles and Eugene were off Doreen's radar.

Leslie popped his head round the corner and nodded at Doreen.

"Ah, the girls have arrived. I'll go meet them. Remember, Jasmine is for you, Charles, and Claudette for you, Eugene."

Sam backed off a little. He was keen to see how this drama played out.

Doreen left the lounge. The boys were silent. You could feel the tension. Then she swept back into the room, followed by Jasmine and Claudette. She stopped to allow the boys time to look at them.

Time stood still. Sam was gobsmacked. Charles and Eugene had seen it all in Asia, or so they thought.

Both girls put on a sexy body pose, arms spread, with a 'do you like what you see' look. Charles' mouth was open. Eugene tried to look cool and relaxed.

Danny's money had been well spent. The girls looked sensational.

"Close your mouth, Charles, and order some drinks." Doreen lit the fuse.

"What would you like to drink, girls?" somehow Charles got the words out.

"Two vodka and tonics please. Can we have doubles?" Jasmine asked.

Charles would have bought quadruples; he was already besotted!

Roger contained himself and poured the drinks.

"Now Claudette, this is Eugene. And Jasmine, this is Charles. They are both very shy so be patient with them."

Roger and Sam burst out laughing.

Doreen continued "And this upstanding young man is Sam. He's mine so keep your hands off him."

The girls laughed, and Jasmine said "Maybe next time, Sam?"

"Now I want to have a private word with Sam about a BMW car, so we're going to sit over there. You guys get to know each other, the night is young. Roger will put any drinks on your tab. Is that okay, Charles?

Charles, keen to assert his status and importance, could only answer "Sure is." He nestled closer to Jasmine, who had already sensed rich pickings. Roger had been primed to put only tonic in every other one of the girls' drinks. Charles and Eugene were lambs to the slaughter.

As they sat down, Doreen eased forward, within touching distance. She was about to sow a seed.

Sam was in her web, his attention mainly directed towards her dress rather than her story. Doreen sensed it and backed off a little.

"Sam, can I talk to you in confidence?

"Of course, do you have a problem?"

"No, not a problem, more a need for some experienced guidance. I want to expand my business and broaden what I have to offer."

Sam raised his eyebrows. He had a limited view of Doreen's talents. She certainly filled an excitement void in his life. Tracie was a voluptuous girlfriend and customers loved the view. However, she was not the sharpest tool in the box, and at times quite boring. Sam was attracted to Doreen's physical qualities and her streetwise confidence. She turned him on physically and mentally.

"If I can help, I will."

Doreen was making progress. Time to launch an attack.

"I want to increase what I have to offer. My wellbeing tent at Sports Day was extremely popular with the locals, and I started to understand some of the personal anxieties that many of them suffer from. So I want to develop that side of my business. I have some premises in mind. I can't tell you where, as they aren't available yet, but I'm looking for some form of sponsorship. Not an investment, but a mutually beneficial sponsorship."

"Money's tight now, Doreen. What d'you have in mind?"

"I need a sponsored car with the sponsor's name and my Wellbeing name on either side. The sponsor will get the benefit of the advertising. The status of the car will add value and authenticity to my new business. There could be other benefits to the sponsor of a more personal nature." Doreen relaxed, crossed her legs, and thanked Danny for the script.

Sam usually answered very quickly as he was always dealing with salesmen trying to sell him advertising space or cheap loans, but Doreen's mention of personal benefits intrigued him. His last visit had cost him almost $500.

"If I'm reading your proposal correctly, you're looking for me to provide you with a sponsored BMW?"

Doreen remained silent. Danny had said, don't jump in too quickly.

She jiggled in her seat, and Sam said "I suppose I'm involved in personal benefits?"

"You most definitely are."

"If I agree to provide you with a car, you will be responsible for all the extras, meaning the signage, yours and mine, on the car. We can arrange that, but you must pay. Let me come back to you with a quote. I'm not saying yes. I'm just considering it."

"Understood. Now let's join the others." Now Doreen knew she could seal the deal.

The girls had wrapped themselves around Charles and Eugene. Claudette had her hand looped through Eugene's arm and was playfully tugging him, occasionally whispering in his ear. Jasmine had pulled her bar stool close to Charles and was sliding her hands up and down the top of his thighs; occasionally one hand would slide down the inside. Each time it did, Charles nearly overbalanced on his seat.

"Well, you guys seem to be getting on really well. Are you ready to eat or would you prefer bar snacks?"

"Bar snacks," Charles cried in soprano as Jasmine's hand ran down his inner thigh.

"Maybe it's a good idea to relax a bit, ladies, the night is young." Doreen sent out the signal and the girls reacted.

"Pass the menus around, Roger, please. Can I suggest we all order some different finger food that we can share? I'll start with spicy chicken wings. Write the order down, Roger. Who's next?"

Sam ordered small sausage rolls and the girls chuckled. Charles wanted a steak. Roger reminded him steak was not finger food.

"Okay, I'll use a fork then, Rodney."

"Just get him a steak, Roger. After all, he's paying," Doreen urged.

Eugene ordered spring rolls with Asian dressing.

"Well, you would, wouldn't you?" said Charles.

"Now how about something light and tasty, maybe some prawns — don't want to spoil your beautiful figures now." Charles waited as the girls smiled at each other and nodded approvingly.

"There you are, Rodney; did you get it all down?"

"It's Roger, sir, and yes, I'll take the order through to the kitchen now. Then I'll suppose you'll be wanting more drinks?"

Doreen smiled. She had grown close to Roger, almost motherly, especially as he was planning to visit Filippo in Italy.

The food was met with great gusto. Charles considered a repeat order, but Jasmine's attentions curbed the thought.

Doreen had set a time for the girls to think about luring Charles and Eugene back to their rooms.

"Maybe suggest a walk outside for some fresh air, then back to their rooms?"

Sam was relieved when both couples excused themselves. He

was getting tired of Charles and thought Eugene was boring.

Doreen sensed this and moved closer to him. "I hope you're not thinking of excusing yourself, young man. I don't expect we'll see them again. Pull up that stool and let's move to the corner of the bar.

Sam was reassured and decided to stay the night. Doreen was ahead of him.

"I hope you don't mind, but I felt so bad that you had to pay almost $500 the last time we stayed together, so I've booked and paid for the room this time. It's on the second floor away from those crude Americans. I'm sure you'll like it. King-size bed and champagne. Okay?" Doreen ticked all the boxes. "Now just order some drinks, I need the loo."

"Drinks are on the house, Sam." Roger ticked another box.

"Ready to go, Leslie?" Doreen asked as she strolled through reception.

"They've just gone to their rooms and I've started the recording."

Doreen disappeared into the ladies and Leslie sent an SMS to Danny. "Roll out the barrel."

"What did that say?" Janice stared across the table. Danny passed his phone over to her. "Roll out the barrel? What does that mean?"

"I met two guys at Fred's the other day who were a musical duet. I asked what their theme tune was and they said 'Roll out the barrel'. They're obviously playing somewhere tonight and wanted to let me know."

Janice swallowed the story, hook, line and sinker.

"Maybe we could use them at the end-of-year ball?"

Danny wriggled a little bit before answering. "I'll check next time I see them. I know they work overseas as well." That might deflate Janice a touch.

Doreen returned to her bar stool and nestled closer to Sam. A free night had nailed it for him, and why not relax and enjoy the ride, so to speak?

CHAPTER 70

SUNDAY AT FRED'S

DOREEN OPENED A LITTLE LATER THAN THE PREVIOUS Sunday. She had texted Danny saying Sam was slow to rise and she had left him to breakfast alone. She would be there by 9am. Before leaving she had noticed Charles and Eugene going for a pre-breakfast walk.

"Go and get the videos, Leslie. I'll keep an eye on those two." Doreen saw them disappearing down the lane. They would be back in about 20 minutes. Claudette and Jasmine had, under strict orders from Doreen, left before the Americans woke up. Leslie had given each of them an envelope.

Leslie said "Better check the recordings worked."

"Okay, but be quick. We've got about 15 minutes." Doreen watched for them by the door while Leslie pressed the play button and sat back.

Thirty seconds of silence followed before Leslie cried out "Bloody hell," and then held his hands to his face.

Doreen turned sharply. "That worked okay then. Put them in an envelope and give them to me. We can do it again tomorrow or Tuesday."

Danny was at Fred's on time, and Doreen put the kettle on.

"The videos are in the envelope, Danny. I haven't watched them, but Leslie has. He's still in shock, he may need medication."

Danny smiled. "I'll look at them later. What did you tell the girls?"

"I said to make sure they get a second session with the boys, either tomorrow or Tuesday night. That should give us enough material to interest the police."

"When are you seeing Sergeant Phillips again?"

"Tonight. It's his day off tomorrow, so I've booked him a room. I'll mention something later."

"What about the Americans? Me and Sam are taking them out for dinner after showing them round his dealership." Doreen had covered all the bases.

"What about Phillips?"

"His shift doesn't finish until 10 tonight, so Leslie will show him straight to his room on the second floor. I'll meet him there."

"Excellent. By the way, how did you get on with Sam and the BMW?"

"He's producing a quote for the signage on the car. If I agree to pay for that, he'll sign the car over to me. He also asked me what colour. What do you think?"

Danny thought for a moment. "Maybe a colour that shows off the signage clearly and isn't too bright. Know what I mean? White, or maybe that light-coloured metallic green I saw on his forecourt. A BMW 3 series would be a good choice. Best not to grow too quickly. You may want to consider asking the Americans to help with the signage costs — you could have Griffin promotional leaflets for your clients."

Doreen's eyes lit up. "Now there's a thought!" Danny always had answers or suggestions. "Great idea, darling. I'll have to raise the issue when Sam isn't there."

"You don't have a lot of time, so I suggest you have your bank account details on you. If they agree to help, they could transfer the money immediately from their iPhones." Danny made it sound so easy.

"How are you going to get Sergeant Phillips interested in what the Americans might be doing?" he asked.

"I've told the girls to stay over with the Americans on Monday night and have breakfast with them. Sergeant Phillips will join me for coffee in the lounge. I've asked him to come in plain clothes, not uniform, because I don't want to arouse suspicion. He'll get a good look at them both with Jasmine and Claudette, and then I've told the girls to take a 14-day break away from here when the Americans are arrested. I'll give them $500 each to disappear. Can you help with that?"

"Sure. It's a good idea to have them out of sight. After all, they're not doing anything wrong. They don't know about the video recordings, nor should they, and we may need them again down the track. Maybe they could learn Italian?" Doreen laughed.

"The Griffin has two cleaners from the Philippines who will find the videos in the rooms and inform the police," Doreen confirmed.

"How do you know that?" Danny queried.

"Because there will be a contact number on them offering a reward and the number will go through to Sergeant Phillips' personal mobile phone. The cleaners won't know he works for the police. He'll advise them to hand the videos in to Leslie in reception, who will seal them in an A4 envelope marked for Sergeant Phillips. Leslie will give them a small reward and I'll contact Phillips later in the day to stoke the fire and maybe meet for drinks."

"Excellent. It's a simple plan and I like simplicity. When Phillips has the videos, we want him to take Charles' and Eugene's passports from Leslie. Can you make sure Leslie has them ready, and perhaps remind Phillips?

"Yes to both, Danny. Phillips will be smelling promotion. I told him last time we met that I was looking forward to the day he became Inspector Phillips."

Danny laughed. Doreen was so streetwise. Every time she and Phillips met the noose tightened a little. Not only was Doreen driving the relationship, but she also had overall control. She could end it any time with a threat of exposure, but for now Sergeant Phillips had a key role to play.

"I'm involved in the governors' tour of the school on Wednesday. I can't get out of it."

"I know, Sam told me. He's going as well."

"Tell him not to drink the tea when we go into the science labs. It won't really be tea. It's not dangerous — just sends people a little daft. You know, giggly and touchy."

But Danny did not know whether to tell Carol or not. If he did, he was really admitting guilt.

Sanjira was sworn to secrecy. She was just using the lab to settle her curry pots before freezing them.

When Danny stood up to go, he asked Doreen to keep him informed of everything by text. "Just text 'Roll out the barrel' if things are going well and let me know which night the girls will be back at The Griffin."

"I'll do that now. Let me text Jasmine."

Doreen typed in the question, and within seconds "Monday" popped up.

She replied "Make Monday a special night. See Leslie before you leave."

"Thanks, will do."

Danny stood in the precinct. Janice was, as girls tend to do, revising hard for the exams, so she was off Danny's radar and not a threat. That left Carol. He mused over yes or no, then sent a text "Free now, coffee at yours?"

"See you soon. C" came the reply.

CHAPTER 71

PREPARING THE WAY

THEY MET AT THE USUAL SPOT IN THE PLAYGROUND ON Monday morning.

"It all went well over the weekend. Doreen and the girls did their job. The girls will be back with the Americans tonight. The first recordings were made, and tonight we should get the second ones. That should be enough. Any questions? No? Okay, let's slip back into school mode."

They all nodded in agreement, and Danny looked at Jordan, who sort of communicated without doing so — a kind of facial body language.

Monday moved slowly, and morning assembly covered exam preparation and the governors' tour. Pupils were reminded of the school's dress code and that they must present a disciplined and well-dressed picture to the outside world. Bartholomew was heading towards a happy retirement, a reflection on his achievements, and maybe some recreational fishing. Mrs Bartholomew was already planning his post-school curriculum, since not much was going on at home.

Danny dropped into the staffroom at lunchtime and had a quiet chat with some of the more vulnerable staff. He timed leaving to make sure he met Alice Brown at the door.

"After you."

"Thank you. Quite the gentleman." Alice tucked her books under her arm and squeezed through.

"I see you teach economics and social studies, Miss Brown. Not my strongest suit, I'm afraid. In fact, I'm a bit concerned about how I'll cope with pensions, tax, etc., when I leave."

"Can I help? Why don't you make a short list of your key concerns and I'll look at them for you?"

"That's really kind of you. I noticed you're free for period 7 on Thursday. Maybe we could meet then?" Danny was enjoying this.

"Why don't I come to your office on Thursday? Just put your questions in my pigeonhole between now and then."

"Will do, Miss Brown. Thank you so much."

Miss Brown wondered how he knew she had a free period on Thursday, but he seemed a nice boy and was helping with her discipline issues.

Sato went in to see Danny with a financial reconciliation.

"Better than I thought, Sato. When we're in position to move in for The Griffin, what should our strategy be?"

"You mean other than blackmailing Wilson?"

"That's a done deal. I mean in terms of producing figures — projections, I think they call them." Danny knew exactly what he meant and so did Sato.

"I've been doing some work in that area, and if we file Doreen's contributions under 'Wellbeing' we have a positive cash flow projection. What I need is a copy of The Griffin's annual accounts for the last three years. If they show a downturn, then we put in a lower bid."

Danny called Leslie. "Hi, Danny here. How quickly can you get me a copy of The Griffins last three years' accounts?"

"They're on the computer, Danny, but I need a password. Charles has it. He usually gives it to the accountant a couple of times a year. It's not only for the accounts, but also staff records, customer profiles, etc."

"Thanks, I'll have a word with Doreen. When she gives you the password can you run off two copies of the accounts for the last three years and put them in an envelope marked for Sato's attention? Text him when they're ready. Bye for now."

Danny texted Doreen "I need two copies of The Griffin's financial accounts for the last three years. They're on the Griffin computer, but Leslie needs the password from Charles. Can you get it and forward it to him?"

"Will do, darling."

Danny smiled. He had caught Doreen in a cheeky mood.

Sato stood up to go. "Everything else is good. See you around."

Their relationship pleased Danny. The positioning was perfect, their roles clearly defined and their mutual respect was based on their ability to get a job done. They operated perfectly together or apart, and the timeline for their relationship had no limit. Sato would go to university and become the accountant for Always Tomorrow, which would, of course, own The Griffin.

Doreen made sure she was at The Griffin when Charles and Eugene got back to get ready to go to see Sam. As they came into reception, Doreen was berating Leslie about his bloody computer.

"Hey you guys, what's all the noise?" Charles smiled as he said it.

"It's your fault. You're the owner. All I want is to book some flights to Europe and it won't give me access. Anyone would think I was trying to rob a bank." Doreen put on her 'I'm seriously annoyed' look and Leslie looked positively frightened.

"You need a special password, Doreen," Charles confirmed.

"Well, don't just stand there. What is it?" she demanded.

"Put your hands over your ears, Leslie, and look the other way." Charles mouthed Oklahoma to Doreen. "I can change it before we leave," he said to Eugene.

"Thank you. Hallelujah, I have access. Now, Leslie, turn around and get to work on these flights for me. I'll be in the lounge de-stressing. Joining me, boys?" Doreen wiggled off, thinking now let me see if I can find some flights to Italy for Roger, and they followed without a word.

Leslie had the accounts printed off in seconds and put them in an envelope marked for Sato's attention. He texted Sato.

Sato smiled as he received the text. He would get an Uber out to The Griffin after school and pick up the copies.

Danny never dwelled too much on the past. He was very much here and now. However, even the here and now group must occasionally deal with little irritations. Potter was one and, come Wednesday, he would be scratched away so to speak. Most of Danny's little irritations were of his own making though. Janice he considered a genuinely nice comfortable girl to be with. He wasn't committed, but he enjoyed her company now and again. The problem was, he knew Janice had designs on him and, to a degree, had got under his skin. At present she was preoccupied with studying, but what when the exams were over?

Carol was exciting. Probably older woman syndrome, he thought. A 19-year-old boy in an intense relationship with a single older woman who has her own apartment and car. What wouldn't the other guys in Year 12 give for that?

Sex with Janice was warm and affectionate – with Carol it was raw and raunchy, and no questions or pressure.

What about Alice Brown, the young first year teacher? Danny was not even looking for a third female partner; she had just fallen at his feet and he had picked her up. The rest was to follow, and he should prepare some questions for her visit. The personal details, such as was she in a relationship and did she live alone, would all come out naturally.

Late Monday evening, Danny received the text he expected from Doreen, 'Roll out the barrel', which meant the girls were tucked up with Charles and Eugene, Leslie had pressed the record button and Sergeant Philips was waiting to be fed!

Danny lay on his bed, his arms behind his head, contemplating the future. It excited him. He had recently read a magazine article about Richard Branson who had begun his empire-building at a similar age and was now a billionaire with his own island in the Caribbean. With a smile he turned on his side and fell asleep.

The next morning he texted Doreen "Can you arrange for Fred to be somewhere else if I come about 5.30, just before you close?"

Doreen texted straight back "Will do Danny. Roll out the barrel."

He watched as she ushered the last few customers out. "Fred's at the wholesalers. I altered the stocktake chart, so he's gone to stock up. He won't be back. I'm locking up."

Danny appreciated that. "Can you update me? Have the girls been paid and left for a couple of weeks? Did the recordings go ahead? Are the cleaners picking up the videos? Does Leslie know what to do? How did Sergeant Phillips react?"

"Wow, slow down. Firstly, the girls did the business. Leslie paid them and they've moved away for a couple of weeks. I'll let them know when to come back. The cleaners did the rooms at about 11 this morning, found the videos and handed them in to Leslie. I'm assuming they phoned Sergeant Phillips, but I'm not sure."

Danny raised his eyebrows. "Can you phone Phillips? Just tell him how much you enjoyed the night and see if he wants to talk about anything else?"

"Good idea. Maybe better to text him first, he could be in a meeting."

"Put some thought into the text," Danny urged.

Doreen went off to another table and began to text. As she came back her phone rang 'private caller'. Doreen was used to this as many potential clients didn't want their numbers seen, so she answered confidently.

"Can we meet at eight tonight? I need to speak to you about a personal issue. Car park at the end of the precinct would be good. I'll be in a private car."

"Yes, see you then." Doreen stared at Danny.

"Phillips?" Danny asked.

"Yes, wants to talk about a personal issue. I reckon he's had the phone call from the girls. I'm meeting him at eight tonight, and not at The Griffin."

Danny took a positive view. "At least he can say that all his visits to see you were cover for an underground crime he was investigating. He's now perfectly placed to arrest Charles and Eugene on suspicion of using The Griffin for illegal prostitution. I'm sure you'll make him aware of that."

Doreen smiled. "By the time I've finished with him he'll think he's Inspector Clouseau."

Danny laughed. "Can you ring me after your meeting? I'd like to know that phase one has gone successfully before the governors' tour."

Doreen was careful to arrive 10 minutes late for her meeting with Sergeant Philips in the car park. The last thing she needed was to be seen loitering in a public place. As she crossed the road a pair of headlights flashed once and she went over and got into the passenger seat.

Sergeant Phillips drove off. "How exciting. Are you going to put the flashing lights and siren on?" Doreen laughed and took the sergeant's arm.

"I've got in my possession two videos of a very graphic nature of sordid goings on in rooms at The Griffin."

"Well, we did get quite excited."

"No, not of us. They feature the two owners you pointed out at breakfast, presumably with two call girls. What concerns me is that they may be distributing this material widely and that The Griffin could be a front for a bigger call girl operation?"

"Well, that does mean of course that your bookings can be justified, so you're safe." Doreen eased the pain and that was reflected in the sergeant's reaction.

"Good point. Thank you." Phillips steered the car into a private driveway and switched the engine off.

"Surely we're not ... "

"No, it's just a safe place to talk. My colleague's away on holiday."

Doreen began to plot the course for Sergeant Phillips.

"Look, this is the opportunity we've been talking about. Uncovering this crime, whatever it turns out to be, is the one that should get you promoted to the rank of Inspector. It's fallen right in your lap. Strange it should happen just as the owners arrive."

"Do you think that they're directly involved?"

"Just look at all the porn you can watch on your laptop. Someone has to produce that."

"How long are they staying?"

"Two more weeks. Better act fast. Why don't you check if they have any criminal history in America? That would strengthen your case" Doreen was almost reading a script.

"I'll do that back at the station tonight."

"Then confiscate their passports. To be held subject to a police enquiry into graphic pornographic videos which the police have in their possession, featuring the owners of The Griffin motel. At least they won't be able to do a runner back to America." Doreen paused for breath.

"If they have some previous, you have them. For fear of not being able to return to America, they will spill the beans on whoever is involved both here and overseas. You'll be flavour of the month, so to speak."

Sergeant Phillips thought about it. He had never opened a case before, other than arresting a few local petty thieves. This might be an international crime. And if anyone wanted to know why he had spent a few nights at The Griffin, he now had a pretext.

"Okay, I'm going to drop you off at the car park. Then I'll check on our American friends for any previous misdemeanours back home."

"Go nick them, Tiger," Doreen said. "Ring me later with any news. Do you want me to stay at The Griffin tonight and keep my eyes open?"

"Good idea. I'll drop you there instead." Phillips was starting to see the bigger picture. No more wandering the streets, calming drunks down on Saturday nights. Bigger crime-solving, and probably plain clothes. A smart suit and an unmarked car.

"Right, let's go."

Doreen was quiet for the 10-minute drive to The Griffin.

"Don't forget to ring." Doreen opened the door and Phillips sped off.

"Just a single tonight, Leslie, away from you know who." Doreen went into the lounge.

"There she is, the lovely lady, now what would you like?" Charles didn't need to ask as Roger had almost finished pouring.

"Thanks, darling. Now what have you two been up to?" Doreen perched on her usual stool and looked at the boys.

"Well, we've been discussing maybe buying a couple of Sam's BMWs and shipping them home."

"Wow, you have been busy. What a lovely idea. Can Sam ship them?"

"That's what we need to clarify. By the way, did that small transfer arrive in your account okay, the one for the signage?"

"Ooh, almost forgot about that. Let me have a look." Doreen rummaged in her bag for her smartphone and logged onto her bank account. There, third from the top of the list transactions, was $3,000 transferred from the account of Charles Jackson. Doreen leaned forward and smacked a big kiss on his cheek. "It has, my darling, thank you so much. Next time you're over we'll arrange some special treatment for you both." Eugene smiled; he hadn't quite recovered from Claudette's previous special treatment.

Charles ordered more drinks and Eugene loosened up. The noise level increased but not enough to drown out the sound of a police siren getting louder as it approached. Doreen froze for a moment. Surely Sergeant Philips wasn't making a move this soon?

The reception doors flew open and she heard a policemen ask for the lounge in a strong, forceful voice.

"Through there." Leslie didn't hesitate.

Two burly constables entered, followed by Sergeant Phillips. They positioned themselves either side of Charles and Eugene. Doreen made to move but they gestured for her remain sitting.

Roger was about to ask if anyone wanted a drink, but had second thoughts.

Then Sergeant Phillips stepped forward. "Charles Jackson and Eugene Danner, you are under arrest for the production and distribution of material of a sexual nature. I must remind you that anything you say may be taken down and used as evidence against you in a court of law."

Doreen was taken back by Sergeant Phillips' arrest style. She found his directness quite a turn-on. Maybe he could come back later.

Charles and Eugene were speechless. Charles thought it was a practical joke at first, but a look into Doreen's eyes made him think again.

"Please come with us, gentlemen." Both men were led out of the lounge and through reception. Leslie handed Sergeant Phillips both passports as he left and the red and blue lights of the police car lit up the forecourt as Doreen began to text Danny 'Roll out the barrel'

CHAPTER 72

THE GOVERNORS' TOUR

DANNY BRIEFED THE CREW ABOUT THE OVERNIGHT happenings, and Sato confirmed he had picked up two sets of The Griffin's accounts.

"You two can begin putting together a list of people who might rent rooms at The Griffin when we take possession," Danny suggested to Chris and Jeff.

"I'm touring the school with the governors this afternoon, so we'll meet tomorrow morning." Danny had had a quick word with Sato before leaving.

"Have you had time to look over the accounts?"

"Just briefly. Basically, the place is on a downslide. Turnover is dropping year by year. I'll make a list of areas we could take advantage of and definitely improve."

Now Danny could focus on the governors. He had decided not to advise Carol not to drink the tea. He didn't want her to suspect anything, but if she had already tried marijuana she would be able to cope. Bartholomew had agreed the route and so the grand finale would be in the science lab.

One by one the governors arrived and were ushered into Bartholomew's office. Janice had produced snacks and soft drinks. Tracie had insisted on coming with Sam as she suspected he had female interests elsewhere. Danny thought the more the merrier and was delighted Sam was worried about her being there. Joan Webster brought a small flower arrangement, which she called 'The Bartholomew' and placed it in the middle of his desk so a few petals fell colourfully across his inkpad. Gerald Trapper thought about clearing them but couldn't control his hands.

"Have you anything a little stronger?" Trapper asked Janice. Bartholomew intervened, "There's some sherry in the bottom cupboard, Janice. Mr Trapper may like a small glass." Janice eased Mr Trapper towards the cupboard and Tracie, feeling a little out of place, asked for one too.

Danny and Sam shared a knowing look, and Miss Stanger looked disapproving. Carol was the last to arrive and Janice gave her a lukewarm welcome. Danny tried the American version, "Hi, Miss Whittleston," but that looked and sounded stilted. For once his instinct had let him down. Janice frowned, and then changed her look to 'be careful, I'm onto you'.

Once again, Bartholomew rescued Danny.

"Firstly, may I thank you for attending our annual Governors' Tour. I appreciate you are all busy people and to take time out to recognise the work our pupils and staff are doing is very much appreciated. We will present you with a cross section of both the ages and the abilities of our pupils, and we have not simply chosen the most talented and best-behaved classes. Finally, a huge thank you, Joan, for this beautiful floral arrangement, aptly named 'The Bartholomew'." Joan blushed as Sam initiated a controlled round of applause, but Miss Stanger said "We'd better get on, Headmaster, time is precious."

"Yes. May I suggest our school captain lead the way? Over to you, Danny."

"Thank you, Headmaster. We'll visit the study classrooms first, and then the art and craft block, before finishing at the science block for a well-deserved cup of tea, which Janice and Kate will make for us.

Janice cringed. That was news to her, and why was he being so smarmy?

"Now, this is class 10A and one of our Year 1 teachers, Miss Brown, is teaching economics. Good afternoon, Miss Brown, do you mind if our governors look at some of the work your pupils are doing?"

"No, not at all, the class is working very diligently today." Alice smiled at Danny.

"I see a couple of the boys have black eyes. Probably going too hard on the playing fields, eh?" Mr Trapper joked.

Danny smiled at Miss Brown.

"Such an attentive, well-behaved class, Miss Brown. You must pop into my shop and I'll give you some flowers." Joan's compliment caused Miss Brown to blush.

Danny sidled up to each of the boys sporting black eyes and applied a firm grip to a shoulder. Good to see you're playing hard and fast boys. His grip reinforced Jordan's application.

"Let's move on, we have a few more classes to see in this block." Danny ushered them all out, himself last so he could smile at Miss Brown. "See you tomorrow."

"Most definitely," came the response.

Trapper was really taken aback by the number of boys in the various classes who had facial injuries, black eyes, swollen lips, and even the odd limp.

"We do have some robust sporting types, Headmaster."

Danny smiled, and Bartholomew knew his henchman had paved the way for a trouble-free tour.

"Now we are entering the domestic science block. Here pupils can study woodwork, metalwork and learn how to cook wonderful pastries. In fact, here are some already prepared for our visit." Danny pointed to an assortment of odd-shaped biscuits. Janice squirmed. Who did he think he was, some TV presenter?

"I don't think my teeth can cope with crunchy biscuits," said Trapper.

"Mine can." Sam butted in and grabbed the two biggest.

Tracie said she liked the ones with the hole in the middle filled with jam, "so I can put my tongue in and wriggle it around."

Miss Stanger cringed and Joan Webster giggled, before nibbling away like a little hamster.

Throughout all this Bartholomew kept a watchful eye on Danny and his girls, Janice and Miss Whittleston. Both relationships were a potential threat to a successful governors' tour. Danny, however, seemed in complete emotional control. Maybe he had arrived at a decision on one or the other, or maybe Miss Brown's positive response lay in his relaxed manner? Either way, the tour was progressing nicely.

"Finally, in this block we visit Mr Atkins' woodwork class. Here mainly boys, although more girls are opting for woodwork, can learn how to make very useful household items like the wooden coat hanger mountings which are so useful when you come in from a walk on a cold winter's day and need somewhere to hang your coat." Danny smiled at the group and Gerald Trapper and Joan Webster both nodded in agreement.

"It was very cold yesterday, Gerald, around lunchtime," Joan said.

"Did you have a tot by the fireplace?" asked Gerald.

Mr Atkins listened intently, while trying to make eye contact with Carol. How could she not be aware of him? His fluorescent green bow tie was almost hypnotic.

"Now, Mr Atkins, what are the class making today?" Bartholomew changed the subject.

"Well, Headmaster, they are making a kitchen utensil holder."

"What a good idea," said Joan, "I'm always rummaging through drawers looking for my spatula or whisk."

"Maybe I could give you mine, Miss Webster? The demonstration one."

"That's very kind of you, Mr Atkins."

"And maybe I could carve your initials in the corner: J.W." Atkins laughed and gave her a little nudge.

"That would be lovely. My word, Headmaster, we are having a wonderful tour."

Janice could not cope with much more of this, but Danny was wallowing in it all. He knew Bartholomew was happy, and that was the key to his continued success.

"Now our final visit is to our science laboratories. Sanjira, one of our Year 12 girls, will guide us through the various labs, and I believe she has also produced some scientific refreshment. I'm not going to say any more, but I am told it is rather special." Danny wandered off and the governors followed like lemmings.

"How exciting, Headmaster," Joan enthused.

"Will the refreshment be alcoholic, Danny?" Gerald needed a tot.

"I'm sure we can find something to warm your palate, Mr Trapper." Danny was loving this.

Throughout all this Carol had kept a stony silence. She knew Bartholomew was aware of her relationship with Danny, and the fact he had not spoken to her about it suggested he was happy with the bigger picture, Danny's control of the school. Hopefully her job would not be jeopardised; after all Danny would be leaving soon, and out of Bartholomew's sight and thoughts.

Sanjira was waiting for them at the entrance to the science labs. Following a text message from Danny, she had several face masks to hand out to the governors, just to create a little mystique. Potter loved Sanjira's interest and leadership, and he was already wearing his when the governors arrived. He looked like the Lone Ranger.

Sanjira handed out the masks, and Gerald Trapper managed to put his on upside down and hooked it limply over one ear so that it hung precariously down half his face. Miss Stanger lunged at the loose end and scratched his cheek, and Joan Webster applied tissues.

Tracie had pulled hers over her eyes and was on the verge of a panic attack until Sam stepped in and pulled it down a few inches.

"I think we're ready for the tour," Danny said.

Potter was already on the move. In Lab Number 1 pupils were working carefully with small blow torches, Bunsen burners and test tubes.

"Don't get too close, Mr Trapper, you don't want to get singed," Joan said. She was alive with interest. Miss Stanger was always a split second behind her.

Danny signalled to Sanjira to go make the herbal tea.

"Come this way please." Like sheep into the pen, the governors followed.

Potter took over in a vain attempt to assert his status and knowledge. "Here we have pupils learning how to blow glass and make glass shapes. Some are making animals from 3D pictures, and others ornamental shapes for the mantlepiece. We allow the pupils to take their creations home after they have been assessed. Over to my left you can see some of our regional award-winning shapes. We are considered one of the leading schools in the area when it comes to artistic design and creativity."

Bartholomew stepped in to endorse Mr Potter.

"We are incredibly lucky to have Mr Potter leading our science department. We only appoint the most accomplished young scientists, and many of our most talented school leavers go on to work in industry at the forefront of new product development. Now, I believe we are going into the back labs to sample some of Mr Potter's herbal tea."

Tracie was becoming increasingly excited. She had linked arms with Gerald, and both seemed a little giddy. Maybe it was the sherry.

Sam was pleased that Gerald was getting the attention, not him.

"Ooh, it's dark in here, Mr Potter." Tracie laughed and gripped Gerald a little harder. "Stay close to me, Mr Trapper. Be careful where you put your feet. What's that smell?"

"The lovely scented smell is from our herb plants and the more exotic smells are from Sanjira' s curry pots, over there in the corner. Sanjira tells me they need somewhere to settle before going in the freezer. We like to help our pupils," Mr Potter explained.

When Danny saw Sanjira was ready to serve the herbal tea he nudged Mr Bartholomew. He was keen not to be connected to the herbal tea.

Bartholomew took the hint.

"Ah, here comes the herbal tea, everyone. Produced from our very own science laboratories. Please take a cup and let's toast Mr Potter and our pupils in Year 12 who have grown and made it. To Mr Potter and the girls."

"Hear, hear," cried Joan a little loudly.

This was all falling into place perfectly, Danny thought. He smiled as he raised his cup to his lips and pretended to sip. The others were gulping away merrily.

Danny sent a quick text to Jeff "Is your mum here?" Seconds later his phone pinged "Yes."

"Why don't we sing, 'For he's a jolly good fellow'?" suggested Mr Trapper, beginning to shuffle his feet. He almost trod on Tracie, who had started to giggle. Joan Webster was staring hard into her cup and trying to suck the leaves. Miss Stanger's eyes seemed to be bulging, and the entire group started to shuffle their feet.

"My word, that is rather pleasant. Any chance of another cup, Sanjira?" Bartholomew led the charge. "Anyone like to join me?"

There were two yesses, three raised hands and a couple of silly smiles. "Same again then, Sanjira, and a big mug-full for our host, Mr Potter." Potter was smart enough not to refuse Bartholomew, especially in front of the governors. Danny tried to avoid Carol's stare. He knew she suspected something. She knew Danny disliked Potter intensely. Pillow talk didn't lie, but what was he up to, she wondered, even as she began to feel a little light-headed herself. The second round of herbal teas arrived, and Sam suggested Mr Potter make a toast. Danny raised his cup and smiled at Carol, who hesitantly joined in.

What followed next could have been a scene from *The Walking Dead* or a Pilates session gone wrong.

Firstly, Deputy Headmistress Stanger reached forward with both arms to touch the wall, not realising she was four feet away, not three. She splattered against the wall face first and slid southward. The crumpled collection of arms and legs had Tracie giggling madly. Potter rushed to pick her up but lost his sense of direction and veered left into the Bunsen burner cupboard. Bartholomew was desperately trying to clean his glasses and focus. Danny texted Jeff "Send mum to science lab now." Joan said "Let's waltz" and she and Gerald were wrapped in each other's arms trying to dance. Gerald wanted to tango and they looked like Mrs Wobbly meets Mr Stick Insect. The inevitable happened and they collapsed on top of Miss Stanger. Sam was holding an unlit blow torch to his lips and pretending to be Elvis. He got as far as just 'can't help believing', then burst into laughter. Carol was fighting hard to stay normal, having realised what was happening, but previous experience suggested she would lose the battle. She too started laughing.

Sanjira, under Danny's direction, had left just before the fun started.

Janice and Kate were speechless, not knowing whether to try and pick some of the governors up or help Mr Bartholomew. Elvis seemed to be okay, having moved on to 'Love me Tender', sung with one arm wrapped around a drooling Tracie.

The sight that greeted Jeff's mum was akin to a scene from Dante's Inferno, with everyone out of control, some unable to speak. Jeff had told his mother to bring a medical bag but she quickly decided an ambulance would be more useful. She worked out who could be helped and who was better left alone, and Elvis was in the latter category.

Carol was desperately trying to point an accusing finger at Danny but couldn't get the direction right or any sensible words out. Her arms waved about like windsocks at an airport.

Bartholomew, with Janice dabbing his eyes with a wet cloth, was beginning to see shapes and couldn't understand why Miss Stanger was sitting on the floor when there were plenty of stools.

He heard the ambulance as it came up the school drive. Members of staff had received a text message earlier saying "School closes one hour earlier today. Please ensure your classes leave in an orderly manner", which somewhat contradicted the way the governors were about to leave.

The ambulance driver and two paramedics slammed the brakes on and rushed into the science labs.

"Ignore Elvis for the moment. Just get these three off the floor and into the back of the ambulance. They thought they were drinking herbal tea, but it's marijuana, and I suspect it's the first time for all of them," Jeff's mum explained.

With a derisive laugh the driver said "Because it's use of a banned substance we will have to inform the police."

Danny stepped in. "I am the school captain and I have a number for Sergeant Phillips as we have met at social functions. He will understand the situation and knows our headmaster, Mr Bartholomew, the gentleman over there trying to put his glasses on correctly. If you call him, I'm sure he will advise discretion."

"Thank you, good advice. Now let's get these people into the ambulance. Usually takes about three hours for the effects of marijuana to wear off, then they can take a taxi home." The paramedics began lifting governors off the floor, and linked arms with those still standing.

"Come on, Elvis, let's go for a ride."

Sam was well into 'Suspicious Minds' as he climbed into the ambulance.

Janice was torn between marvelling at Danny's calmness and control and wondering whether he had orchestrated it all. Although Sanjira was missing when the uproar began, Miss Whittleston leaving in the ambulance was some consolation for Janice.

Danny texted his crew "Meet at Fred's 5pm", then turned to Janice and Kate. "Wow, that was exciting. Would you like a coffee? Let's go to the staffroom — it will be quite empty. Or my office?"

Kate declined and Janice preferred Danny's office. She wanted to ask a million questions, but the thought of Danny concocting outlandish stories deterred her. Maybe a quiet word with Sanjira would explain .

CHAPTER 73

DANNY AND DOREEN

DANNY WAS AT FRED'S 15 MINUTES EARLY. HE WANTED A quiet word with Doreen.

"Do you think you could put a note in Punter's letterbox, briefly explaining what has happened at The Griffin? Don't sign it. I'll see he finds out about what's going on at school, but make sure he doesn't print anything. I'll feed him some ammunition at the right time." Danny the mastermind was back in charge of proceedings. "Any news from Sergeant Phillips?"

"Yes, he wants to talk to me tonight, to see if I know what's been going on."

"Good. You may want to say some Italians came over and stayed at The Griffin. Just flavour the possibilities so to speak. And can you contact Mr Wilson and tell him you desperately need to see him as someone has been filming sex scenes of unsuspecting couples at The Griffin and the police have video evidence. He'll be mortified."

"I'll do it now," Doreen enthused and picked up her mobile. She was relishing her involvement with Danny.

"Hi, sweetie, hope you're not with someone. Can we talk?" Have you heard the news? The police made some arrests last night at The Griffin. Apparently, someone has been making video recordings of couples having sex in two of the rooms." Doreen stopped for breath.

There was a deathly quiet.

"Hello, sweetie, are you still there?"

"We had sex in rooms at The Griffin." Somehow Wilson got the words out. His entire career was on the line, not to say his pension and investments. The bank would sack him immediately and at his age he was unemployable. Plus, The Griffin was deeply indebted to the bank, and domestically the publicity would end his marriage.

"Do you want to meet me at The Griffin tonight? I'm seeing Roger and Leslie there. They'll know what's going on. Also, remember Danny the school captain? He's a good friend of Sergeant Phillips. I'll get in touch with him. He may be able to find out some details." Doreen winked at Danny.

"Yes, I'll be there. I'll nip home first. Be there about 6.30." Wilson's brain was scrambling. There was a myriad of problems. The headline in the local rag was the most worrying.

Danny put his head round Punter's door. "Major drug story emerging at school, Colin. It'll leak out, but don't print anything until you speak to me. I'll get an update. Speak tomorrow."

Danny had lit the fuse. Punter needed a headline as business was at a low ebb and Mildred was turning the screw.

Doreen arrived early at The Griffin and briefed Roger and Leslie.

"If you want to keep your jobs when this is all over, keep your mouths shut. Don't talk to anyone, understood?" Doreen could not have been clearer. Both men nodded in agreement.

"I'm meeting Mr Wilson from the bank at 6.30, and afterwards Sergeant Phillips. Neither will be staying, so no rooms required. All else remains as before."

"Hi, Mr Wilson, please go through. Doreen is in the lounge bar." Wilson thanked Leslie, trembling at the prospect of his being interrogated by the police and telling all.

"Hi, sweetie, G&T?"

"Better make it a double."

"Ooh that bad is it? Here, take a stool and relax. Things are never as bad as they seem." Doreen was in for the long haul with Wilson. He wasn't close to a nervous breakdown, but panic attacks were on the menu.

"Can we sit away from the bar in private?"

"I think that will only draw attention to us, especially if the police come." Doreen fired a tiny bullet and it hit the target.

"Surely they have the culprits. Why would they want to come back?"

"Leslie says they were here all day checking all the rooms."

Wilson went white!

CHAPTER 74

THE AFTERMATH

DANNY AND CREW MET IN THE SCHOOLYARD THE following morning as though nothing had happened.

Bartholomew was staring out of his office window feeling extremely vulnerable. The paramedics' phrase "We will have to inform the police because illicit drugs are involved" had settled in his brain. In a few minutes he had to take assembly. How much of yesterday's debacle had leaked out? Neither of his lieutenants could get on the stage, let alone run the show. Miss Stanger was gaunt and ghost-like, Potter a mumbling wreck. Bartholomew's entire career was on the line and he could envisage the headlines ... "Science labs a drugs nest." He couldn't understand so much of what had happened. How had the herbs become marijuana? His only link was Sanjira. Surely not her? Carver didn't take a science subject and kept away. Potter was floundering.

Bartholomew went into the assembly hall. Many members of staff wouldn't look at him. Rumours filled the air. Pupils in Years 11 and 12 sniggered and nudged each other. The Asian girls displayed smug confidence, occasionally glancing at Potter. Payback was complete.

Following the assembly, Bartholomew returned to his office and his two lieutenants joined him.

"The police will need to examine the science labs again. I have asked them to come after school. They will need to re-interview each of us, although they are convinced we are not growing and supplying illicit drugs. The question remains how the marijuana plants came to be there and who was responsible. Once established, they will proceed with some form of prosecution. Internally, because the governors are involved, we are free from immediate dismissal. However, I am duty bound to inform the education authorities." Bartholomew looked at the others. His analysis sent shivers down both their spines and neither had any answer.

"Should we get the Union involved?" Potter asked.

"Do you want to risk the publicity?" Miss Stanger replied.

"What about local publicity? Punter's *Advertiser*. He could ruin us," Potter added.

"For now, I think the best thing is for you to return to working your normal timetables. I will let you know when the police plan to arrive." Bartholomew ushered them out.

Danny heard the headmaster's door shut, left it a few minutes, then knocked.

"Come in. Oh, it's you, Danny. Have you heard anything? Is what happened public knowledge?"

"Someone has spoken to *The Advertiser*, and Mr Potter's name has been mentioned as the mastermind, the teacher who is growing marijuana in his labs. I have been to see Mr Punter and told him to hold off putting anything in this week's *Advertiser* until the true facts are known. I told him he could get sued for fake news." Danny took a breath.

"However, someone must be responsible and, as it happened in the science labs and Potter is Head of Science and deeply involved in growing the marijuana, he will be charged for sure. Can I talk privately to you, sir, and in confidence?"

"Yes of course." Bartholomew needed something, and quick.

"I know you have benefitted from my time as school captain. The school is a far more disciplined place, and the staff are happier, as are the governors — especially yesterday afternoon. And I know you are aware of some of my relationships with females and have kindly trusted me to behave respectfully. I am grateful for your confidence in me. I would not want you to suffer because of some misdemeanours taking place in the science labs.

"Both of us are in our final year." Bartholomew looked alarmed. "No need to panic, sir. One of the cleaners knocked your resignation letter onto the floor by accident and wanted to throw it away but checked with me first. I would like us both to finish on a high, so to speak. A good friend of mine is in a relationship with Sergeant Phillips, who is conducting the investigation. He is married. I know Sergeant Phillips reasonably well and feel sure my friend and I could talk to him sensibly and ensure you are vindicated, and a victim rather than a willing participant.

"I can also see that when Mr Punter writes his article next week, he further absolves you of any knowledge or involvement. He has access to all police arrests, so we cannot expect him not to write about the incident. The only person to carry the can will be Mr Potter as Head of Science. To minimise the effect publicly, I suggest you advise Mr Potter to resign for health reasons. He will then have to fight legally and medically to protect his pension. This will read more favourably in the press. I'm sure the governors will agree. Mr Trapper would not want this occurrence to feature on the next council meeting's agenda. Sam Johnson thought the whole thing hilarious, Joan Webster is your number one fan, and I will speak to Carol Whittleston. All bases covered.

Bartholomew took a few moments to take in Danny's analysis and proposal.

"Why would Punter play ball, Danny?"

"He's sees ladies of the night, and if Mildred found out his days would be numbered as well as parts of his anatomy. He knows I know, so relax on that score, sir.

"If you're happy with my recommendation, you should contact Mr Potter ASAP and get his resignation. Mr Potter and I do not get on so, please, no mention of me. I will speak to Sergeant Phillips before your meeting this afternoon and arrange to meet Mr Punter tomorrow morning. Shall we say I have a dentist's appointment?"

Bartholomew felt physically uplifted. The survival pathway was clear.

"Of course, have the morning off if you need to. I'll see Potter after lunch."

"Can you text me the outcome? I'd like to know before I see Mr Punter."

Danny leant forward and, for the first time in their relationship, they shook hands.

Bartholomew slumped back in his chair, then got up and headed for the drinks cabinet and something a little stronger than sherry.

Danny texted Doreen "I need to speak with Sergeant Phillips before he sees Bartholomew after school. Please arrange."

Barely a minute had passed when a text returned. "He will meet you in your office at 3.45pm. He will be in plain clothes. Tell the receptionist."

Danny smiled; he loved her style. The meeting with Sergeant Phillips fitted in perfectly as he expected Alice Brown to knock on his door in period 7.

"Hi, remember me?" Alice poked her head around Danny's door.

"Of course I do. I was about to roll out the red carpet. Come in, take a seat. Can I get you some coffee?"

"Just a small one. Milk, no sugar, please. May I ask you a question?"

"Definitely, but I've no plans to settle down." Danny stared at Alice, who blushed just a little.

"No, it's educational. Well, almost educational. Did you arrange for two of my class to behave when the governors visited?"

"Let me think. Yes, I did." Danny chortled and Alice shook her head but smiled.

"Did you have to hit them?"

"Certainly not."

"Who did then?" Alice queried.

"In the real world, Miss Brown, we have to make judgements. I liked you from the first moment I saw you. I know it's your first year and you're not much older than me. I didn't see why you should have to put up with a couple of delinquents. So I handed the discipline down the line to a friend, nay associate, of mine. He did what was necessary. I apologise if I have offended you in any way, but I like your smile." Danny handed over the coffee.

Alice was temporarily dumb. Danny's answer was both honest and complimentary. He continued "You will have no trouble from them in the future. If you do have any trouble in any of your other classes, please let me know. Some of the younger kids are just cheeky."

"Someone told me that one of the Year 7 boys was left hanging upside down from the school gate. Was that you?"

"He was a bully. I loathe bullies, Miss Brown."

"Call me Alice, at least when we're alone."

"Thank you. I'll try to remember." Danny was ready to move on.

"Danny, you told me you had some issues with your economics lessons. I also studied accountancy, so I may be able to help." Alice offered.

Danny's eyes lit up. Had another piece just fallen into The Griffin mix?

"Well, you probably heard the story going around school of a serious incident yesterday in the science lab during the governors' tour?"

"I have, but I dare not ask, not in my first year."

"Wise! Sergeant Phillips, who arrested Mr Potter and the governors, who were all high on marijuana, is due here in a few minutes to interview me so, unfortunately, we don't have the time to talk right now. Can I suggest we meet after school next week at The Griffin motel, say Monday, 4.30pm? I'll have had time to make some notes and we can relax in the lounge. It's very private, and hopefully this issue with Mr Potter will have blown over."

Alice was a bit taken aback but said yes without thinking.

Danny immediately got to his feet; no point dwelling on a win, he thought. "Can I text you a reminder?"

"Yes, that's okay."

"Is your number on the staff list?"

"I think so. Take it now. Have you got a pen? 0488 113 422."

"Great, something to look forward to," said Danny as he moved towards the door.

Alice slipped away down the corridor to the staffroom. Bartholomew heard Danny's final goodbye, thought about some mischief, then decided to text instead: "Potter will hand in his resignation tomorrow. Headmaster".

Danny had finally removed the thorn in his side. Now he had to reposition Sergeant Phillips.

"Hi, Danny, Sergeant Phillips is here. He has a meeting with you, I believe?"

"Yes, he has. Thank you, Mrs Peters. Come in, Sergeant Phillips. Would you like a coffee? I know you're meeting Mr Bartholomew later; we had a chat this morning. We have a good working relationship."

"How do you know Doreen?" Sergeant Phillips tentatively edged forward.

"I got her the job at Fred's café and we've been good friends ever since. I don't have a problem with her past or present." No point messing about, Danny thought.

Like the scene in the film *Heat*, where Al Pacino and Robert De Niro face off in the café, Carver and Phillips held each other's stares.

"Now what do you want to see me about?" Phillips broke the ice.

"I spoke at length with Mr Bartholomew this morning. He's been my headmaster since I came to school here in Year 7, and he retires this year. He's helped me through some difficult times and he had no prior knowledge of what was being grown in the science lab. He was merely fulfilling his role, escorting the governors on a tour of the school. I would hate him to be involved in any subsequent prosecution. You may want to focus on Mr Potter." Danny resumed the De Niro stare.

Sergeant Phillips stood up, thanked Danny for his time and left the room.

Danny thought about it. Would I have just stood and left? Maybe I would.

He heard Mrs Peters take Sergeant Phillips in to see Mr Bartholomew and decided he needed to speak to Doreen.

"Can we chat at the café in 10 minutes?"

"Make it 20, and I'll get rid of Fred," came the response.

It was five when Danny arrived. There were only a few singles scattered at tables around the room and Doreen cried "Five minutes, then I'm locking up."

Danny sat down at the corner table with his back to the others, and the door was closed, locked and the closed sign swung over.

"I've had a brief chat with Sergeant Phillips. I don't want Bartholomew included in the investigation."

"What did he say?" Doreen asked.

"Nothing. He just stood up and left."

"Good, he doesn't want to begin a dialogue with you. I'm seeing him tonight at The Griffin for an hour only. We thought it wise to keep it professional. I'll get an answer for you. Now, how do you want me to play the American story?"

"Check with Sergeant Phillips to see if you can visit Charles and Eugene in the next few days. You need to ask some personal questions about room hire, etc. I want you to paint a serious picture. If they're found guilty of a criminal offence their passports will be kept and jail is a real possibility. Tell them the bank manager came to The Griffin to discuss reducing the size of their loan because of a poor set of accounts."

"So the solution to their problems is the immediate sale of The Griffin to you, the return of their passports, and return to America with no possibility of coming back here?" Doreen smiled. "Whatever happened at school yesterday worked well for me. Sam phoned to say he was agreeing to my request for a sponsored car and I should go in on Friday to decide on a colour and discuss the signage. Leslie is designing my Wellbeing logo." Doreen was alive!

"Wow, great news! By the way how's Wilson?"

"He's mortified. If the police find any more videos his whole life will be over. The implications are too horrendous to contemplate."

"Good. Next time you see him, tell him you have a possible solution, but you need some delicate information, i.e. the amount of the Americans' bank loan. Tell him you know of a potential buyer who could take The Griffin over and put an end to any police interest in guests who have stayed there. Tell him his reservations were recorded on his credit card, so they know he has stayed there. His wife wouldn't be happy to know that, especially if she received a video recording. Don't say you can make it all go away, just paint a scenario." Danny sipped his coffee and Doreen smiled.

"Could be a good week for us both, Danny. What colour did you suggest for my BMW?"

"I suggest something low profile that would highlight your

Wellbeing logo — maybe white or that metallic light green?" Danny raised his eyebrows "Well?"

"I'll make a decision on the day." Doreen had never had it so good.

"Text me tonight when you've seen Phillips. Go easy on him. That promotion's just around the corner." Danny stood up and squeezed Doreen's shoulder as he went by.

Doreen remained seated. She'd seen many false dawns, but Danny had entered her life unlike anyone else. He used her in a way she understood, in a way that always benefitted her, and he put her first. He had renewed her self-esteem and acknowledged her natural cunning. A new BMW, 'Wellbeing' premises and an opportunity to run her life on her own terms almost brought a tear to her eye.

Then she jerked back into the present and began cleaning tables before heading off to The Griffin.

CHAPTER 75

DOREEN PAINTS THE PICTURE

"WHAT DO YOU THINK OF THESE TWO DESIGNS, DOREEN?" Leslie called as Doreen went past.

"Bring them through. I need a G&T desperately. Double usual, Roger, please."

Roger was on it like a flash and Leslie came in with an A4 envelope.

Doreen brushed some beer mats aside then laid the designs on the table. Roger put the G&T down at arm's length. Doreen took a gulp and looked skyward — thank you, Lord, thank you.

"Leslie, these are particularly good. Let's see, what do you think, Roger? I know, let's write down the ones we each prefer in order, then compare notes. There are five designs, so list them in order of one to five, with one being the best and so on."

Roger passed around pens and bits of paper.

"Okay, turn your papers over. Ah, we all agree on number three. Now here's the next question. What would be the best background colour for number three? Write that down. Two whites and a red, interesting. I'm going to Sam's on Friday to pick a colour. Can you reprint the logo on white, red and maybe light metallic green, Leslie, please?"

Leslie left and Roger refilled Doreen's glass just as Sergeant Phillips came in, in plain clothes.

"Promoted already, I see. Like the suit. Very AFP."

Phillips couldn't help laughing. "Scotch, please with some water."

"My tab, Roger." Doreen switched from Wellbeing car mode to gangster's moll.

"Now what have you been up to today, super sleuth?"

Phillips poured a little water into his scotch and waited for Roger to move to his stool at the end of the bar.

"I met with your friend Danny. Very streetwise young man. I think I can trust him, but only on your recommendation. Do I have it?"

"Of course. He has created an opportunity for me which I want to talk to you about, but not tonight. Well, maybe a little. How are your investigations progressing?"

"Forensics swept through all the rooms, and thankfully only the two rooms occupied by the Americans have used video recordings."

"Phew, that's a relief. Did they cover both floors?"

"Yes, we can relax. Fortunately, the rooms we used are in your name."

"Bravo, you're in the clear." Doreen planted a kiss on his cheek and Roger slipped off his stool.

"It would appear so. Our investigations are ongoing. We can hold both the Americans for a further four days until we get records back from Oklahoma or they confess to further crimes. At this point they are certain to be charged with creating illicit sexual material privately obtained. We would like to speak to the girls involved, but suspect they are on the game."

Doreen probed for a bit more.

"If they're found guilty, will they serve their time here or in America?"

"They will have their passports red-coded and then it's up to the Americans."

"Can they receive visitors?"

"Yes, but only by arrangement. Why, would you like to talk to them?"

"Well the staff are concerned for their future and can't be seen entering a police station or prison. Between me and you, Leslie on reception says the recent sets of accounts are extremely poor. I would like to ask them a few questions just to reassure the staff." Doreen pitched the appeal perfectly: soft and sincere.

"Oh, and which of these do you like? Leslie designed them."

"Number three."

"Excellent, and on which background?"

"Metallic green."

"Perfect, thank you. Now can you arrange a visit for me?" Doreen looked intent.

"Let me text you a time tomorrow when I've spoken to the duty officer. Now, are we eating? I'm starving!"

"It's either love or food with you, Sergeant. Pass me the menu, Roger, we're eating at the bar. By the way, what's happening at the school? Who's responsible?" Doreen switched tack.

"Well, thanks to your friend Danny it seems the headmaster is in the clear. All fingers point to Mr Potter, the Head of Science. Was he growing the marijuana deliberately or was it a genuine mistake? I've since heard he has offered his resignation and, as the school governors were involved, we may not proceed and leave it to the education authorities to impose any discipline. Now what are we having?

"You choose, I must powder my nose, darling." Doreen left and began a text message to Danny from the ladies room. "Bartholomew in clear. Police may not proceed as Potter has resigned. Bye for now."

Danny rolled over on his bed and smiled at the text. Good girl, he thought.

Before falling asleep, Danny listed his priorities for the following day. He had to talk to Punter and the Italian restaurant owner. Bartholomew had authorised his taking the morning off. Plus, he had to face Carol. That made him smile.

CHAPTER 76

DANNY TAKES CHARGE

DANNY KNOCKED ON PUNTER'S DOOR AND WALKED IN.

"Hi, Danny, glad you're here. I want to speak to you about a couple of stories. Firstly, the school issue. Is it true marijuana was growing in the science labs?"

"Yes, it is, but I don't want you to publish a negative story, because Headmaster Bartholomew is retiring at the end of the year. He's been good to me — and you. One plant out of a batch of herbs was found to contain illicit leaves thought to be marijuana. Is that clear? There's another story about to break which you may feature in, so please listen carefully. Police have arrested the owners of The Griffin motel for videoing guests who were engaged in extreme sexual behaviour with local call girls. The police are conducting a forensic sweep of all the rooms and contacting everyone who has booked a room there over the last six months."

Punter collapsed and Danny flicked the 'Back in 10 minutes' sign across the door.

"When will the police finish their investigation, Danny?"

"I know Sergeant Phillips. I'll contact him later today. If the police have your name, just admit to staying there and having some company. There's nothing wrong with that." Danny had established complete control over Punter.

"I'll see Sergeant Phillips keeps your name out of the press. You wouldn't want Mildred to find out."

Danny looked at Punter's trembling hands. The mention of Mildred had induced the shakes.

"If you're in the clear, I'll help you put a story together and make sure it gets massive exposure. Sales will increase for sure. By the way, what rent do you pay for this shop?"

"$4,000 a month. You can see why I need good stories, Danny."

"I'll be able to help you when this issue with the school is all over. I'll text you tonight when I've spoken to Sergeant Phillips. Is that okay?"

"Yes, please do."

Danny flicked the sign back to 'Open' and left.

CHAPTER 77

MASSIMO CRESPO

MASSIMO CRESPO WAS AN EXPRESSIVE FIRST-GENERATION Australian. The years had rounded his shoulders, he was too fond of his own pasta and at 90 kilos he was sadly out of shape. However, when dressed in his favourite cooking apron with scenes from Milan and Rome, he became the true Italian chef. He welcomed every patron like a long-lost member of his family with arms open and a beaming smile, and escorted them joyfully to their table. His niece Christina gave out the menus and took the orders. When the place was empty, she played INXS and Powderfinger, and as guests arrived she flicked the switch, and Pavarotti or Bocelli changed the mood.

Lately there had been a decline in trade. An increase in the number of fast-food outlets in the precinct was tempting patrons to stay local and not take the short car ride to Massimo's Italian on the edge of town.

"I am a so glad to see you, Danny. Thank you for dining at my restaurant with your beautiful young girlfriend. Did you like the pasta?"

"Massimo, the pasta was, how you say, fantastico!"

"Danny, you are always welcome, but I may not be here for much longer. They put the rent up again and everyone uses Uber Eats now for burgers and fries. It makes me incredibly sad."

"Very soon, Massimo, I may be able to help you. I want you to be the best Italian chef in the state, making the finest Italian food. First I have to complete a few transactions and then you and I can have a talk."

"You sound like the Mafioso, Danny. I hope you will treat me fairly. I am not a young man."

Danny laughed, he loved Massimo and his jovial personality.

"I have to go now. I'll get back to you very soon, so keep cooking and remember my favourite dish is pork risotto." Danny winked and stood up, and Massimo embraced him.

Danny decided to walk back to the precinct to give himself some time to think. Firstly, I'll put Bartholomew at ease. He began a text. "Spoke to the police and *The Advertiser*. All good, no need to worry. Speak this afternoon. Danny".

Bartholomew read the text several times searching for a hidden meaning, then convinced himself it was true. The pressure eased and he sat calmly, his future still secure and on track.

Danny looked at his iPhone and contemplated contacting Carol. Phone or text? Positive or negative? He put the phone to his ear and waited for her to answer.

"I thought you'd never call," she said.

'I've had a few issues to deal with since your arrest."

Carol laughed. "Were you behind the marijuana plants?"

"Of course not. When did you realise it was marijuana?" Danny was always worried about calls being recorded.

"Very quickly. Immediately after the first taste. My voice still croaks a little."

Danny relaxed and made the conversation personal. "I find it very sexy. Keep croaking."

Carol knew he was responsible, because Danny had mentioned Potter in bed.

"Where are you now?"

"I'm walking back to Fred's. Bartholomew gave me the morning off to secure his pension and ensure the publicity is kept to a minimum. What are you doing?"

"I'm about to leave and meet you for coffee at Fred's." Carol giggled childishly.

Danny loved the roguery — and the challenge of living on the edge!

Fred was chatting to his customers when Danny walked in. "Take a seat. Having a day off?"

"No, I've got a meeting with the careers lady here in a few minutes." Fred wasn't convinced.

Carol had never been to Fred's before, and came in tentatively peering around the room. She spotted Danny in the far corner. "There you are, tucked away out of the public eye. You can see the whole café from here, just in case anyone dodgy comes in."

"Take a seat. Would you like a coffee?"

"Cappuccino, please."

"Usual and a cappuccino, Fred, please."

"You know, this is the first time we've met in public. Aren't you scared of being seen?" Carol searched for a weak spot.

"No, Fred thinks you're the careers lady from school."

"Well, I am, and my other career is hanging out with you, physically and emotionally. Are you sure you asked for cappuccino?"

"This is Fred's not Giuseppe's in the Piazza Bra, Verona." Danny surprised himself — talking to the Italians had left its mark.

"Ha, love it! Now, did you orchestrate yesterday's charade just to get back at Potter?"

"Promise not to tell?"

"I promise."

"Yes, I did," Danny whispered across the table.

"Well you are a clever boy. I wonder what else is circulating inside your lovely head. I suspect that was not a one-off. What's next? Are we empire building?"

"Yes, we are. Would you like to be part of my empire?" Danny joined in the game.

"Most certainly. It's a long time since I've had so much fun. Are you going to tell me, or do I have to guess?"

"You know me very well, so have a guess. Or maybe a few guesses."

"Hmm, you're definitely not the type to be ordered around, so an apprenticeship is out of the question. An office job would be too constraining. You must be the main man, so you are probably putting everything in place for when you leave school, but what, I wonder? You get on very well with Sam Johnson, but selling his cars — that would be temporary. He likes you — and Elvis."

Danny smiled. He had yet to speak to Sam. Maybe he should send him an Elvis greeting card?

"Very good so far. I have my mind set on a little place on the outskirts of town. Maybe we could meet there tonight for dinner?"

"Oh, exciting. Where do you have in mind?"

"Massimo's Italian, down near The Griffin motel. Can you pick me up?"

"I can, but you should consider driving lessons and save for a car. You could borrow mine when I'm in school."

Danny was aching to laugh, but restrained himself.

"That's exceedingly kind of you. Can you pick me up here at 7pm? I'll book a table."

"Sure can — see you later." Carol left and Fred cast a knowing smile at Danny, who ignored it and made for the door.

"See you, Fred, stay happy."

CHAPTER 78

THE VISIT

DOREEN PEERED INTO THE LONG MIRROR IN HER BEDROOM. Despite a chequered lifestyle, this was a new horizon. She pulled and tugged at various items of clothing. Her dress was much longer than usual, a mixture of black and beige. Then the decision to remove the skirt and replace it with black trousers. A liberal amount of makeup and jewellery. High-heeled shoes were replaced by more modest ones.

Time to book an Uber. Doreen tapped in Albury Police Station.

Mohammed was very welcoming, but couldn't avoid saying "Do you want me to wait outside? You wouldn't want to stay there overnight." He thought it was funny.

"Ha ha. Just visiting a friend who made a mistake."

Doreen thanked Mohammed for the ride and headed towards the blue light above the door. It did occur to her that some of the policemen there might have been or were clients. Too late to worry about that. Boldly she pushed open the door and headed for the desk. A characterless face forced out the words, "Yes, madam?"

"Doreen White. Sergeant Phillips has arranged a visit to see Charles Jackson and Eugene Danner." Doreen was nervous.

Characterless looked at his work sheet.

"5pm, Doreen White. Yes, you're down here. Please take a seat and I'll arrange for the gentlemen to be taken to the interview room."

Two minutes later, two younger policemen popped their heads around the door. One of them Doreen recognised, and he disappeared quickly. The other was about to ask her a question, then had second thoughts.

"Okay, Doreen White, you can come through. Firstly, please hand over your bag. You can collect it before you leave. Just go down the corridor to Interview Room 1. You have a maximum of 30 minutes." Characterless watched as Doreen reached the door to Interview Room 1 and went in.

Charles and Eugene looked dishevelled. Neither had shaved, nor slept by the look of their sagging, dark eyes.

Doreen attempted to generate a smile. "Well, don't you two look terrible. You could at least have washed." Neither smiled, so Doreen chose another route. 'Do you know if you are going to be charged?

"No, we have heard nothing other than police are continuing their investigation. Do you know anything?" Charles almost pleaded for an answer.

"Well Leslie and Roger asked me to come and see you. They're worried about their futures and dare not come on their own. The police have interrogated them, and both denied any knowledge of the videoing. I have a friend in the police who says, if you are charged, you could have your passports impounded until the trial — and that could be months away. That would upset your plans to return to America. The best you could hope for is bail, but I'm not sure how much that would be. The bank has also been in contact with Leslie. Seems you are behind with your loan repayments for The Griffin." Doreen painted a very gloomy picture.

"One of the reasons Eugene and I came over was to try to renegotiate our loan with the bank. Given our current circumstances, that might prove a little difficult." Charles began to prowl around the room.

"You say you have a friend in the police? Can he help?" Eugene asked.

"I've spoken with him, and for you to be set free they really need to find the guilty party. Is there anyone over here or back home you've upset, because this looks like you've been set up. Do you owe money to anyone who might have done this?"

"No, we just have this debt problem with the bank. We know banks will repossess if funds don't meet the debt. It's highly unlikely they would renegotiate the loan now, especially if this made the newspapers." Eugene was being very realistic.

"Look, our 30 minutes is up. I'll try to get to see you in two days' time. Until then, try and put together an exit strategy. One where you can leave the country immediately. A friend of mine knows the bank manager very well and he has some influence over him. I'll talk to him tonight. At least we can find out the bank's next move. Is that okay?" Doreen had joined the links in the chain.

"They can only hold you for three more days without charging you. I'll come back tomorrow or the day after."

She opened the door just as Characterless arrived.

"Just wait in reception, Miss White, and I'll give you back your bag and mobile phone."

Doreen sat in the Uber and began texting Danny. "Painted the picture for the boys. They're desperate. I'm going back in two days."

Danny had two days to manoeuvre into position.

CHAPTER 79

DANNY'S PLAN

CIAO, MASSIMO. PLEASE MEET CAROL, MY CAREERS OFFICER from school. We want to discuss my future over one of your wonderful pastas.

Massimo thought otherwise, but was his usual charming self and couldn't refuse, "piu bella di Madonna, Danny." He took Carol's hand and gently kissed it before leading them to a quiet table under subdued lighting.

"What a charming man. What did he say in Italian?"

"He says you are more beautiful than the Madonna," Danny smiled.

Carol thought Danny might have fed Massimo the script earlier, but either way she liked the sound of it.

"If you like risotto you could do worse than order the pork risotto from the specials board, it's my favourite." Danny was in control.

"Okay, let's have two of those. Now let me buy the wine. Maybe a bottle of Barolo?" Carol was ready to begin her interrogation.

"So, what is your master plan, Mr Carver?"

Danny loved her frankness. Direct and sexy, he thought.

"I'm going to buy The Griffin and this Italian restaurant. Then I'm going to close the restaurant down and move it to the motel, Massimo with it."

Danny took a sip of his wine. Carol wondered for a moment whether he was joking, but no — she knew him too well. If he wasn't joking though, how on earth was he going to do it?

"I take it you're serious?"

"Very much so." Danny stared into her eyes.

"I take it you have a plan?"

"Very much so." Again, the stare.

"Do I figure in the plan?"

"Very much so." This time a glint in his eyes.

"Would you mind telling me how I figure in your plan?"

"I want you to take an office in The Griffin and run your business from there. I have some ideas about how you might broaden your range of products and services, but we can talk about that later. Do you like the risotto?"

The last thing on Carol's mind was the risotto. Her head was in a spin.

"Yes, the risotto's fine. What does Massimo think of your plan?"

"He doesn't know yet."

Carol nearly choked. How could this brash, soon-to-be-19-year-old be so confident and, more to the point, how had he found his way into her bed?

"The wine's lovely, Carol. Good choice." Danny decided he'd said enough.

"When will all this happen?"

"It's happening as we speak. In a few days it will all be over. Then it's down to people like yourself to decide. Maybe we should wander up to The Griffin after dinner and I'll show you the office I have in mind for you?"

"Why not? The world's your oyster. Does Richard Branson know about you?" Carol decided to go with the flow. This was the most exciting thing that had happened to her in the last five years.

"One more thing. The tiramisu is to die for." Danny redirected the conversation. "Do you watch MasterChef?"

"Only when I'm not moving office and changing the world."

Danny laughed as Massimo cleared the table.

"Two of the world's best tiramisus, Massimo, please."

"For you and your beautiful companion, compliments of the house."

Carol concentrated on the rest of the meal and wondered how the night would end. It wouldn't do any harm just to drive up the road and see what Danny had in mind.

Leslie welcomed them, and Carol noticed how readily and easily Danny fitted into the environment.

"I just want to show Miss Whittleston the spare office down the corridor. Can you give me the key?"

Leslie didn't ask any questions. He just handed the key over, and Danny set off down a corridor marked admin.

"Don't worry about the admin sign, that will come down. Here we are." Danny unlocked the door and allowed Carol in first. "We'll repaint and furnish to your requirements. Quite spacious, isn't it? And there's a lovely view over the rear gardens."

Carol thought for a moment. Is this really happening? I'm on a roller-coaster and can't get off, or can I? Why am I accepting all this from a 19-year-old?

"Are you okay?"

"Yes, fine. Just taking it all in. Can we have a coffee in the lounge and talk about this?"

"Good idea."

Danny handed the key back to Leslie and headed for the lounge, Carol following him.

"Well, what do you want to talk about? First, let me order two coffees."

Carol noticed how everything was so easy for Danny. He just signalled to the barman and coffee was on its way.

"I see opportunities, Carol. I put a strategy together and go along with it. Plus, certain key people are vulnerable, such as the owners of this motel."

"Where are they?" Carol was curious.

'We passed them on the way to Massimo's. They are in the cells at the police station. Something to do with videoing sex scenes here in the motel rooms," Danny explained nonchalantly.

"Where are they from?"

Danny smiled, "Now you're getting there. Oklahoma."

Carol thought for a minute. "How can you take advantage of that?"

"I have to frighten them into selling me the motel at a greatly reduced price. Then I can get them released and they can fly home."

"That simple?" Carol was smiling at the audacity of this.

"Yes, I have something on all the key players, plus I made a lot of money gambling on Sports Day. I advised an overseas group of Italians and they won big and gave me 20%. Sam Johnson helped me pull that off."

"You still need the bank to agree, and you're only 19." Carol said a little smugly.

"You see the lady sitting at the end of the bar?

Carol turned to look. "The one that looks like an older call girl?"

"Don't stare. The bank manager visits her quite regularly, here at the motel. He pays for drinks and a room. He's currently on the verge of a nervous breakdown as he thinks he's on one of the videos."

"What!" Carol was beginning to untangle Danny's strategy.

"I think he would be extremely grateful to anyone who could make his problem fly away to Oklahoma. Do you like the strategy?"

"Dare I ask who at the police station is about to be manipulated?"

"You dare, and the answer is behind you. Don't turn round. He may also want the owners to fly back to Oklahoma and have the charges dropped."

Carol took a sip of her coffee. She could now understand how she had become embroiled in Danny's charisma. This was a very charming and devious young man.

"Can you drop me off near my place on the way back, please?" Danny asked.

"Of course," although Carol was secretly hoping they might be going back to her place. Danny continued to surprise her.

CHAPTER 80

CLOSING IN ON THE DEAL

DANNY WAS HAPPY WITH THE POSITIONING OF THE KEY players. The Americans, Wilson at the bank and Sergeant Philips all had a lot to lose. Doreen was on fire. She was harnessing all those street smarts she had learnt from risky days and nights. Danny had provided her with a golden pathway to security, and she was not going to blow it, so to speak. All she had to do now was paint a fatalistic picture for each of them and Danny's strategy would fall into place.

Danny had to maintain calm at school. Potter had resigned. Bartholomew had fended off questions from inquisitive parents and given Danny a list of them. Danny contacted each personally.

"Thank you for your support, Danny. The incoming calls have stopped, and the pressure has eased." Bartholomew gestured for Danny to sit down.

"I'm seeing Colin Punter at *The Advertiser* this afternoon. He'll have to refer to the incident, so I'm going to write the piece for him.

I'll make sure you come out of it in a favourable light, sir." Danny played the school captain role perfectly.

"That's exceedingly kind of you. I can placate Joan Webster and Gerald Trapper. The other governors are still in shock, apart from Sam Johnson, who thought it was hilarious." Bartholomew was beginning to feel more at ease.

Danny stood up to go. "I should have a class exam revision period. Could you explain my absence please?"

'Of course. Please text me after your visit to *The Advertiser*." Bartholomew got up and held out his hand. Danny shook it firmly.

Colin Punter, the world's most boring man, was at his desk when Danny walked in.

"Are you free for a few minutes?" Danny asked.

"Yes, it's very quiet." Punter needed a story. Of course, yes was the only answer Danny would have accepted and why he had flicked over the 'Open' sign to 'Closed'. Punter knew it was about to become profoundly serious and personal.

"I want to help you write Thursday's front page article for *The Advertiser*, but first I could murder a coffee?" Danny flashed one of his I've-got-you smiles.

"How's Mildred? Did she enjoy Sports Day?" He was slipping into gear.

"Yes, she made a lot of money for the butchers. Her hot dogs sold really well." Punter handed him the coffee.

"I loved her bandana and the way she wielded the carving knife — more like a machete, very barbaric and intimidating. I can see why no one refused her hot dogs. By the way, are you still visiting that lady from Fred's café?"

Punter lay back in his chair.

"I want to, but I'm scared to death Mildred may find out. She comes in here every now and then, and if I'm not around there'll be a public enquiry when I get home." Punter had come to realise it was pointless trying to fool Danny.

"I can help you with that problem. And this problem — the rent that is. Now let's get on with Thursday's article." Danny reached into his pocket.

"Here's the headline." He gave a piece of paper to Punter: *Wise and alert. Bartholomew saves the day.*

Punter studied it. "Infers quite a lot, Danny. I like it."

"Good, let's get writing."

Thirty minutes later the article was finished.

"Now I'm going to text it to Bartholomew for his approval, and then you and I can talk seriously about your future." Danny copied the article and sent it off with a "please confirm immediately."

"Very soon I will be able to offer you a rental property for a lot less than you're paying now, not too far from here. You will find it will satisfy both your commercial and nocturnal needs, so to speak." Punter knew not to interrupt. "Would you be interested in having a preliminary look?"

"When did you have in mind?"

"In about 10 minutes I want to show you something to your advantage. You will be out of here for about 20 minutes. First, I just need to pop across to the butchers and thank Mildred for her contribution to the school fundraiser."

Punter suspected Danny was clearing the way for whatever he had in mind.

As Danny left a text arrived from Bartholomew. "Great article, thank you", and he smiled to himself as he crossed the road. Mildred was dressing the window: lamb chops to the right, sausages to the left and a plastic sheep and pig in-between.

"Just looking in to say hello. I'm taking your husband out for a coffee. We need to discuss his article about the school. By the way, I prefer the blue bandana, the red one was a bit too abattoir!"

Mildred thought for a moment, then worked it out. "Oh, I see.

Do you think it scared a few people away?"

"Only the squeamish," Danny laughed. "At least you made some money, and the school will use you again. Better go now, I think the old man will be ready."

"You got the last bit right. There's more life in this mince." Mildred waved her machete and smiled. She liked Danny.

Leslie handed over the admin corridor keys, and Danny walked Punter towards an unused office.

"This is the one I have earmarked for *The Advertiser*," he said confidently. "A third less rent than you're currently paying. Lovely view over the gardens. Use of the lounge area to meet with clients, ample car parking and, most importantly, two kilometres from the butchers in the precinct. You'll be able to use all the new office facilities and equipment and you may also want to use the motel's other facilities from time to time." Danny smiled, sales pitch over.

Colin Punter liked everything Danny had said. The picture was easy to understand. When would the office become available, he wondered and, more importantly, how was Danny going to get the owners to agree if they were locked away or back in Oklahoma?

"Danny, when you say you have earmarked an office for *The Advertiser*, are you planning to work here after you leave school?"

"Not at all. I'm planning to buy the motel. That's why I can offer you a bright future, stress-free. I can also offer you a lead article about what has been happening at the motel and all the new and exciting changes taking place under new ownership. We shall expand our interests into Europe, starting with Italy where you will open a property office, selling Australian properties to Italians and Italian properties to Australians. You will have to travel between the two of course, and on certain visits may take some company with you. Nudge, nudge, wink, wink."

Danny took a step back and watched his plans ferment inside Punter's head.

"When will all this happen?"

"Within the next week, and I need a provisional yes from you on the office, so I don't offer it to anyone else. I'm sure you can see the potential."

See the potential? Punter was on the verge of an orgasm. Mentally he was settling down in business class on an A380.

"Yes, I'm in." Punter was raring to go.

"Great. Let's get you back to the shop." Danny lobbed the keys at Leslie and Punter, who had started the day at a height of 195cm and had now reached 205, lurched behind. He suddenly had a tomorrow, and the prospects on all fronts excited him.

Danny had a few hours to think about his meeting at The Griffin with Alice Brown. He had decided not to go back to school that afternoon and texted Bartholomew asking to be excused. So he went to Fred's where Fred and Phil were working their way through Saturday's horse racing, and Doreen joined him.

"Time's running short," said Danny. You're going to see the Americans tonight, aren't you? Paint a bad picture, stressing that you've spoken to the bank and, given their predicament, it's highly likely they will repossess The Griffin. The bank may seek further monies too, if The Griffin is sold at a discount. Do you still see the Commercial Finance Manager, the one above Wilson?"

"Of course, and he pays well."

"Good. See Wilson again and paint a deteriorating situation. Say some additional material of a sexual nature has been found. Then arrange a meeting with the Commercial Finance Manager, but don't tell Wilson."

Doreen listened attentively, then said with unexpected shrewdness "Since we first met, Danny, you've treated with me with respect and politeness. No man in my life has ever been so considerate. I know I pay a commission for contacts, and I'm comfortable with that because in my profession it's better to be safe than sorry. The more I know of the clients' backgrounds the safer I feel. I know your plans, and I like the idea of having my own Wellbeing office at The Griffin.

Until now you've worked like a mastermind, manipulating and operating behind the scenes — very successfully I might add. I can do everything you ask of me and make everyone feel extremely vulnerable but, I think, if we are to take the final step and make this happen, you must front up to both the Americans and more importantly Wilson and the Commercial Manager. You can offer them all an exit strategy that they can't refuse. You control the local media and should tell them that, and that you have additional video material which could become public."

"I'll get Sato to compile a spreadsheet of all parties who have agreed to take an office or workspace," Danny said immediately to Doreen's surprise, "And an itemised revenue list. We have a valuation. I'll meet with Wilson and the Commercial Manager and make an offer for The Griffin. We already have a considerable sum in the 'Always Tomorrow' account. Can you arrange that meeting for me?"

"Sure, I'll do it today."

Danny had to match Doreen, so he texted Alice Brown "Sadly, I have to cancel this afternoon's meeting at The Griffin. I'll text you shortly to reschedule." Alice felt a little miffed at the postponement.

Doreen rang Wilson and Danny rang Sato and reminded him "Don't forget to put the two pokie machines in the itemised revenue column."

"I have, along with the pool table."

Danny smiled. Sato was ahead of him.

Doreen said "10am tomorrow at The Griffin."

"Is Wilson contacting the Commercial Manager, or are you?"

"He is. I'll ring him in a few minutes just to make sure — the Commercial Manager, that is."

Danny texted Sato to invite him to the next day's meeting with the financial projections for Always Tomorrow and Sato texted by return "All done. See you at The Griffin tomorrow."

"I think you should be at The Griffin tomorrow taking coffee in the lounge," Danny said to Doreen. "Just to remind them of the potential disaster if their extracurricular behaviour becomes public. By the way, what's the Commercial Manager's name?"

"Selwyn Driver."

"What?"

"That's his name, Selwyn Driver."

Danny stood up. "Text me when you've finished with the Americans. Might be a good idea to meet Sergeant Philips later."

"Might be," she agreed.

CHAPTER 81

DOREEN BACK AT THE CELLS

DOREEN DRESSED QUICKLY IN THE FIRST GARMENTS SHE found in her wardrobe. She contemplated her make-up, then remembered the young shy-looking policeman who had looked into the waiting area and put on the dark red lipstick.

"This way, Miss White. You know the drill. Just hand over your bag. Constable Pickering will look after it until you return." Characterless churned out the script.

Doreen smiled directly into the young constable's eyes. He reached for her bag and she slipped a business card into his hand.

"Second interview room on the right. I'll collect you in 30 minutes," Characterless continued, leaning on the desktop.

Doreen went straight in and said "Have you guys got access to some cash back in Oklahoma? I hope so because you're going to need it."

They looked shocked and she continued "The bank is going to repossess the motel, and that will leave a deficit, between its value and what you owe them. So, it's in the bank's best interest to keep you here in this country, which may put pressure on the release of your passports. Plus, it appears new videos may have come to light. Relax, a friend of mine has them, but if the police get their hands on them, you're finished."

Eugene, the financial arm of the partnership, stepped in.

"How much?"

"A minimum of $200,000."

"When?"

"As soon as the bank repossesses The Griffin."

"How do we know this isn't some giant scam?" Charles asked.

Eugene glared at him. "I'm assuming the bank manager is a client, Doreen?"

"Yes, and his immediate superior Selwyn Driver, the Regional Commercial Manager is too."

Charles had nothing to say.

"How do you know the police will release us?" Eugene asked.

"Because the police sergeant is a client, right, Doreen?" Charles had worked it out.

"Within three days you could be on a plane back to Oklahoma."

A voice from down the corridor shouted "Two minutes remaining."

"Okay, I'll arrange for $200K to be tele-transferred tonight to The Griffin's account. Can you speak to the bank, your friend and Sergeant Philips?"

"Will do. This should all be over within 24 hours. I'll be back tomorrow evening."

Doreen closed the door behind her and set off down the corridor. Constable Pickering returned her bag and business card with 'I'll be in touch,' written on the back.

In the car park, Sergeant Philips was leaning against his car.

"Can I offer you a lift back to the motel, Doreen? We can chat in the car."

"That would be really nice. Yes, please."

On the way back, Doreen explained she had contacted the two girls who appeared in the video, who apparently had some more videos, which included her and clients. "I told them both that if they return the videos I won't contact the police. Blackmail is a criminal offence."

"The best thing you and I can do is to get those two Americans out of the country. *The Advertiser* can still print a story highlighting how you exposed an international sex ring. That will be enough to get you promoted. If not, let me have the name of your immediate superior."

Philips turned into the car park, came to a halt, and looked at Doreen.

"When do you want me to release them?

"Day after tomorrow. They're transferring money to The Griffin account from Oklahoma. Can you ensure they get access to a computer if they need one?"

Philips smiled and drove off.

"He's at the bar," Leslie said as Doreen walked in.

Wilson was red with anxiety, having waited for over 30 minutes. Roger smiled at Doreen and reached for the gin as she let rip. "More videos have surfaced. The two call girls are threatening blackmail."

Wilson turned crimson with fear.

"Are you talking to them?"

"No, a mutual friend is."

Wilson put two and two together and came up with Danny Carver. Hence tomorrow's meeting.

"Any advice?"

"Repossess The Griffin tomorrow. At present the Americans are tele-transferring 200K to The Griffin's account. That can go towards the loan. It's all they have."

"I can't do this without my Regional Commercial Manager's permission," Wilson frowned.

"You can get it now. He's just coming through reception." Doreen stood up as Wilson spun round, and there was Selwyn Driver, equally crimson.

"I'll leave you two to have a brief chat. Shouldn't take long to reach a conclusion. I'm off to powder my nose." Doreen winked at Driver and left the room.

"Your usual scotch, Mr Driver?" Roger asked.

Wilson froze, and then the penny dropped: Selwyn was a client.

"Danny Carver is intending to buy The Griffin. He and his cohorts have an account, 'Always Tomorrow', with a substantial amount on deposit and I suspect he's the one with the additional sexual material. I suggest we repossess The Griffin and take the $200K. The police have no further sexual material so will have to release the Americans. Doreen will drive them to the airport and get access to all the videos, which will become ours once Carver owns The Griffin." Wilson was somewhat relieved, Driver less so.

"Who does this Carver think he is?" Driver was about to launch into a venomous tirade when Wilson explained ...

"He's the one who holds our careers, pensions and reputations in his hands, and that includes our marital status, which would evaporate in the hands of our wives. We would be homeless and jobless. I'm not sure I could handle that."

Doreen returned looking refreshed and nodded at Roger, who reached for the gin.

"I was thinking of submitting an invoice for $5,000 for facilitating the $200K transfer. Let's call it a finder's fee. Are you comfortable with that boys?"

"Do we have a choice?"

Doreen laughed and ordered — "Drinks all round, Roger, please."

CHAPTER 82

DANNY TAKES OVER

10AM, AND WILSON AND DRIVER WERE SITTING AT A TABLE in The Griffin lounge. Doreen was perched on her barstool with coffee and a magazine.

"Let's get this over with as quickly as possible." Driver was feeling the pressure.

Doreen glanced over occasionally and crossed her legs. Wilson was praying no one he knew would walk in. As much as they wanted to find a solution for the bank, they couldn't. They were in uncharted waters, both personally and commercially. The implications of getting it right so it would go away or getting it wrong so it lingered long and hard sent a chill down Driver's back. Wilson was trembling and his coffee cup shook whenever he took a sip.

Danny met Sato in reception, glanced quickly over the itemised revenues and projections, smiled and they both walked confidently into the lounge.

Driver started to stand up, but then felt subservient and sat down again. Danny went straight over to Doreen and kissed her on the cheek, which didn't go unnoticed and just emphasised the dilemma Driver and Wilson were facing.

"Coffee, boys?" Roger asked.

"No, just water. Can you bring it over to the table with the two gentlemen, please?" Danny walked across to Driver and Wilson, and Sato followed. This time they stood up and everyone shook hands.

"You're a very determined and savvy young man, Danny," Driver complimented him.

"Not sure what savvy means, but I do like to take advantage of opportunities and, as Mr Wilson will verify, your bank is already benefitting. Always Tomorrow has a considerable sum on deposit and I have introduced several new customers — one of whom is close by." Danny smiled knowingly at both men.

Wilson was keen to move on.

"We all know the situation we're in. What are your plans, Danny?"

"Always Tomorrow wants to buy The Griffin. We understand you are about to repossess, and I have arranged for the current owners to transfer $200K from Oklahoma to The Griffin account. This is a gesture in lieu of the mortgage, and to ensure charges are dropped. Then they can get their passports back and go home." Danny waited for the dust to settle.

"How confident are you that the police will free both Americans?" Driver needed reassurance.

Danny turned and looked at Doreen who winked and crossed her legs. Driver and Wilson shuffled a little uncomfortably in their seats.

"I have access to additional video material of a sexual nature which could implicate prominent local people. I also have access to and control over the local media."

Danny glanced at Sato. "Money arrived this morning, Danny."

Driver looked at Wilson, who didn't know but offered to check.

"No need," said Driver, "I'm sure Mr Sato knows. I'm presuming you are about to make an offer for The Griffin, Mr Carver?"

"I have an offer in mind, but first you may wish to look at this list of secured itemised revenues." Danny handed over a folder marked secured incomes, lease options and agreements.

"Anyone can produce a list of names and companies, Mr Carver."

"They can, and that is why I have put a contact name and telephone number at the side of each. You are free to contact any or all."

Driver passed the list to Wilson, who confirmed that 75% of them banked with them.

"Those that don't bank with you will, as part of their lease agreement, have to relocate to your branch." Danny was closing all exit routes for Driver and Wilson.

"And your offer?" Sato handed another folder to Driver who, bank-trained, remained deadpan. Wilson glanced at the figure.

"This represents an overall loss to the bank." Driver looked at Wilson.

Danny said nothing. He knew they would be thinking it through. He glanced at Sato, who produced another folder titled Griffin Financial Projections.

Danny held onto it but face up so both Driver and Wilson could see the title.

"I suppose that is your pièce de résistance, Mr Carver. No doubt it will show how you will repay the loan you are seeking to purchase The Griffin?" Driver reached for the projections. "I suppose we could call your bluff and walk away."

Wilson cringed and Danny remained calm and non-committal until Wilson had worked his way through the projections and confirmed "the lease agreements cover the loan repayments, so it is a viable commercial proposal. I suggest we prepare a letter of terms."

Driver looked at Danny. "I'm assuming you will destroy the videos in our presence or hand them over once the sale has been completed?"

Danny stood up. "Could you please drop the letter of terms off here tomorrow morning? I will ensure the Americans are released, the videos secured and the case closed." Then he shook hands, first with Sato and then with Wilson and Driver, before going to join Doreen at the bar.

Doreen smiled at Wilson and Driver as they left the lounge. Sato said his goodbyes and followed them out, and there was a brief silence.

"You did well," Doreen said. "Their body language told the whole story. You'd do well on the streets."

Danny smiled. "Getting you off the street has been my masterstroke! When do you get your new BMW?"

"As soon as we move in here."

"Can you ask Sergeant Philips to get the Americans released? Tell him I have a story that will stand him in good stead and support his promotion. I'm off to school to fiddle my exam results. Talk later. Oh, and don't forget to get the videos."

Doreen watched him leave, especially his bottom, and sighed — another time, another place maybe.

CHAPTER 83

THE THREAT ON THE HORIZON

ALL THE PIECES IN DANNY'S JIGSAW HAD FALLEN INTO place. The Americans bad been released and were heading home. Doreen had the videos. The bank had fulfilled its obligations, much to the relief of Wilson and Driver. A takeover completion date had been set for three weeks' time.

Punter's article, astutely written by Danny, had raised Sergeant Philips status, not only in the community but also professionally, so that he was now Acting Superintendent Philips.

Sam Johnson had made his lawyer available to Danny free of charge as thanks for the inside information Danny had provided before Sports Day.

Doreen now drove the streets rather than walked them in her new sponsored BMW, metallic green. Her established client list had been damaged and mentally bruised, but they were too safe to lose, so the process of gradually enticing them back into the web had begun. New clients included Constable Pickering.

Justine and Claudette were back in town and available for special assignments.

Bartholomew told Danny that Potter had taken a teaching position 60 kilometres away in a small country town.

Danny had still not rearranged his meeting with Alice Brown, but he did glance across when he walked out of the economics exam. Alice pretended not to notice, but her body language gave her away ... and Danny knew it.

All the new offices at The Griffin had been let.

Punter was relocating *The Advertiser*.

Carol Whittleston had a Careers Adviser office.

Doreen took a bigger office with a massage area and wellbeing couch for personal chats.

An anteroom to the lounge had been offered to Mr Foster, just in case he decided running a TAB betting room was more exciting than teaching French. Short odds suggested he would.

Massimo Crespo, the Italian restaurant owner, had provisionally agreed to move his restaurant to the motel. Danny was keen to let Sam Johnson's lawyer handle the transfer. Massimo was initially overly cautious, but the numbers were extremely attractive. His fixed costs would be halved. He would own half the restaurant so long as he signed it over to Always Tomorrow when he retired. Danny was keen for Massimo to develop a new menu and take on two school leavers to train in Italian cooking techniques.

Sato had an accounts office which he could use while he was at university.

Chris had a clearly defined role: to increase corporate business at The Griffin and persuade more companies to hold functions there. Danny was keen to engage with the local community and encourage them to use The Griffin to promote their own businesses. Mr Woo had already agreed to a 'How to cook noodles' evening, using The Griffin's kitchen and staff.

Jeff would supervise internal maintenance and security. This ensured Jordan Smith could be called on to oversee behaviour at all functions.

Woodwork teacher Mr Atkins had agreed to do all internal repairs. The chance to stay close to Doreen was too attractive to ignore.

Mohammed, the Uber driver, became The Griffin's first choice ride share operator.

Sam Johnson would place a BMW car in a prominent position on the forecourt.

Danny had plans for a grand opening night. Invitations would go out to all school staff and sponsors, including the governors. All Year 12 parents would be invited. Massimo would engage Fred and Mr Woo to produce an evening of Asian and Mediterranean food.

Roger and Leslie were to remain, which would make the transition of ownership seamless.

Danny still had his personal life to sort out. Or did he? His ability to operate on the edge meant there would always be personal issues. Plus, he loved the challenges.

Janice had decided to go to a university far from Redberry. Danny said that would let him concentrate on running The Griffin and that he looked forward to visiting her. Janice took that with a pinch of salt.

Carol was of commercial value and he loved the raunchiness of their relationship. He found her very sensible and good to bounce ideas off.

Alice Brown was the new kid on the block, so to speak. Danny had yet to put his toe into the water, even though it looked very inviting.

Carol helped Danny organise the opening night party. Bartholomew and Mr Trumper received invitations, and the night before the opening Danny saw everyone involved, including Ronnie Rickets, lead singer with the Meltdowns, a local pop group who were appearing live. He spoke purposefully and covered in some detail how he wished the night to develop.

After a few questions Danny thanked everyone for their support and asked Roger to open a couple of bottles of champagne to "toast The Griffin and all who sail in her." Bartholomew looked at Trumper, and the two wise old men smiled knowingly. Between them they'd spent over a hundred years teaching, and had never encountered a student more astute or streetwise than Danny Carver.

Danny circulated among the champagne drinkers and then took Leslie to one side.

"Who's the old guy sitting at the table by the window?"

"His name is Salvatore Pappalardo, he's from Sicily. He would like an introduction."

"Mr Pappalardo, I believe you would like to meet me."

"Your success has not gone unnoticed, Mr Carver. When you have finished winning over the masses, I would like to sit and talk. Maybe over lunch on Thursday?"

Danny smiled, "Thursday it is."

ABOUT THE AUTHOR

Mike Penistone is best known as the 'Global Rugby Coach' from his years coaching Rugby League and Rugby Union in the UK and Australia, and latterly through his global Rugby Coaching Consultancy, establishing and conducting coach education programs and advising clubs and teams how to get the most out of their players and coaches alike. His experience extends all levels of the game, from U7s through to elite international players at the highest level, in both the northern and southern hemispheres.

With an educational background and a Bachelor of Education degree from Keele University, Mike has a unique ability to connect and communicate with players of all nationalities and playing abilities. He is a genuine coach educator.

With a resulting insight into the 'young adolescent male' and a degree of 'Danny Carver' in his own character, Mike was inspired to write his light-hearted coming of age tale, '*Keeping it real*'.

In his first book '*The Global Rugby Coach*', Mike shares his passion, humour and knowledge of the game he lives and loves.

'*Keeping it Real*', Mike's first novel and prequel to '*Pulling Strings*', introduces us to Danny Carver and his crew, and their emerging talent for turning every opportunity to their advantage.

The third book in the trilogy '*Taking the Lead*' is soon to follow.

Made in the USA
Monee, IL
15 April 2021